The Family Business

Michael Ponzi

PEGASUS BOOKS

Pegasus Books
3338 San Marino Ave
San Jose, CA 95127
www.pegasusbooks.net

First Edition: June 2014

Published in North America by Pegasus Books. For information, please contact Pegasus Books c/o Caprice De Luca, 3338 San Marino Ave, San Jose, CA 95127.

For all intents and purposes, this book is a work of fiction. Any resemblance ta any actual persons, livin or dead, events, or locales is entirely coincidental. We *mean* it! And also, no animals was harmed durin the production of this book. Some names have been changed to protect the privacy of individuals.

Library of Congress Cataloguing-In-Publication Data
Michael Ponzi
The Family Business/Michael Ponzi – 1st ed
Library of Congress Control Number: 2014933487
ISBN – 978-0-9910993-7-5

1. DRAMA / American / General. 2. FAMILY & RELATIONSHIPS / Humorous. 3. TRUE CRIME / Organized Crime. 4. PETS / General. 5. SOCIAL SCIENCE / Conspiracy Theories

10 9 8 7 6 5 4 3 2 1

Comments about *The Family Business* and requests for additional copies, book club rates and author speaking appearances may be addressed to Michael Ponzi or Pegasus Books c/o Caprice De Luca, 3338 San Marino Ave, San Jose, CA, 95127, or you can send your comments and requests via e-mail to cdeluca@pegasusbooks.net.

Also available as an eBook from Internet retailers and from Pegasus Books

Printed in the United States of America

For my Ma

*Who will literally kick your ass
if ya give er any grief!*

Today, I settled all *family business*,
so don't tell me that you're innocent.
Admit what ya did...

Michael Corleone
The Godfather, Mario Puzo

The Family Business

The Family Business

Hi, my name is Michael Ponzi, and I'm Italian. Well, I guess I'm only half-Italian. My ma is Irish, ya know, from a very traditional Irish family of *cops*. Her father was a super-cop actually—ya know, the kinda FBI/RICO underhanded cop the government puts out there ta take down the mob—which is why it was kinda ironic that my ma and dad ever got tagether in the first place!

You see, my dad, Dominic Ponzi, was in the mob for as long as I could remember. My ma hated it, but I remember, as a child, my dad takin me ta Vinny's on Jackson in Hoboken. It was the typical smoke-filled room, with a crazy assortment of wise guys and "made" men, eatin the spectacular meatballs, or *polpetti*, that Vito's ma came in and made every Tuesday and Thursday.

His two younger sisters, Gianina and Lolita, *taught and trained* by their mother, worked in the kitchen. Gianina did an exceptional *Frutti di Mare* that was so good it was said old man Luchessi had a guy from Brooklyn murdered for takin the last servin that he'd called dibs on.

Lolita, who was three years older than me, did the *cannoli*, which my dad always got for me. I can still remember it now—so light and crispy, and the sweet ricotta fillin—ta this very day I've never had anything so delicious and mouth-waterin. But I'm Italian and we're talkin about food.

Anyway, when my dad took me ta that place, I was always impressed by the level of respect he got from all the guys in there. There was Tommy Rotten, officially second-in-command, who always wore a rose in his lapel—he absolutely *loved* my dad. Then there was Fat Tony, Tommy's son, who was actually anorexic on accounta his domineerin ma. And there was Alphonso the Brain, who could remember everything—numbers, names, what you were wearin, what you said and when and where you said it—everything.

But some of the guys in there were scary, like Jake the Ass, which was short for "assassin." He was a big guy with big hands and feet—like size sixteen, I think. I remember—all his teeth were silver, like the guy in the James Bond movie. I didn't know back then he was a killer, but he and my dad always took a moment ta have a business meetin in whispers in the corner booth in the back. By the time I was a young teenager, I was hearin rumors that Jake Soranno had murdered over eighty people—under family orders, and I got the feelin he enjoyed his work.

Then there was Marcelino the Dwarf, though he wasn't a dwarf. No, he was actually a midget, and he never let you forget that. Born into the Carzano crime family, he was the boss the neighborhood and much of the whole state. What he lacked in height, he more than made up for in—how did they say it?—*coglioni?* Nevermind the translation, but he was a tough character.

Folks in the neighborhood said he was the family member who called the hits on Nick the Greek and rival crime boss Bruno Casanova. An immaculate dresser, Marcelino once had a man shot in the knee for steppin on his size five, extra-wide Fratelli Rossettis. And he loved his family. You could pop off all the *short* jokes you wanted ta about im, but say somethin about his family, and you'd find yourself in the company of angels, with dirty faces... and dirty hands, because I was sure Marcelino had *them* in his pocket too.

Vinny's

"How long has it been since I had ya in here, Michael? Nine, ten years?"

"More like seven, Dad, give or take a few months. I came ta visit after college. Ya remember."

"I say ten years!"

"No, Dad, maybe it was eight. Let's just go in."

We were right outside the front door when he stopped.

"So what are ya? So *smart* now? My father and me, we bust our asses sendin ya to a big, fancy college, then ya disappear and come back thinkin ya know more than everyone else? And you're the one who ain't had a job in three years!"

"It's the recession, Dad, and the Republicans. I've been lookin for work five days a week for the last four years."

My dad looked back over his shoulder, lowerin his voice.

"And it don't take a college genius ta know ya get married first, *then* ya have a kid. I coulda helped ya out if I knew where ya were. I don't know where ya go. Ya have this way of just disappearin. Ya keep your ma worried sick!"

Inside, it was like old times, except everyone was older, which kinda made it different, I guess. But other than that, it was just like old times, except they had a big screen TV with cable, and yeah, *Family Guy* was on. Ya know, the episode where Stewie goes "all-gangsta" on Brian? That episode was on—my favorite of all time. But other than the fact that everyone was older and they had a big screen HDTV, and the fact that Vito was dead, it was just like old times inside the joint.

Lolita was there, with a big kiss and a warm plate of *cannoli*. When I was a kid, I had this sorta crush on Lolita, but she had married Lorenzo Lipps, which wasn't really his last name. They called him that because he had the biggest lips you ever saw on a white guy, or at least an Italian. His real last name was Volpe, which Lolita only sometimes used.

My dad told me Lorenzo got himself shot and killed by the husband of his mistress, so Lolita was single again. The rumor was that she was secretly seein Carlito the Ass, who was the illegitimate son of Jake the Ass, by a Puerto Rican mistress. So Carlito was always kinda an outsider. He just didn't come across as *one* of us. I don't know. There was somethin, well *different* about im.

"Michael!" my dad warned. "Ya don't let her put her *tongue* in your mouth like that when she *kisses* ya. Jake and I have been best friends for a long time, and we don't need bad blood between us."

Lolita didn't get that. She had her hands and tits all over me. I'd get her off me and go across the room ta have a conversation with another old friend, *specifically* ta get away from her, and it would be minutes before she'd be on me again.

"I still can't believe you, Michael! So grown-up, so handsome! You act all shy, but I hear you have a kid, so I know there's a stallion pinned up in there somewhere."

The door opened at the exact moment that she patted my ass, so I was sure he saw it. Carlito stood there, glarin at me. It had been years since I'd seen him. Back then, we were the same size, but he had gotten huge—it had ta be steroids. Now he was six-five and almost as wide as the door. Defiant, Lolita looked up, smiled at him and sashayed back ta the kitchen, exaggeratin the hip sway for my benefit.

Carlito Soranno walked right up ta me.

"Michael Ponzi. I hear you've come back ta join your dad in the business. For your sake, I hope you've gotten over your faintin spells."

Carlito, who had apparently followed in his dad's footsteps, was definitely an "ass" before he was an assassin. He was one year younger than me, and I was stuck with him when our fathers went out ta do their jobs. He had serial murderer written all over him from birth, but once he did it himself—in a mirror, with a sharpie when he was eleven, right on his forehead—he wrote "serial murderer."

You know how they say serial murderers start out their careers with helpless animals—stray dogs and cats? Well, it was true in Carlito's case. When he was nine, he swallowed a toad, headfirst, just ta do it. He almost choked ta death. It just puffed up in his throat. He hadda go ta the hospital an all, but that was just the opener. When we went ta the lake, Carlito fed the ducks and geese rat poison for the hell of it, and durin the brief time he thought he wanted ta be a doctor, he performed lizard and mice autopsies with a scalpel, only after he executed them with the guillotine he made in his garage.

As he got older, his obsession with killin grew more perverse. He went after kittens and puppies, parakeets and turtles. He was just such a heartless bastard, even as a teenager. One time when we were in the ninth grade, we went to see my Aunt Rachel, who lived in the country, on a farm. I protested ta my dad from the beginnin, insistin the notion of Carlito on a farm with livin animals was crazy. But no one listened ta me.

Auntie Rae's husband had this big prized bull, with these gigantic prized balls. They were makin ten, fifteen thousand a year studdin this bull out. So I go inta the barn, and Carlito had somehow got behind this bull and duck taped an M-80 firecracker ta its nuts. When I saw what he had done, I panicked, ignorin my own safety, and tried ta rescue the bull. *Too late!*

Before I knew anything, I was covered in blood and bull ball bits and I couldn't hear anything. I could taste that bull's balls in my mouth! And when I looked ta the bull as it slammed around the pen, blood gushin, I fainted from the trauma. And just so you know, the bull didn't die. The vet came out and injected him with all kinds of pain killers and sewed him up. My uncle, of course, was pissed—until Jake the Ass came out and paid him somethin like a hundred twenty thousand for the damage done ta the bull, uh, and the horse.

When Carlito was sixteen, he went to a juvenile detention center for beatin up an old lady who wouldn't let go of her purse. That was the last I saw of him, but I heard stories. My dad said he got out and tried ta straighten up. He even got married and had a kid, but he was in trouble again before he turned twenty—that time for beatin a boxer ta near-death because he couldn't be persuaded ta throw a fight.

At twenty-four, Carlito went ta go work for Marcelino the Dwarf, next ta his father, which was a pretty natural fit, I guess. The thing that bothered me personally about im, was that he was kinda cross-eyed—not completely cross-eyed, but just enough ta where sometimes he was talkin ta ya and lookin somewhere else. So for seven years Carlito was an assassin for the mob, which I heard he was very good at. My dad said The Dwarf was singin his praises.

So we're standin there, talkin, and The Dwarf comes up ta us. First, he rears back and just wallops Carlito in the gut. There was a pause, and then they both just cracked up, laughin. So I'm thinkin we're gonna have some real problems if the midget tried ta hit *me*

like that, but this was Marcelino the Dwarf we were talkin about—
he was the head of the Carzano crime family and was runnin half
the whole state, and parts of New York too. He was like God.

I remember thinkin, 'if God wants ta punch me in the
stomach, maybe I better let im.' So I stood there, cringin, ya know,
bracin myself.

"Aww, I won't waste my energy on you, College Boy!"

He had ta reach up, but he elbowed me in the stomach
instead. It hurt, knockin the wind outa me, but I pretended not to
feel it.

"I'm here because my dad said I'd needed ta talk ta ya if I
wanted ta join the business."

The Dwarf smiled, displayin the gold inlays on his teeth.

"I knew that before *you* knew that, Michael. We'll talk in the
booth."

Marcelino was actually kinda good-lookin for a midget. Unlike
the dwarfs, whose hands and feet are regular-people-sized on a tiny
body, midgets are a little more proportional. Dwarfs have big heads
and weird, half-goofy faces. I guess that sounds prejudiced, but I
just thought midgets were better-lookin than dwarfs. Marcelino was
all-midget, though they called him "The Dwarf."

At four-ten, The Dwarf was just a shrunk-down, miniature
man who reminded everyone that the only body part that *wasn't*
proportional was the "lady-killer" part in his Armani slacks. He had
a good-lookin face, and his hair was jet-black, showin signs of
grayin at the temples. Accordin ta my dad, The Dwarf was fifty-
eight, with a tall wife and five "regular-sized" children.

At his size, he was bound ta have some height complex issues,
and he did. The booth where we sat was engineered so that *his* seat
was elevated ta the point that he was lookin *down* at me, like
suddenly he was towerin over me.

"And you're sure this is what you want ta do, Michael? Ta
become a killer?"

"*Si, Padrino,*" I answered, bowin my head. "I have thought
long and hard about it. My papa always said, 'a job is a job, and we
do what we gotta do ta take care of our families.'"

Somber, he took his time, steeplin his fingers and sighin,
cheeks puffed out like Don Corelone's, but when I looked down,
his tiny feet didn't even reach halfway ta the floor. He was like a

little kid, sittin in a restaurant booster seat—little legs stickin out down there. I couldn't help but laugh ta myself, but I got scared cuz I think he *saw* me laugh. He continued.

"That's commendable, Michael. Family is everything. I would do *anything* for my family, and if something ever threatened or harmed the family I love, there is nothing I would *not* do."

I nodded in agreement.

"*Padrino*, my papa's gettin old. Ma's been on his ass about retirin. I figured it was time for me ta take over the family business."

The Dwarf smiled.

"Ah, family, yes! Do you know how far our families go back? How long our families have been workin together?"

"I know my dad works for you, and he worked for your dad, Marco Bello."

"It goes further back than that, Michael. Carlo Pietro Giovanni Guglielmo Tebaldo Ponzi was your great uncle, once removed. Him and my grandfather were close friends. Of course you know about *him*, Carlo Ponzi?"

"Only that I am related ta him, and that he was famous for makin money."

"He was a rare *genius* ta be admired. An immigrant, he came to America from Lugo, from Italy, with two dollars in his pocket. And by his own ingenuity, he went from penniless to a millionaire in fifteen years, and that was the 1920s. *Postage Supply Coupons*—go figure! Carlo Ponzi—he was a very clever man. That is *your* family, Michael Ponzi—genius is in your family make-up. Unlike dumbass Carlito out there, who comes from a family of thugs. And you wanna be a *killer*?"

"Like my father before me," I nodded.

Lookin back ta his tiny feet stickin out there, his legs weren't even long enough ta bend at the knee! I had ta cover my mouth ta disguise my near snickering.

"What? You think I'm funny? Funny how? Tell me what's funny."

I wasn't goin down that path, so I completely shut it down.

"No, nothin, *Padrino*. I'm just happy, happy ta be gettin in the family business."

"And your father? You *know* for a fact what your father does? You know that?"

"Most of his life, he's kept it from me. But I know, and I want ta follow in his footsteps."

"Guns, knives, poisons? You know how ta use those?"

"Yeah," I answered. "Besides that, I have a PlayStation 4 and an X-box, and I've mastered *Grand Theft Auto V*, *Mortal Kombat* and *Call of Duty, Black Ops II*—all at the highest difficulty levels. I think I even set a few online records."

The Dwarf started at me, contemplatin.

"Ya know, Michael, once you start in this business, there's no turnin back. You mess up—I can't help ya. You'll have ta answer ta the family, and you know that might have deadly consequences."

"I know about that. I accept the risk."

"And your father is in total agreement about this?"

"Of course! *Padrino*, I've been strugglin the past three years, and I have a little girl now. I went ta college ta become a writer, but no one's hirin. My ma, she wants me ta be a teacher, but that's not me. I'm a killer, and I'm ready ta get started."

Marcelino sat back.

"Your little girl—she lives with her mother, Maria. Are you sometime gonna *marry* Maria?"

"No. Maria hates me, and I hate her. Besides, she's not my type."

"Not your type? She's my cousin Umberto's granddaughter. What *is* your type?"

"I like black chicks."

The Dwarf nearly choked on the smoke from his cigar.

"Black chicks! Are ya crazy? Black chicks are nothin but trouble! Whatsamatta you?"

"Why? Tell me why you *say* that, Padrino. Do you *know* somethin about em? Why trouble?"

"Well, maybe not for black guys, though maybe some black guys would say otherwise. But for you, black chicks would be trouble. You're Italian—well, half-Italian, and Italian and black don't go together. And married? It's… it's like socks without shoes. I'm serious!"

"*Padrino*, I'm sorry," I reassured him with a wink. "Calm down. It's not like I said I was gonna *marry* a black chick. I just like em, that's all."

"Ah, I get it," The Dwarf smiled. "Well, why didn't you *say* so? Big asses, brown skin, luscious lips... Between you, me and this booth here—I kinda like em too."

On the way back ta the house, I noticed a black car followin, lurkin about three ta five car lengths behind me and my dad, turnin when my dad turned. You know, stoppin when he stopped.

"Do you *see* that, Dad?"

"Stop lookin back and use the *mirrors*, ya moron. Of *course* I see it. They've been followin me for the past two months."

"Who is it?"

"I've been wonderin, but I can't be sure. If I had ta guess, I would say it's maybe one of your *ma's* relatives. My guess would be FBI. Maybe your cousin, Patrick."

I squinted inta one the mirrors, tryin ta make out the man behind the wheel.

"Definitely a government suit, but I don't think it's Patrick. What do you think they want?"

"My only guess: I did a job about six months ago. Actually, the job came from a U.S. congressman who was havin problems with his wife—in this case, the so-called 'problem' was named Pierre—or somethin else French. Anyway, this congressman was tired of comin home and findin Pierre in bed with his wife. He threatened her many times, but she wouldn't listen. Every time he turned his back, she was sneakin Pierre inta the bedroom."

"What a slutbag!" I sighed.

"So he called me and asked if I could take Pierre outa the picture, ta which I said, *for the right amount of money, I'd take King Kong outa the picture*! He paid me fifty thousand without blinkin, and two days later. *Pop! Pop! Pop!* Pierre was no longer sleepin with his wife."

"Serves em both right."

"Oh, I didn't kill the broad—the contract was on Pierre. Needless ta say, the wife didn't take it well and suspected right away that the congressman was involved. After filing for divorce, she called the police and the FBI, insistin her life was in danger. And ta tell the truth, it *was*."

He checked the car in the rearview mirror before makin a sharp left, across traffic.

"Turns out that when I was in the house, some hidden surveillance camera snapped a picture of me—somethin that has never happened before—and the broad *had* it."

He made a sharp right onto a back-way entrance to our neighborhood. The tail was gone.

"The Dwarf wasn't too happy about that. It threatened his whole operation. So he sent Jake the Ass, and I guess Carlito—Carlito the Ass—ta clean things up. But by the time Jake blew up the wife's apartment, she was already in a witness protection program. The Feds were sniffin around after me, but only ta get me ta turn evidence on the congressman, who has been a gigantic pain in the President's ass for the last two years."

He pulled inta the driveway.

"Like *that'll* ever happen!"

My Ma

At the dinner table, my ma couldn't eat for all the sobbin.

"So we, your grandfather Guido and us, we sent you ta this special, top-notch college, and the best you can do is be a killer, like your father here?"

"I didn't *say* that, Ma!" I offered in protest.

"You didn't *have* to, Mikee. I have sources too, and I heard you were down at Vinny's this afternoon ta get The Midget to put you ta work."

My father corrected her.

"It's The Dwarf, Claire. The *Dwarf!*"

"But I thought you said he was a midget, and *not* a dwarf?"

"He *is* a midget, but they just *call* him The Dwarf. Marcelino wants everyone ta call him The Dwarf."

"Then why don't they call him The Midget. It goes better with his name. Don't you think so, Mikee? Marcelino the Midget sounds a lot better than Marcelino the Dwarf, especially when he *is* a midget, and *not* a dwarf."

My father wagged his head.

"Claire! A man oughta be able ta be called what he wants ta be called! And Marcelino wants ta be called The Dwarf."

"Uh-un! It don't make sense. You told me last Christmas that, right in the mall, Marcelino had a Santa's ass kicked and had him defrocked down to his underwear for calling him a dwarf, because he insists he's a midget."

"He did, because Marcelino *is* a midget. That ignorant Santa called him 'a' dwarf, which he isn't, because Marcelino knows what he is, which is absolutely a midget. And it was especially offensive comin from a Santa, who should have *known* better. Marcelino wants ta be *called* 'The' Dwarf, as long as everyone understands what he really is, which is a *midget!*"

My mother looked toward my dad, disgusted.

"Santa has *elves*, Dominic, not dwarfs. Marcelino should have known better. But the truth is, and don't get mad at me for sayin it—Marcelino looks more like an *elf* that either a midget *or* a dwarf. He really should think about calling himself Marcelino the Elf."

My father finally lost it.

"Claire! For the love of God! Elves aren't even *real!*"

He stopped suddenly, seemin a little confused as he whispered the aside ta me.

"Right, Michael? Elves aren't *real*?"

"Midgets, dwarfs, elves—they're *all* little people, but right, Dad. Elves aren't real... except for on the movies and on the North Pole."

My mother just sighed aloud.

"You *see* what you're getting yourself into!"

In an attempt ta change the mood, my father placed a reassurin hand on my mother's clinched fist, strokin gently.

"But sweetheart, every cloud has a silver linin. The business is slowin down a little from all the competition and Obamacare and such. It ain't big enough for both me and Michael, so I'm gonna spend maybe a month trainin him, and when I think he's ready, I'm gettin out of the business and then we can go to Italy! The Dwarf said I would be eligible for 401K benefits and retirement startin in November anyway. I figured now's as good a time as any. I'll get out while I'm still healthy and unindicted."

She shook her head, givin up.

"So *you'll* be out of the mob and Michael will be in. You're going ta turn our son, our *only* child, inta a killer?"

"It's the family business!" my dad said, "In the words of a famous Corleone, 'Don't ask me about my business, Claire! Don't ask me about my business! Enough!'" he shouted, slamming the table.

She sighed.

"Eat your meatballs, Dominic. They're getting cold."

He tried ta hold character, but his timin was off.

"All right. This *one* time—this one time I'll let you ask me about my affairs."

She patted my hand.

"You *see* what you've gotten yourself into?"

Fishin with Asses

The drive out ta the lake took four and a half hours. Jake and Carlito, who had the boat, led us up the road for the last five or so miles.

"Tell me somethin, Dad. Why aren't you an Ass?"

"I don't know, Son. I don't really get out ta church that much, but I try to apply the *Golden Rule*. You know—*he who has the gold makes the rules*. So I just try ta be a nice guy."

"I'm not talking about that. Jake gets ta be an Ass, which is short for '*As*sassin,' and short for '*As*sociate,' he told me. That's true, right? And Carlito gets ta be an Ass, after only seven years in the business. So why didn't you ever go for bein an Ass?"

"Oh, that."

My father looked at me, his eyes becomin a little moist.

"I guess I really *wanted* ta be an Ass when I was your age, but my dad, Guido Ponzi, said in words I will always remember: *Blaze your own unique path, son, no matter how stupid it seems.* And that's what I did."

I spoke up as my father blotted his eyes with a handkerchief.

"Ya did fine, Dad. Ya did *Nonno* proud. But I definitely wanna be an Ass," I insisted. "I'm gonna learn this business and get real good at it. You should have seen me on the PlayStation last night. I've got ice water runnin through my veins! I can't wait ta get out there and shoot someone for real!"

The four of us were on an eighteen-foot aluminum fishin boat with a small outboard motor. Jake supplied the poles, while my dad stopped at the bait store ta get extra tackle, fishin licenses, beer and the other stuff. When we got a half mile from the shore, the three of em started gettin their poles ready. They were old hats, but I hadn't been fishin in years.

"So what are we goin for? Perch? Walleye, Pike, Salmon?"

Big Jake, who already had his line in the water, called out the answer.

"On red worms? Are ya nuts? We're goin for sunfish."

"*Sunfish!*" I moaned. "Ya mean we got up at four in the mornin and drove five hours ta catch sunfish? Bluegill? Really?"

"My boy and I *always* go for sunfish," he shot back, offended, "since he was little. Fish is fish. You somehow got a problem with sunfish, Michael?"

But before I could open my mouth, my dad did that "dad thing"—a single glance most kids understood that said, "Shut the hell up!"

I got a pole and started settin it up. It was hook first, or two, if you wanted two hooks, and then the weight at the bottom. The bobbin went last, at the top. I was ready. So I had scooched over ta where they had the bait, fingered through the dirt and grabbed a red worm, ready ta put it on my hook, when suddenly somethin hit me.

That hook looked really *large* in comparison ta the size of the worm! That would be like stickin a piece of metal the size of a large fence post inta a skinny human and threadin it through the body. It was weird. I baited hooks all the time when I was a kid, and I never thought about the worm, but just then, it hit me.

I shrugged and stuck the worm with the very keen tip of the hook anyway, ready to skewer it through him, but then that worm started squirmin like crazy, and some icky yellow juice—some kinda worm blood, started oozin outa the wound.

When I looked out the corner of my eye, I got this feelin Carlito was *lookin* at me, enjoyin the micro-torture, just waitin for me ta stick the poor worm again. I didn't want him ta think I was a sissy, but I couldn't stick that worm again, so I pretended ta drop it.

"Dammit!" I exclaimed, cleverly. "These worms are too little! Tiny! And I forgot my glasses. Couldn't someone have gotten *bigger* worms! Dad, where are those *rubber* worms you got? Let me get one of those."

We had fished for about thirty minutes before we got any bites, and then it was like gangbusters—for everyone but me, with my rubber worm. Carlito was like a big kid. He got all excited every time he caught a fish.

We each had our own buckets, which we filled with a little water, except for Carlito, who didn't bother. He just threw his fish in an empty bucket ta let em flip and flop around in there, suffocatin, I guess, gaspin with those little fish mouths.

"Hey, all that floppin is startin ta get annoyin, Carlito. Why don't you just put some water in your bucket already?"

"Cuz I like ta watch em die, *pauroso*! That's the whole point of it. I don't *eat* em. I never eat em."

He smiled, sadistically, lookin slightly ta my left.

"I like ta listen ta the sound of sufferin. What are you gonna do, Michael? Faint?"

He caught a few big ones, but most of the ones he pulled up were under six inches—and he even kept the ones that were two inches! My dad and Jake caught a few, but after an hour or so, it became clear the whole fishin trip was for Carlito's benefit, so he could get his jollies watchin fish die for nothin on a Saturday mornin.

When my bobbin suddenly sank and disappeared, I thought I was hung up, but then I felt somethin tuggin ta the right, and then ta the left.

"Ya *got* somethin, Michael! It's something big! Set your hook!" my dad yelled. "Set the hook, for God's sake!"

Instinctively, I jerked the tip of the rod up, felt for movement and began the process of tirin the fish out and reelin it in. The process took about five minutes, and we were all surprised when I got it up. It was a huge, largemouth black bass—had ta be eight or nine pounds! And it was a clean snag—right through the upper lip. So I grabbed the fish by the gill plate, dislodged the hook and eased it back inta the water.

"Michael! What the hell are ya doin? That fish is gonna get *away!*"

"I'm puttin im back, Dad. I don't want ta deal with this guy. Besides, I *hate* fish! I'm allergic ta raw fish."

"Then give it ta *me*, Mikee!" Carlito pleaded, like when he was a kid. "I just wanna watch it die."

Fortunately, the fish struggled, violently spankin its tail down on the water in the moment I released it.

"Dammit! He got away!" I sighed. And then to Carlito, "Shoulda told me earlier."

I was discreet about it, but I fished with a bare hook for the rest of the six hours we were out there. Carlito was beside himself and angry with me. He went ta fishin with a second pole, strugglin with his cross-eyes ta bait the hook with a skinny rubber worm, but nothin bit for him.

"Close one eye, Son," his father always said ta help him see better. "Just close one eye!"

Later, as we were hitchin the boat ta the trailer in the dark, preparin ta head home, Carlito pulled me aside, still fumin about the fish I released.

"The Dwarf doesn't *know* you, Michael, but I do. You wanna be an Ass, but you don't have Ass *in* yas. You faint! You ain't up for the job, so you're gonna mess up, and when you do, rest assured, *I'll* be the one to come for ya. That fish got away, but can't wait ta watch *you* die instead!"

Welcome ta the Family

Back at Vinny's on Monday mornin, my dad and I had a meetin scheduled with The Dwarf. We were at the booth where tiny Marcelino held court, his shiny little shoes danglin off the edge of the seat. He had on an outfit I was just about sure was a kid's suit I saw in the Macy's ad on Sunday. But he sat there, distinguished, grayin at the temples, glasses pushed down his nose, studyin some papers in a folder he had opened.

"Okay, so it's like this, Dominic: I know ya don't usually take the small jobs, but ya got your boy along, and I thought I would give ya a little somethin ta get im started out, ya know, cut his teeth, taste some blood."

Turnin toward me, The Dwarf removed his little glasses ta share a personal opinion.

"Your father's a *legend*, Michael. Dominic the Vet, they call im. Consummate professional, highly-respected by bosses from here ta Palermo. Your dad's one-of-a-kind, believe me. I owe him my own special gratitude for takin out Johnny Romano and The Chimp. Has he ever told ya that folks, even the big governments—they fly im around the world ta take cara touchy little problems when they come up? Naw, he wouldn't tell ya, cuz he's too modest!"

Replacin the glasses, he turned back ta my father.

"Anyway, Dominic, I got this job for ya in Manhattan. It's on 59th. Ya did a job on 44th, what—two months ago? This one's not the same kinda problem, but it's an actual nuisance. The neighborhood boss didn't wanna get involved at first, but it's gotten outa hand. Everyone's complainin. The problem—name is Ziggy, and he's black. If ya go inta that neighborhood, be careful, but listen around and you'll find im—beady-eyed black bastard! Accordin ta the contract, ya hafta shoot im, right in the head, right between the eyes, and ya gotta cut off his balls. The job's gotta be done by Thursday. And make sure ya get those balls. *Capiche?*"

My dad nodded as he accepted the envelope stuffed with cash—fifty crisp, uncirculated, one-hundred-dollar bills.

I sat there amazed. I was more excited than a bar of *Dove* soap in Lolita's shower. I could not believe I had finally entered the *true* underworld. Lotsa guys I grew up with, friends of mine—they bragged cuz they were involved in the petty stuff—robberies, scams and phony, irrelevant crime. They only *thought* they were mobsters, *but this was the real shit!* I had just witnessed a boss, the head of the Carzano crime family, order a hit! And not only that, I was gonna be partially *responsible* for killin the bastard. And the best part of all: The Dwarf was *payin* us ta do it!

When I was younger, my ma always warned me about gettin involved with the mob. She told me The Family was full of "no-goodsters," who would smile and hug ya one day, and put a knife in your back the next.

She never trusted Marcelino, from the time he stole her lunchbox when they were in the fifth grade. Almost a foot taller than he was back then, she kicked his little ass pretty good. That's when he swore on his mother's grave he would someday make my ma pay. *That's* why she was so worried about me gettin mixed up with the guy.

Far as I could tell, The Dwarf had gotten over it. After all, his family had employed my dad for as long as I could remember, and his dad before him. Our families had history, all the way back ta Carlo Ponzi. My dad, after all, was a respected hitman for the mob! Ya messed with him, ya got whacked! And on that day, I became a part of the family business. I was a hitman, a paid assassin, a killer, a hired gun—and if Carlito wanted a piece of me, I knew me and my dad could take out him and his dad just like that, any day of the week!

After The Dwarf slipped outa the booth with an unsteady thud, he stood, extendin his right hand. That's when my father signaled ta me that I should bow and kiss the ring on his finger. It was uncomfortable at first. I had ta bow a long ways down ta reach his little, chubby hand. In fact, I had ta get on one knee, and that's where it looked kinda weird—like I was proposin marriage or somethin. The shiny gold ring musta been his father's, who was a regular-sized man—cuz Marcelino had gold tape or somethin else added ta it ta make it fit.

"Welcome ta the business, Michael!"

It was one of the happiest days of my life, as I had finally fulfilled my destiny. Like my father before me, and his father before him, I had taken up life as a killer for the greater good, for order among the ranks, for mob justice in the United States of America!

It was obvious that Lolita saw the little ceremony in the back between me and The Dwarf. She was lookin good, and I could tell by the way she squirmed and groped, brushin up against "the *perpendicular*," that she was happy ta see me.

"Michael... Congratulations! I *saw* that back there! Wow, looks like you're in?"

I backed a little, lookin around, tryin not ta draw too much attention, but I nodded, speakin in a quiet voice.

"Yeah, I'm in with my father till I get a little more comfortable—ya know, get a few kills in under my belt."

"It's a bloody business," she whispered, seemin a little turned on, glancin down. "Are you sure you're up for it?"

"Are ya kiddin?" I sighed. "I was born ta do it. Killin's in my blood, followed by ice water."

She was mashin her big boobs against my arm.

"Ooh! I *like* that, sweetie! Can I buy you a drink ta celebrate?"

But even before she could turn and order, the bartender put my drink, an Irish whiskey with a Jägermeister chaser, right on the counter in front of me.

"It's on the house. Congratulations, Michael!"

It was like one of those movies. I could almost hear the music—the mandolins, the piano, the violins in *tremelo*. As I moved to the front of the restaurant, everyone I passed had a hand extended. Walkin up there, I must have heard "Congratulations, Michael!" fifteen or twenty times in various accents, rangin from Brooklyn ta Bronx, from Newark ta Yiddish. Some of the old guys kissed me, on the cheek, on either side. I'll admit I stood a little taller. It was a proud moment.

Lolita took a break and sat at the barstool next ta me, her hand on my thigh. She had wine and she wasn't subtle in any way. I knew what she wanted, yet at that point, I wasn't sure if she wanted me for *me*, or if she wanted me because of my new status. My dad gave me one of those looks from the booth where he sat with Jake, but I brushed it off. It was my special day, after all.

"I'm off in an hour, Michael. So why don't cha come on over ta my place? I'll make you a special dinner and you and me can celebrate in a more... personal way. I promise—I'll feed you somethin much more delicious than the *cannoli* ya like so much."

I'll admit I was tempted, but my dad probably wasn't gonna go for it. And then there was the matter of the rumors.

"What about Carlito? Carlito the Ass. Everyone's talkin like you're *his* girl."

"Everyone's *talkin* like you're gonna faint doin your first hit job. Am I supposed ta believe *that*? Does this 'everyone' have a name? Is it Carlito the Ass?"

Point well taken.

"I guess so. But you *have* gone out with him?"

"Yeah. I'm a single woman. What do ya expect me ta do? Sit at home seven nights a week?"

"Well, did *he* make it past, ya know, sample the *cannolo*?"

She slid closer ta me, her wet lips touchin my earlobe as she spoke.

"Now *that's* a very personal question, sweetie, but I'll answer it because I like ya. Yes, he went beyond the *cannolo*… one time, but I was drunk so it didn't count. I wasn't impressed."

She sat back in the barstool, sippin her wine.

"My state of intoxication didn't matter ta him. He's been crazy over me ever since. But that was it. He hasn't had a second helpin, cuz I ain't that kinda girl. Don't *hafta* be."

Lolita was hot—in a category all her own!

Women and Cats

Most of us guys, we know some women call us dogs, which alotta us actually are—hound dogs, junkyard dogs, mange-eaten mutts, wolves, bitches, leg-humpers, companions and loyal friends. We know where we fit it.

Men are dogs—which means women are *cats*, in the various classifications, since all cats ain't the same. So, first ya got the *alley cats*—ya know, the young, pretty, slutty women who are always hungry, always wantin ya ta buy em somethin or pay off a bill, always in the food-and-shelter mode, and money, especially cold cash, is like *catnip* ta this breed! Oh, they'll give ya a good time if they think they can get somethin out of it, but they're not loyal. They've always got *somethin* workin—some bad boy *tomcat* hidin around the corner, while they take ya for everything they can get. Sometimes *alley cats* get confused with *feral cats*, who are just plain crazy.

Then there's the *house cats*—clean, attractive, well-mannered and well-groomed. They're breeders and they put out, but only if you're takin good care of em—a home, a car, a sense of belongin and maybe a little romance. They like shoppin, especially if you're payin. Of course, ya gotta accept they might give ya a litter of *kittens* or they might bring one with em when they move in. If they're good-lookin, they're the ones guys refer ta as MILFs, but underneath it all, they've got sharp fangs and claws, just like the rest of their kind.

Next, ya got the *cougars*—the older broads with a little mileage on em, maybe a kid or two, an ex-husband or ex-boyfriend, pretty decent-lookin for their age, good for slutty fun but probably not for marriage. Early on, they'll lie and say they're independent, but that's an illusion that won't last. They've finally discovered themselves and what they want. They're lookin for love and security. They want a partner, and if you're around long enough, they'll eventually wanna get married.

And ya got the *pumas, or panthers*—even older broads, with fangs showin—probably with grown kids and grandkids and well-established, ya know—with a house and discretionary cash, which they've learned ta use as leverage, or bait. They've mastered the game of seduction, though they've lost the goods ta actually seduce a younger man. They're usually in the female mid-life crisis, a little insecure and desperate, saggin in a few places, but some are still doable, even with the lights on. Pumas are always quick ta give it away, and sometimes they'll even pay ya ta take it.

But finally there's the *jaguar*—not some young, skinny, inexperienced, clueless bimbo or a stretched-out, toothless tiger, but a woman, sportin all her body parts ta perfection and knowin how ta use em. She's not a MILF, cuz she's even better. She ain't got/don't want kids and ain't the marryin type, but she's the ideal mixture of independence, sleekness, beauty and danger, with much larger hidden claws and fangs. She's a sexy predator and she knows it. She can be naughty or nasty, dependin on her mood, but she's quiet about things, never puttin what she does *out* there, and she is *always* in charge, unless *she* decides otherwise. If a jaguar decides ta devour ya—ya just lie back and enjoy the ride.

Lolita Cardullo wasn't just a jaguar—she was the queen of beasts. Yeah, yeah—most women are haters when it comes ta jaguars, but inside they *know*. Sure, they know. Their problem is— no matter what, a woman can't *make* herself inta a jaguar. She's gotta be *born* that way, a freak of nature, but God ain't fair. So, whether women liked Lolita or not, it was hard for a man ta resist her, even me.

****

I arrived at her house a little after six, a bouquet of red roses tucked under my left arm while chokin a bottle of *Chianti* with my right hand.

"Michael! Come in! You're a little early. Oooh flowers! How sweet!"

The atmosphere inside the small, cottage-style house held a spicy scent that initially pervaded the senses, fillin my nose and lungs with warmth and carnal excitement. Lolita wore a full-length silk black robe, providin no clue about what was underneath it. Only her face and neck were exposed, and her hair was pinned up.

Her manicured hands were soft and moist from body oil, scented with lavender. I inhaled deeply as she touched her smooth cheek against mine, kissin me once on each side. She was so beautiful! I wanted ta devour her on the spot, but I kept my cool.

She thanked me for the roses and went for a vase. As she reached up ta the top cabinet shelf, I could see she was wearin black satin stilettos—and stockins with that French-heel thing that some experimental women wore.

"*You* open the wine…" she flirted as she slid an opener in my direction. "And *I'll* finish getting ready for you."

The table was set for a candlelit dinner, with two huge, ball-style crystal goblets, which I filled ta about a quarter-full. I could hear Lolita in the bedroom doin somethin—I don't know, but it sounded like somethin rattlin along the floor. I sipped the wine and nodded approval, my senses on edge in anticipation of overload.

When she came out, the robe was gone and her dark, curvy hair was down. Her soft, honey-brown shoulders were bare, except for the tiny tattoo of a red and black scorpion on the left. The black lace corset held two flawless, round 36D mounds of succulence firmly in place while narrowin her already tiny waist. She wore a black pencil skirt with a slit, exposin a garter belt that secured gossamer black stockins, which were little more than a sexy shadow on her shapely, sculpted legs.

Sittin across from her, I enjoyed a sultry leg show as we sipped wine and sampled calamari and shrimp appetizers, along with fresh oysters on the half-shell. Slippin off her heels, her feet played in my lap, teased and stroked, all while she smiled and flirted with me. Only then did I notice how well-shaped her lips were, and how white and perfect her teeth were. She worked in a restaurant for her family, but if she wanted to, she could have been a movie star, an international sex symbol, like Marilyn Monroe.

"I'm *horny* for you, Michael. I've wanted you in a bad way since we were teenagers. I'm gonna *tear* you up tonight!"

It was too good ta be true. I almost lost it in that moment. I had ta push her feet outa my lap ta avoid a misfire.

"Let's just skip the dinner for now, Lolita, and go right ta dessert."

Her huge bed was the centerpiece for the room. Of course it was brass, king-sized, with pillows and a canopy made from sheer silken material, which was draped along the sides ta enclose the sensual arena. She led me in and pushed me onta the mattress before pouncin on me. Straddlin me, she pinned my arms at either side, kissin me with passion. Sittin back, she ripped my shirt open, sendin buttons flyin all over the room.

"First, I'll have my way with you, and *then* you can have your way with me!"

And before I realized what was happenin, I felt the metal snap around my wrist, and then the other wrist. The other ends ta the cuffs were quickly attached ta the metal bed frame. She obviously had a little practice, but I was enjoyin her aggression, and she was talkin nasty ta me, tellin me how she was goin ta take me, and use me and torture me.

She snatched off my belt and ripped off my pants and shoes before cuffin my ankles ta the frame at the foot of the bed. I felt vulnerable, but I was ready for all she was gonna give me, and she had just settled on the perpendicular when I heard a bang, and then a second bang, and then the sound of someone kickin in her front door!

"What the hell!" she exclaimed as he leapt off me and sprung for the bedroom door. Furious, she charged out inta the apartment, slammin the door behind her.

"How *dare* you come over here and kick down my door! The Dwarf's gonna *hear* about this!"

The argument was loud enough for me ta follow through the closed door.

"How could you *do* this ta me, Lolita? You've got a *man* in here, don't cha? After all I done for ya!"

"What the hell are ya *talkin* about, Carlito? You've never done nothin for me, cuz I ain't never *asked* ya ta do nothin for me! Get outa my house, now!"

"I see two wine glasses, and a table set for two. Who's *here*? Who *is* the bastard? I'll kill im!"

I got a little nervous at that point. I mean, I wasn't exactly in a position ta *defend* myself if he came in the room.

"I *love* you, Lolita!"

"For Christ sakes, Carlito! There's *nothin* between you and me—never has been, never will be. You're a big dumb oaf, a lummox. You're not my type, and if you don't leave this very second, I'm gonna call the cops, and then I'm gonna call my uncle Marcelino ta tell im what ya did tonight, violatin my space like this!"

"Who's here? Who *is* he?"

Seconds later, the bedroom door exploded open.

"*Michael!* You little bastard! I shoulda *known*!"

It was probably one of the most embarrassin moments of my life. All I could do was look at him, vulnerable, and then ta my suddenly shrunken perpendicular."

"It's probably not—" I stopped. "Yeah, it probably *is* what you're thinkin."

Hands ta his face, Carlito started bawlin like a little kid, tears runnin down his face and snot on his lip.

"What are you doin here? She's in love with *me*! This ain't fair! I liked her *first*! And she never made dinner for *me*!"

"That's because you're just not her *type*, Carlito," I offered, tryin ta comfort him. "You got lucky once, but I think you're just a little outa your league with this one."

Big mistake!

Just then, he spotted her caddie, full of novelties and black leather props. Takin a braided spanker with a wide flap, he approached me.

"Oh *yeah*, Michael? So now you're in the big league and *I'm* in the peewee league? I know what you're up to! You're doin is tryin ta take advantage of my girl cuz she must be drunk! Ya pervert!"

"Carlito?" I begged as he approached.

"So ya like it rough, huh? Then let's play ball!"

With that, he whacked me with that spanker, right where the perpendicular sat out there, shriveled and exposed. I screamed, naturally, and then he whacked me again, and then a third time. It's one thing ta whack it yourself, but ya don't want some other *guy* ta come in and whack your tallywhacker! By then, Lolita had managed ta come between us, darin Carlito ta hit her with that thing. Receiver ta her ear, she had The Dwarf on the phone.

"Yeah, Uncle, Carlito just kicked down my door and disrespected my privacy. Now, bein my *favorite* uncle, I told him he might wanna take that up with you!"

Carlito was on the phone for a total of fifteen seconds before he apologized and begged Lolita for forgiveness. I didn't receive the same consideration, even after the injury he inflicted on me.

"Of course, ya know this means *war* between us, Michael. Ya stole my girl. I'm gonna kill ya first chance I get."

Lolita tried ta rekindle the sexual discovery after Carlito left, but I was in pain "down there," due ta Carlito whackin my Peter

Johnson. I insisted for her ta un-cuff me, but she kinda ignored me. I tried ta let her down easy.

"Started out pretty good, Lolita. But maybe some *other* time! Jeez! Can ya un-cuff me, please?"

"I don't *know*. It seems like I got the upper hand here, and I kinda *like* that."

"This isn't a game, Lolita," I laughed, nervously. "I need ya ta un-cuff me, right now!"

"No. I don't want ya ta go, and you don't get ta tell me what ta do. From what I can see, you're powerless, my victim, so it looks like *I'm* in charge here. It's a good feelin. I get ta *take* what I want. I like this. I'm the predator, and you're the prey."

Pluggin inta the power supply, she held up a sizeable Black & Decker power tool.

"We never got a chance ta play with the sander or any of my other toys!"

Before I knew anything, she was on me again, straddlin me, grindin on me and takin me, against my will. After she had her way with me, she started usin some of her power tools on me. But by that time, I was a little sore and irritated, protestin out loud.

"You can't *do* this ta me, Lolita! Whadaya think you're doin?"

"Consider it *rape*! I'm *takin* what I want. Take *this*!"

As a jaguar, she knew what she was doin. I fought against her, but she took complete control of me, seemin more turned on the more I protested. She knew how ta make my body *do* things, and then I would hafta brace myself as she *took* it from me, drainin me, wave after wave, in every copular way she could. She made me do things that night that I had no idea my body was capable of doin. Oh, and I could tell she was enjoyin the experience of bein completely in control, but it was more than that.

"Michael! Baby! Ooh! You are *so* good! The expressions on *your* face and all! The panic, the anger! Ooh! I'm comin again! You taught me tonight that I've been goin *about* it all wrong. I'm *not* a giver. I'm *not* some piece of ass. Instead, I *want* a piece of ass. I'm a *taker*! I'm a predator. I take what I want and I enjoy it! And you make it so excitin! I want *more*!"

I had no choice. She took it from me all that night. After five hours, when she was partially satiated and she un-cuffed me, I was putty in her hands as she continued ta use me in position after position. I had never felt so taken advantage of in all my life! She was a greedy, insatiable cat! And finally, when she was through with me, she allowed me ta escape her claws, with all my body parts intact.

"I swear I've never had it so good! You are *great*, Michael. I can't wait ta get some more of you! You're my *bitch* now, ya understand?"

I had no idea how ta answer that question as I collected my clothes and put them on, still traumatized by her unusual degree of aggression.

"Whatever you say. Can I please *go* now?"

She grabbed my butt, pullin me close.

"You're in the family now, and you're the best piece of ass I had in all my life. I ain't lettin you get away! Ya understand?"

"Yes."

"Just so ya know. So I'll expect ya back here tomorra night, ready ta go."

"Anything you *say*!" I replied, though I knew I had no intention of goin back.

"You work for the Carzanos now, and ya got *one* job as far as I'm concerned. I'm a taker, and you're the man I wanna take, at least for now. Welcome ta the family, Michael Ponzi!"

First Job

On Monday mornin, my dad and me went ta the gun store, gettin ready for the hit on Ziggy. Until then, I had never owned a gun, but all that was about ta change.

"Congratulations, Michael! May I introduce ya ta the TAR-21, an Israeli assault rifle, with a built-in laser and Mars red-dot sight, excellent for shootin around tight corners. If you're like your dad, you will need such a weapon."

Jimmy the Weasel was an old friend of my father, but not because my father had known him a long time. He was just *old*, and missin his left arm, right at the shoulder. My dad warned me not ta stare, but it was hard *not* ta, with Jimmy wearin a wife beater. His arm got shot off in Nam, and accordin ta my dad, after the arm was gone, Jimmy took five shots ta the torso and legs tryin ta rescue a buddy, a black guy. It's why he was in the wheelchair.

He came back home ta a hero's welcome, but it wasn't long before they forgot about him, and I mean *everybody!*—friends, family and the government he got wounded for. The only thing he knew was guns, so he opened a store. He had connections, so he could get cha any gun ever made.

I leveled the TAR-21, peerin through the sight.

"Not bad, but I kinda prefer the M27—better all-around assault rifle. The SMR ain't bad either."

"SMR? Lissen kid—there ain't no such thing as an SMR! Frickin SMR? What the hell are ya talkin about?"

"It's, it's a rifle, an assault rifle," I stuttered, "with ya know, Reflex Sight, um, Fast Mag, Quickdraw—"

"No," he interrupted, "I *don't* know. I know every gun that's ever been made, and there ain't no SMR!"

He wagged his head, his white ponytail swishin.

"Waitaminute—don't tell me—ya've been playin some frickin *video* game, right?"

"Uh, right," I nodded.

"And *that's* your only experience shootin a gun?"

"Yeah."

He looked toward my father.

"SMR my ass! Better get this one a bulletproof vest."

My dad handed The Weasel an envelope, stuffed with cash, which the old man started countin.

"Waitaminute! I just remembered!" I sighed ta my dad. "I left my wallet in my other pants. I'm sorry, but I didn't bring my ID."

"And?" the older man responded, barely raisin an eyebrow.

"Don't I need an ID ta fill out some paperwork, you know, for the background check?"

My dad and The Weasel just stared at each other for a few seconds before burstin inta laughter.

"This one's a keeper, Dominic," Jimmy chortled. "Better get im a crash helmet too!"

****

We rented a car in Newark, headed up ta New York and drove through the Manhattan neighborhood, lookin for a parkin spot that gave us a clear view of the front of the house. It was startin ta get dark as my dad sat back, pourin himself a cup of coffee.

"*You* wanna take the shot, Son?"

"Not, not this time," I answered, because I wasn't sure I was ready.

"Then switch places with me. You're the get-away driver."

We musta sat for three of four hours, each with a pair of binoculars in our laps. I remember thinkin I shoulda brought a book or a crossword puzzle or somethin. Bored, I challenged my dad ta a game of *I-Spy*, and I was winnin when he grabbed his binoculars and sat up, leanin out the window.

"That's him! He's on the move!"

I focused on the man through the lenses of my binoculars. For some reason, he wasn't at all like I imagined. From what I could see, he had ta be in his mid-fifties, kinda wimpy-lookin. He was wearin a suit and a Fedora, comin out of a nice home ta walk his dog. I remember thinkin: *How was this guy a nuisance? Blastin Michael Bolton too loud on his stereo? Pesterin the neighbors with stock tips? What?* My dad loaded his rifle and aimed.

"Aw, crap! Get outa the way. Move! Dammit!"

"What happened?"

"*Mary, mother of God!*" my dad groaned, returnin the rifle ta his lap. "Neighbor came up, blockin my shot!"

Lookin again through the lenses, I saw the neighbor, but it didn't seem like he was blockin the shot.

"He musta moved, Dad, but the dog is pissin on the neighbor's leg. Looks like a clean shot now."

"No, it's *not* a clean shot," my father said through clenched teeth. "Your first day on the job and you're tryin ta tell me I don't know what I'm doin? Ya think I dunno how ta tell if I got a clean shot or not? *You're* the shot-caller now?"

He shoved his rifle toward me.

"You think it's a clean shot? *You* take it! Huh, Mr. Bigshot College Graduate? You *take* the so-called clean shot! Come on!"

I immediately retreated, takin up the binoculars again.

"No. No, Dad! You were right. It's *not* a clean shot, but he's walkin away."

"So we wait. He's gotta come back sooner or later."

We played *I-Spy* for about thirty minutes, and then we went back ta waitin. As I ate the sandwich that Ma made for my snack, I started wonderin about my father. *He had the shot, a clean shot, but he didn't take it. Was he scared? Was he losin his edge? Was he becomin senile?* After all, it was an easy job—no break-in, no torture, no women or kids. If he had just taken the shot, we would have already been on the way home.

But at that very moment, somethin hit me. I remembered somethin the The Dwarf had said.

"He's comin back!" my dad shouted in a whisper while raisin the rifle. "Get ready ta *drive*!"

"But Dad, I think you got the wrong—"

The shot was off before I could warn him that he was makin a mistake, shootin the wrong guy. That was the thing I remembered. The Dwarf, when he was callin the hit, he said Ziggy was a black guy, but this nerd out walkin his dog was *white*!

"Dad! Ya shot the wrong guy! Ziggy's *black*—The Dwarf *told* us that! Ya shot the wrong guy!"

When I raised the binoculars ta view the carnage, I had the shock of my lifetime.

"What the—? Ya *missed*, Dad! I thought you were a sharpshooter. Ya missed im completely!"

"No, I didn't."

He really *was* losin it! When I looked again, the man was still standin there—freakin out, but he was still standin, and he wasn't even wounded.

"Look for youself, Dad. He's still standin. Ya *missed* im!"

"I don't have ta look. Just drive the car! Get me over there, now!"

I started the car and screeched away, vehicle hurdlin toward the man. When I slammed on the brakes, the back of the car spun around and slammed inta the curb next ta where the terrified man stood. Unfastenin his safety belt, my dad reached for the glove box and took out a huge butcher knife. Stormin out the car, he rushed toward the man, quiverin knife in his raised hand.

I couldn't watch. With a gun, with a bullet, it was just easier, but ta kill a man with a knife, that was a different deal. I mean, where do ya start? Do ya first stab im in the stomach? Or the neck or head or what? No, ya go for the heart, but it's got ribs blockin it. So what? You hafta stab over and over again until the guy falls down, and then a few more times ta make sure? And the blood! Naturally, with all that stabbin at close range, you'd be covered with the guy's blood. What a mess!

"It's *done*! Drive!"

My dad was back in the car, blood all over his jacket. He had a sort of wild look on his blood-covered face as he yelled again.

"Drive, Michael! The cops'll be comin!"

"What's *that*?" I shouted, referrin ta the bloody blob of flesh in my father's lap.

"They're Ziggy's balls!"

I threw up all over the dashboard and I burned rubber outa there, but not without lookin back in the rearview mirror—where I caught a glimpse of the same goofy-lookin man, in the Fedora and suit, still standin there.

****

The Dwarf had a friend in the meat packin business. That's where my dad had ta drop off the balls and where he was able ta get cleaned up. He had brought some extra clothes in the trunk, so he wrapped up his bloody pants, shirt and jacket and put em in the dumpster, already full of bloody aprons and stuff.

So we're sittin on the stoop outside, waitin for someone ta pick up the balls and drop off the money, when I suddenly remembered what I thought I saw in the rearview mirror.

"What *happened* back there, Dad?"

"Whadaya *mean*, what happened?"

"The guy—Ziggy. First ya missed im, and then ya went after him with a knife, and when I looked back, he was still *standin* there. Unless he's the walkin dead, those ain't' his balls back there in the refrigerator. The Dwarf and his friends are gonna know."

My father laughed.

"No, those weren't *that* guys balls! Those were *Ziggy's* balls."

"That *guy* was Ziggy!"

"No, that guy *wasn't* Ziggy! Ziggy was the dog."

I was totally confused, but then it all started ta make sense. My dad didn't miss the guy, because he was aimin for the dog all along! He killed that black *dog!*

"Waitaminute! Are you tellin me that the mob put a hit out on a *dog?*"

He nodded.

"That's what I'm tellin ya. Ain't so strange. Happens all the time. Dogs, cats, geese, alligators, you name it. The mob's the mob. They can put a hit out on anyone or anything they *wanna* put a hit out on. I just do my job."

I was still tryin ta wrap my head around a hitman killin a dog.

"Don't you feel like that's *beneath* you, as a hitman? Killin a dog?"

"It's a *payin* job. First rule of the business, Son—do whatever job they give ya, and let em know ya appreciate the work. Ain't for us ta pick and choose."

I could not believe my father's blasé attitude. He had just killed an innocent dog.

"Why would they kill a dog? Do you *know?*"

"The Dwarf said he was a barker—kept the neighbors up all night, and the boss's ma lived three doors down. Everyone was complainin about Ziggy so much that finally the boss decided ta take im out."

"And why the balls?"

"Boss wanted em as a gift ta the woman who brought the complaint and lived next door. He's kinda sweet on her."

The Chimp

"Is this the first and only time you've ever *done* this?" I asked, incredulous.

"No. No, I've done it plenty of times before, all kinds of animals. One time, it was a chimp, a real-live chimpanzee. Ya see, in that case Johnny Romano, an up-an-comin crime boss from the east side, he got this chimp, who he named 'The Chimp,' and he taught this chimp how ta shoot a 38 Special—took the little monkey out ta the shootin range all the time, until he was a really good shot, a marksman, or maybe a marks-chimp.

"So Johnny takes this chimp with im everywhere he goes, ridin shotgun—he even outfitted the little bastard in a custom-tailored, purple-colored zoot suit. And if there was someone who crossed Johnny or got in his way, he'd tell the chimp ta whack that person. Of course, no one expected it. No one saw it comin until it was too late. So The Chimp took out quite a few tough guys— Iceman Gino, Spider Rocco, Giorgio the Gentleman, Tito Two-Face, Peter Pecker and bunch of other guys before word got out what Johnny was doin, which was workin his way up the ladder ta The Dwarf.

"In the meantime, The Chimp is earnin this reputation as a tough guy. He's knockin folks off, left and right. And allofa sudden, everyone's complainin. A couple of the widows even went ta the cops ta report that a chimp had killed their husbands, but who was gonna believe a cockamamie story like that? I mean, were they gonna put out an APB for a gun-totin chimp in a purple zoot suit?

"So The Dwarf calls me in and tells me about The Chimp. Says he wants the monkey ta go ta sleep with the fishes. He puts me and Jake the Ass on it—Jake ta take out Johnny and me ta take out The Chimp. We waited on em two days outside Johnny's hangout. We knew they were in there, *cuz there was always bananas in the trash bin.*

"After a while, Jake got tired of waitin and decided ta storm the place through the front door. *Bad idea*—cuz The Chimp was waitin for im. He shot Jake in the shoulder, and then in the leg. So I'm out there, and Jake is screamin bloody murder, yellin for back-up, cuz The Chimp's got him cornered. Me and Jake—we take care of each other, see. So ignorin my own safety, I dived through the window and slid behind the counter.

"All the while, The Chimp was shootin at me, and Jake. As I was hidin behind that counter, I was thinkin—*he's gotta stop ta reload, he's gotta stop ta reload!* And when he did, I did one of those Hollywood movie-type flips, and rollin on my back, I shot The Chimp, right in the leg. He fell down, losin his pistol, and when he stood up, he had his arms and hands raised."

"Dominic, 'I *think* he's surrenderin!' Jake called from behind the couch. 'He's givin up! He's got his arms up in the air!'

When I looked, he *did* have his arms up, with no gun in his hands, but I didn't completely trust him. I had read somewhere that chimps could be tricky.

'I'm not sure if I *trust* im, Jake. I heard he did the same thing with Spider Rocco when he whacked him.'

'But *look* at im, Dominic—he's in pain. Ya *shot* im, poor thing! He's just a dumb animal. He don't know any better, and he ain't got no gun.'

"So I was goin up ta The Chimp, my gun lowered, when outa the corner of my eye I saw it. Jake was right—The Chimp's *hands* were empty, but he was holdin a gun with his foot! If his leg hadn't been wounded, he woulda got me, but the wound made im cringe at the exact moment when he shifted his weight. *Pop! Pop! Pop!* It was just enough ta make him miss me. His ace in the hole had always been that he could shoot even *better* with his foot than he could with his hand! but he missed. I reacted with a bullet, right through his forehead. And that was the end of The Chimp.

"It turns out Johnny Romano and The Chimp had a beef a coupla days before about The Chimp's pay in bananas, and it didn't work out so well for Johnny. We found his body, shot in the heart, hangin over a high tree branch in the yard. So ya see, Michael, there's a lot more ta this business than you probably ever imagined."

I sat there durin the entire story, dumbfounded. On that day, I learned that my dad had no problem killin a dog and cuttin off its balls. I also learned that he had been the winner in a gunfight with a chimpanzee. I didn't want ta ask, but I had ta.

"Were there any other *animals*?"

"I had ta take out a fifteen-foot python once—belonged ta some famous Las Vegas magicians. I fed it a frozen turkey, thawed on the outside—twelve pounds. Had no problem swallowin it, but when the snake got it down, and it was goin past its heart—I placed my foot on the snake's back at a strategic spot, and the turkey just froze the python's heart in place. When the turkey and snake thawed, no one was the wiser—looked like natural causes. And then there was this Goose at Central Park, the white one that hissed at The Dwarf's mother on Christmas Eve. I had ta make sure that particular Goose was served for Christmas dinner."

I was beginnin ta see a not-so-good pattern. From what I knew about the business, alotta the hitmen had their specialties. Some liked *the icepick through the temple or the back of the head*, while others liked *piano wire*. Some liked *stranglin people out*, while others liked *pistols, at close range*. Some liked *exotic poisons*, while others liked *sabotage: settin traps, cuttin brake lines and blowin up things*. I was beginnin ta think that my old man was not a fan of the SPCA.

"So you're a hitman, Dad. And you kill *animals*?"

"Yeah," he nodded. "That's sorta my *thing*."

"Have you *ever* killed a human?"

He hesitated at first, and then he leaned close.

"In a word, *No!*"

"Then you're not really a hitman. You're just a doggie destroyer, a kitty killer. You *lied* ta me!"

"What are ya talkin about?" my father demanded. "I never told you I went around killin people!"

"But you said you were a hitman!"

"I am. I paid for a house, I've taken care of your ma, and your grandfather and me—we sent your ungrateful ass ta college for six years—all by doin what we do. I ain't proud of sayin it, but we did it all by bein hitmen for the mob."

"Hitmen kill *people*."

"Not *all* of em. I'm livin proof of that. And now, Son, so are *you*."

It suddenly hit me, like a sack of onions.

"Oh no, Dad! I'm a *regular* hitman. I don't hafta do it like you did. I'm gonna kill *people*."

"Ain't up ta you. We're Ponzis—it's what we do. I do it, and your grandpa did it. So what are ya gonna say ta The Dwarf when he tells ya he wants ya ta whack a pigeon or an alpaca? Nothin! Ya just *do* it. You'll get used ta it, just like I did."

"No, I *won't*," I protested, crossin my arms. "I am *not* killin any animals! No one told me goin in that I had ta do that."

"But you'll kill *people*? Does that make *sense* ta you?"

"In this kind of business," I answered, "a person's gotta assume that the *people* who get whacked—somewhere along the line they musta done somethin ta piss someone else off real bad—stole money, sold bad drugs, killed someone, ratted ta the police—somethin! But animals are innocent. They don't do nothin. What was Ziggy doin? Barkin, cuz it's what dogs *do*! His owners probably left im on the chain all day. *They're* the one's ya shoulda whacked. But for barkin, he gets shot and his balls get cut off? That ain't right! He didn't deserve that."

"What are ya tryin ta do, Michael? Add some kinda *morality* clause ta this business? When ya think about it, they're *all* animals. It ain't a matter of who deserves what. We're part of a system that fixes things when they go wrong. This country's got an animal problem, a serious *animal* problem—and when animals get outa line, people like us gotta take care of it, whether they walk on two legs, or four."

He stood, peerin down the street ta see if the driver was comin.

"Me, I prefer ta deal with the four-legged animals—less hassle. People get upset—some of em highly upset, but ya can spend a few hundred or thousand dollars ta replace a dog or a cat, and it's almost the same—they're even workin on clonin household pets. They can all be replaced. But *humans* are somethin else. I've always thought there was somethin more special about humans. Ya can't replace a father, a brother, a niece, a son or daughter, not even a best friend. No amount of money can buy them back."

"Some people feel the same way about animals," I objected.

"Maybe so, but that's because they lack the ability ta form close bonds with other humans. I've read doctors who say it's a form of surrogacy, but it ain't really the same."

He came back ta the stoop and sat next ta me.

"Besides, for folks who do what we do, whackin animals is less risky. Ya ever see any of the mob go ta jail for killin a cat or a canary? And men who kill men—most of em won't live long enough ta qualify for Social Security. It's a dog-eat-dog world out there. If ya kill people, rest assured people will be out ta kill you. Jake and Carlito, the Asses, they know their card could get punched any day, but you and me—unless were wrestlin alligators or swimmin with sharks—we ain't got nothin ta worry about."

An Offer He Can't Refuse

By the time we got ta the location of the next hit job in southern California, I was convinced I could never be the kinda hitman my father and grandfather were. We flew inta LAX, rented a car, and took a drive ta the coast. It was my first time in California, so I was expectin ta see some celebrities, but the airport was full of regular people. When a lady near the baggage claim conveyer said Jack Nicholson had just passed by, I told her, *no big deal—every time the Knicks play the Lakers in LA, I turn on the TV and there he is!* I wanted ta see someone really famous, like Al Pacino.

We musta drove two hours outa the city when I noticed rows and rows of green plants, stretchin out in every direction. My dad said they were grapeviness and said we would probably go ta winery on the way back.

"So what kinda animal are we killin *taday*, Dad?"

"A horse."

"A horse? I don't get it. What? Is he a *nuisance*?"

"No, he's a thoroughbred, a race horse."

"Why? What he do?"

"He won the Derby."

That was the one thing I didn't like about the mob. I never got the way bosses figured things. I mean, where was the logic in that? What was the point of killin a horse for winnin? If that was the case, what did they do ta the losers?

"So we're supposed ta kill im for winnin?"

"No, we're killin im because the owner of this thoroughbred ranch, some big Hollywood producer—he won't green light a movie for Pauli Mazzola."

"Are ya kiddin? *I* wouldn't green light a movie for Pauli Mazzola," I argued. "Mazzola makes lousy movies. *Kill the Midget* was crap! I'm embarrassed ta say I know im. They want us ta kill a beautiful creature like a thoroughbred horse just so Mazzola can make another crummy movie? I don't get it."

When the phone rang and my dad answered, I knew it had ta be The Dwarf on the other line by the way my father did that funny stutterin thing he did. A week earlier, he confessed ta me that his first impulse was always ta call im Marcelino The Midget, maybe cuz of the alliteration thing—or it coulda been because my Ma always called him "Marcelino the Midget" at home. Apparently my dad had slipped up a couple times in the past and I guess The Dwarf wasn't too happy about it.

"What? *Ixnay on the Orsehay?* We're already almost *there!*"

Change of plans? I thought. *Horse musta been wearin a lucky shoe!*

"Yeah, yeah. He sold him. Ta who? Ta *you?* Really? So we're *done* out here, right? We can come home. No?"

Apparently not.

"Ya want us ta whack a *what?* Are ya kiddin? Are ya crazy? How am I supposed ta *catch* that thing?"

It had ta be somethin faster than a horse. Really?

"Yeah, yeah—me and Michael, we'll figure it out. *Ciao!*"

He was silent as he drove for the next few minutes. I was almost afraid ta ask.

"Okay, Dad. What do we gotta kill now?"

"A kangaroo."

"A kangaroo? Like a hippity-hoppity kangaroo?"

"Yeah, a big red, a kangaroo."

"But don't kangaroos live in Australia? Way in the outback?"

"Yeah," my father answered. "But this big-shot producer— he's got this thing for kangaroos, I guess, and he's got this favorite boomer he named Buster. The Dwarf said we gotta watch out, cuz Buster's got this bad temper, and he's a trained boxer."

I wasn't sure how ta feel. On the one hand, at least I didn't have ta be involved in killin a horse. I liked horses—I had seen em up close—they were beautiful creatures, with big pretty eyes, but I wasn't sure how I felt about kangaroos. I wasn't even a hundred percent for sure that I knew exactly what they looked like.

I knew they had rabbit ears and long legs and pouches for the joeys, but that was about it. Basically an overgrown rabbit. I wasn't exactly sure how big they grew. But this kangaroo, Buster—he had a temper? And he was a boxer? Right! I was the Golden Gloves champion, 154s, right outa high school.

"These things can get up ta 200 pounds, and they can be very mean customers," my dad warned.

"A 200 pound jackrabbit with a bad temper? I'm just glad we didn't hafta whack the horse. A rabbit I can help ya out with."

"Problem is," my dad added, "they're very fast and agile. They can leap maybe thirty feet in a single bound."

"That's impossible!"

"We gotta set a trap," he said, "and when we catch him, we gotta be very careful takin im out."

I guess my dad, after all the years of whackin em, knew a lot about animals and their habits. So after a phone call ta determine where on the property he would find Buster, we traded in the car and rented a jeep. Then we went ta a local sportin goods store a got some camouflage clothin, nettin, rope and a shotgun. When we got back ta the estate, it was just a matter of findin Buster, trappin him and takin im out."

My dad found a narrow area of the property where he thought we could corner the big kangaroo, so we went about riggin the nettin and creatin a stagin area where, if we could get him there, my dad would have a decent shot. Then it was a matter of findin im, threatenin im and forcin him back ta that area.

As soon as we spotted im, we went ta work, shooin him this way, and then that way, drivin him back ta the stagin area. A coupla times he tried ta slip by us, but my dad fired shots at im, tryin ta take im out early. Finally resigned ta his fate, Buster leapt ta the stagin area and waited, huffin and mad as a box of frogs. He didn't cower. Instead, he took a few steps forward, challengin me, dukes up. It was an offer I could not refuse.

"Think ya can take im?" my dad asked. "I could just shoot im."

"He deserves a fightin chance. He just might be two hundred, so he's got twenty pounds on me, and he looks about six-two, but I'm a man and he's an overgrown rabbit."

And so takin off my shirt, I approached im, guards up. We kinda sparred a little at first, walkin around in circles, but then he snorted and lunged at me, flailin his paws, like a bitch, slappin me in the face. Durin the exchange, one of his claws scratched my cheek, drawin blood. The next flurry was a little more even—he got a good jab in on me and I landed a hook and an uppercut, but mostly, we were blockin.

After a minute or so, we started really mixin it up. I woulda floored im if he didn't have that uncanny ability ta throw his head back. I connected though, with a solid right cross, makin him woozy, and then it happened. I was square in front of him, ready ta finish im off, when somehow he leaned all the way back on his tail, brought up his legs, and kicked me, square in the nuts! It was like hittin "fast forward" on the DVD—I went from standin there ta lyin on my back in a fraction of a second. I thought we were boxin, but he went all UFC on me.

Pow! Pow! That was exactly the openin my father needed. Before I knew anything, the shotgun exploded with a cloud of white smoke and Buster was down for the count, and then some. Lookin at the poor kangaroo, I felt sad for him. Insteada bein shot like that, he shoulda been back at home in Australia, fendin off dingos and crocodiles. We had ta wrap im in a big blanket and deliver him ta one of The Dwarf's friends in Pasadena.

My father told me that big-shot Hollywood producer—he woke up the next mornin sleepin next ta Buster's severed head. He said the man freaked out and then he gave the green light so Pauli Mazzola could make another lousy movie. I was sad. What a waste of a life! What a waste of film, and time, and money! Pauli Mazzola and his stupid movies!

Lolita

Back at home, we had an appointment ta see The Dwarf at Vinny's. Naturally, I was a little reluctant ta go, because I hadn't seen Lolita since that night we saw each other. She made me promise I'd come back the next night, but I was traumatized, convinced that if somehow I wasn't up ta a repeat performance, she'd tear it off me and devour it.

I bowed my head and went straight back ta The Dwarf's booth, hopin she didn't see me.

"What's wrong with ya, Michael?" my father asked, as he eased inta the booth beside me. "Ya just disrespected your uncle, Tommy Rotten—he was tryin ta talk ta ya, but ya ignored im. And ya almost knocked The Dwarf down when ya blew right past im!"

Marcelino showed up a moment later, a bit disheveled, but clearly agitated about the near take-down.

"Whatsamatta you? Ran right inta me, ya moron!" he said. "Oh, *now* I remember! Ya were at *Lolita's* house last week."

My dad instantly shot me a disapprovin glare that made me shrink in the seat and The Dwarf wagged his head, curious.

"I donno what ya *did* ta her, but she's all changed—wearnin her hair down an all, and if she was a bold little kitty before, she's a ferocious tiger now. Keeps callin herself a 'taker.' *You* know anything about that, Michael Ponzi? Oh, and I think she's a little pissed off at ya for not callin."

"Are ya *crazy*?" my dad whispered under his breath.

"Ta top *that* off," Marcelino continued, "Carlito's tellin everyone ya stole his girl, that you got Lolita inta that bondage shit that these women are allofa sudden gettin inta, that ya made her tie ya down ta the bed and turned her inta a freak."

My dad bowed his head, almost embarrassed.

"Is this *true*, Michael?"

There could be no satisfactory answer, so I said nothin. I looked toward The Dwarf.

"I just went by cuz she invited me ta dinner. The rest of it was all her. I had no idea! Can you help me out here, *Padrino*?"

"Her mother is my wife's twin sister, so I ain't involved. But I'll tell ya this—if she's anything like her mother, ya piss her off and it'll definitely end in blood: yours. More dangerous than shotguns—all three of em! I told ya when ya started this: ya mess up, and you're on your own. Now let's get down ta business."

He took out a folder, opened it and read, his glasses pushed down his nose.

"This next job is very important, Dominic—highly sensitive, involvin potential consequences for a certain unnamed government official who is important ta the family—ya know, essential ta operations. If he goes down, it'll set us back years and leave us open ta unspecified problems we don't need. *Capiche?*

He slid a thin stack of papers toward my father. There was a photo of a buildin clipped in the front.

"FBI Crime Lab, Quantico, Virginia, Marine Corps Base. Your job'll be ta get in there."

"What are we takin out?" my father asked.

"Beetles."

My father nodded.

"Creophilus beetles? Like last time?"

As The Dwarf sat back, he inadvertently slipped off his perch, disappearin under the table top briefly. When he tried ta right himself, he bumped the back of his head on the underside of the table, and then after stumblin, he bumped his head again. I woulda been dead if I had laughed! He played it off by pretendin ta go back inta his briefcase. When he finally got resituated, he had a picture of a bunch of small green bugs.

"Naw, Dominic, this time it's the Histers—Hister beetles, cuz they're guessin the body was buried in a shallow grave on the government official's property the day before they were able ta get over there ta search the grounds. Usin thermal imagin, they were able ta zero in on a place where they *thought* the missin federal agent was buried. In the dirt, they found maggots and then they found the Hister beetles that eat the maggots. Preservin the beetles in all their stages, they're figurin ta prove the time of death *and* the fact that somethin the size of a man—in this case the agent—was buried out there on the property."

"So we gotta figure a way ta get in there, locate the preserved and the live beetles, and take em out?" my father asked.

"Ya got it! We got the two of you a way in there as janitors. We got location, badges, door codes, everything ya need. All ya gotta do is go in there and do what ya do. Easy money."

When the meetin was over, I tried ta slip out the booth and out the back door, but Lolita surprised me, standin outside.

"Somehow I get the feelin you're tryin ta *avoid* me," she said. "Ya stood me up, and ya won't even answer my calls! As the chick in the movie said it, 'I'm not gonna be *ignored*, Michael!' I'm expectin ya at my house tonight—seven o'clock, ready ta put out. Ya understand? I was *happy* the other night, but ya better show up tanight, unless you wanna see what I'm like when I'm *angry*."

She had me pinned back against the outside wall, her breasts smashing against me, her nose touchin mine.

"Lolita—I can't! I *want* ta, but The Dwarf's got me and my dad out on a job tonight. I, I don't wanna see you angry, but I don't wanna see your uncle mad at you for makin me miss an important job."

I just stood there as she took inventory of my body parts. I pleaded with her.

"Ask The *Dwarf* if you don't believe me! I can't tell you what the job is because it's top secret mob business. I mean, the future of the whole mob is at stake!"

"*Right*—and they got *you* on it?"

"My dad, actually, but I'm on a special, a very special job with him. Ya gotta believe me!"

She was gropin me in broad daylight, in public. No shame.

"I believe you, but there's always *tomorra* night. You gonna come see me tomorra? Ya gonna take cara me tomorra?"

"I will!" I answered, just wantin ta get away from her. "I'll be there tomorrow at seven."

Pinnin my arms against the wall, she kissed me, forcin her tongue inside my mouth.

"Oh, you're so cute! How could I stay mad at you? But you better have your ass over at my house tomorra night, ya *got* it?"

"I got it!"

By that time, I was hopin ta maybe trip and fall into a vat of *flesh-eatin* beetles ta put me outa my misery. Never in my life had I been so terrified of a woman! So ladies—just a word of advice: don't come on too strong. Ya don't wanna be a Lolita!

Pinched!

My dad and I flew inta the airport at Stafford, rented a van and took I-95 north ta the Marine Corps base at Quantico. True ta his word, The Dwarf had us supplied with fake IDs and badges, so we had no problem gettin by the sentries and inta the place. Usin a schematic for the facility and a diagram of the buildin, we located the room containin the vault where the Hister beetles and beetle larvae were stored.

For some reason, my father had been actin a little squirrelly for the entire day, sayin somethin just didn't *feel* right. He explained that he'd been on many jobs, but while everything *seemed* ta be goin perfect, somethin didn't smell right.

"My father always said, *Too good is no good!*" he warned. "*If you ever think it's too good to be true, it is!* I smell a set-up. Your ma had a dream last night!"

We were standin in the vault, where we had just discovered that all the beetles and larvae were missin. When the doors slammed open and a dozen federal agents, armed with semi-automatic weapons and riot gear entered, rifles pointed at my father, screamin orders that we should get down on the ground, we complied.

"Dominic Ponzi!" the lead agent declared. "We've been after you for some time. You are good, but now we got you. Of course we can make this all go away and no one has to know about it, you know, if you *help* us out. We never had any beetles. That was just a story we put out there."

After cuffin us, the agents raised us ta our feet. My dad seemed unfazed.

"Illegal entry? I guess ya got *somethin*, but then I'm just a confused old man who took a wrong turn while drivin and ended up here."

"This is federal property, a military base, Ponzi, and you came in here to destroy critical evidence for a federal trial."

"Ya yourself said it's evidence that *never* existed—right, Genius?"

Lackin a comeback, the agent said nothin, so my father continued.

"So I'm just an old man who got *lost*. Sorry for the trouble. Would ya mind uncuffin me?"

Seemin confused, the agent started talkin on the inline mic attached to his earpiece.

"Yes sir, Agent O'Brien. They're detained. You got em."

He spoke ta the other agents.

"Okay, let's clear out!"

O'Brien? I made the connection as the small militia filed out of the room. *It couldn't be!* But it was. The man who entered wasn't a man at all—it was my cousin, Patrick. My father's instincts were dead-on. From the time Patrick was a little ginger kid, Dad always said he was a *too goodster* who would someday be a big pain in the ass. Alone with us, Patrick smiled.

"Hi, Uncle Dominic. Michael? So I take it you've joined the mob? Ma and Granma will be so disappointed."

Dad was quick ta make a pitch.

"Patrick, obviously there's been some sort of misunderstandin here. We got *lost!* Believe me, we'll *all* be better off if you just let us go. Make up a story—whatever. Just uncuff us and get us *outa* here."

Patrick just shook his head.

"It's not goin to work that way tonight, Uncle Dominic. They *need* you. I don't want to piss Aunt Claire off, so I can let Michael go, but my bosses—they want to make a deal with *you*. And since you happened to get *lost* on federal property, they've made it clear they want to *keep* you."

He turned me around and removed my cuffs.

"Listen Michael, *you* were never here. I'll have a guard escort your van to the front gate and you'll be on your own from there. Consider this a mulligan on the eighteenth hole of the last course you ever want to play. And by the way, I'm tellin Ma on you, and Granma. You're too *smart* for the mob business. Get out before you're in over your head."

So I had ta return the car and fly back ta New Jersey without my father. I wasn't sure who I was more afraid ta talk ta—my Ma, or The Dwarf. Either way, it was gonna be hard ta explain. They were both gonna be mad and they would find some way ta blame me, when the truth was that *someone* had tipped off the FBI that we were comin. And if my father was right about smellin a set-up, someone in The Dwarf's organization was a rat who was workin for the feds.

****

"I was startin to get worried, Michael. Where's your father?"

I had spent the last eight hours rehearsin what I was gonna tell her, but seein the vulnerability in her face, the intuitive discernment that came from bein married ta a man for thirty years, I knew she would be able ta see right through any lie or any excuse. I had ta tell her the truth.

"He got pinched."

"Pinched? What do you mean, 'pinched'?"

"*Arrested, busted, taken down,* I guess. We were on the job, when somethin went wrong. The feds nabbed im. Patrick, my cousin and your nephew—he was in on it. He let me go on your account."

Oh, then came the tears! It ripped my heart in two ta see Ma cryin like that. She lost it—waterworks and snot. I tried ta hug her ta comfort her, but she pushed me away.

"Forty years!" she screamed. "You bastard!"

"What?"

"Forty years! He's been doin the same thing for forty years! And he never had no trouble! But he takes you on *one* job and he gets arrested by the feds! I *told* him this mornin—after I had my dream—the *universe* told me this mob job ain't for you! It's goin ta work out bad for you and anyone who has anything to do with you—until you fulfill your true callin. That goes double for Marcelino the Midget. You have to be true to who you are."

Marcelino! I thought. I knew my Ma would cry, but The Dwarf—he was gonna see the arrest as a liability ta him and the family. I wouldn't ta put it *past* im ta order someone ta take out my dad ta make sure he didn't talk. But he had ta know my father was a professional who was loyal ta the family. He'd never talk! He was too smart for that.

"You go ta see Marcelino," my Ma said. "You tell im he *owes* your dad! His family owes *our* family—alltheway back to your great uncle Carlo. You tell im it's his fault he sent your father into a set-up. You *tell* him that! You tell im your Ma wants her husband back—now!"

"Ma?"

I had never seen her so angry, so threatenin.

"You tell that midget—if he doesn't have Dominic out of there by tomorrow night, I'm comin down there to kick his ass! And believe me, it'll be worse than that time in second grade!"

"I can't tell him that!"

"You *tell* him that!" she demanded. "Tell im I said, 'Don't *make* me come down there!'"

Tommy Rotten

I did not wanna go anywhere *near* Vinny's, for obvious reasons, but I had ta go. After all, my father was in FBI custody, and I had ta get ta someone who had some real juice. The Dwarf was the one who sent us ta Virginia. He set the whole thing up. And so somehow, he had missed somethin—either that or he was in on the set-up in the first place. But why would he do that?

I think I heard somewhere that bosses like The Dwarf—sometimes, when a major figure like my father was gettin ready ta retire—the boss would send im on a job where he would get pinched, so the boss didn't have ta pay out retirement, 401K and health care benefits. It was a win-win between the mob and the FBI. The particular agent could show the top brass that he was earnin his pay and perks, and the boss was off the hook for the retirement.

So I made a few phone calls, and that's when I found out that Tommy Rotten, who was like family ta me, was gay. A year earlier, they say he blasted the closet door clean off its hinges. I never made the connection before, ya know. He always had the rose in the lapel, always wearin cologne, always groomed, and he was always goin on about my dad, always tellin me how handsome he was, but yeah, he was gay, and openly gay. In fact, he was the first straight-up gay mobster I ever met, but he was a tough guy—none of that limp-wrist shit.

Uncle Tommy had real juice, since he was related ta the Carzanos by marriage and ta the powerful Tuscano family by blood. Besides that, he was one hundred percent Sicilian, if there was ever such a thing. He wasn't really my actual uncle, but I had called him Uncle Tommy since I was a kid.

"Problem with The Dwarf and his dad before im," Tommy told me, "is you can't *trust* em. I mean, his dad, Marco Bello, before he retired—Marco Bello was a businessman, respected on Wall Street and all over the place. But the Carzanos as mobsters—ya might as well be dealin with the distant relative who they always brag about. For years they been sayin the Carzanos are somehow descended from Niccolò Machiavelli."

"What? Really, Uncle Tommy?" I interrupted. "Machiavelli from Florence was The Dwarf's relative?"

"Sure as spit was, Michael. Some kinda great, great grandfather or uncle, goin back ta the 1500s. Family's always been ruthless, but throw in a healthy mix of Sicilian blood, and you got Marcelino and his dad, Marco. They look tame, but they're monsters underneath—real snakes, or rats."

"Okay. So goin back, did my ma really kick The Dwarf's ass?"

"Hell yeah! I was there," Tommy laughed. "Cheeky Claire O'Brien! Fifth grade—I flunked twice, so I was there. *I* was the one who pulled her off im. She had im in a headlock, just bustin im in the nose, but that was after takin im down with a flyin forearm and knockin the wind outa him with an inverted atomic drop body slam and a facebreaker knee smash. Yeah, I mean she *really* kicked his ass!"

"So ya think my dad gettin pinched might be payback for that?" I asked.

"Naw! Your dad is just *married* ta your mom. If there was any kinda payback, it would hafta be against *you*, cuz you're her blood. It's gotta be against the blood. Believe me—the Carzanos are my in-laws. I know how Marcelino thinks. With your dad, maybe The Dwarf is doin the same thing that some folks said his dad did before him."

"What's that?"

Uncle Tommy leaned in, lowerin his voice.

"Ya didn't hear this from me, but Marco Bello, ya know the name they call Marcelino's father—accordin ta rumors, Marco Bello was best friends with your grandfather, until your grandfather stole his girl, who became your grandmother. So anyway, while Marco Bello didn't take that too well, they had business together, profitable business. Your dad's good, no doubt, but your grandfather, Guido, was just plain *clever*! *All* the Ponzi's have been that way—clever."

Tommy had ta stop ta daub his eyes on account of the video we were watchin at his house. The movie was *King of New York*, with Christopher Walken playin the drug lord who steals all the drugs, kills all the cops, kills all the bad guys and then dies like a mook in a cab. Tommy Rotten said he'd watched the movie over fifty times, and still, he always cried at the end. I didn't *get* it.

Uncle Tommy apparently wasn't always gay. His wife, Octavia, was a real looker when she was younger, but bein a Carzano, Marcelino's sister, she was a shrew. All I remember from when I was younger is that she complained about everything, from Cousin Tony's weight to Tommy's lack of stamina. By that I'm not sayin it was something about her that turned my Uncle Tommy the other way, but it coulda made him kinda peek across the street.

Anyway, Tommy blew his nose and then continued on about The Dwarf's father.

"If Marco Bello was anything, he was vain. He never forgave your father for stealin his girl. In fact, he always said that if he had married your *grandmother*, Marcelino never woulda been born a midget, which has always been kinda embarrassin ta Marco. If Marco had married your grandmother, then Marcelino woulda been *normal-sized*, and not a midget at all. Marco always blamed your grandfather for that, for Marcelino bein a little man and all.

"When your grandfather Guido wanted ta retire, they say Marco Bello set im up by sendin him on a greyhound hit job in Cleveland, where Eliot Ness had this gamblin sting goin on. So Guido Ponzi just kinda walked inta a set-up—charged and convicted for murderin an FBI informant, when everyone knew your grandpa never whacked a human in his entire life!"

He could tell I had made the connection as he raised his eyebrows, whisperin.

"He got ridda your grandfather, who went ta the pen for life, and Marco Bello never paid out any retirement benefits ta your grandfather or your family. And what really stinks—he never helped your grandmother or any of the family out—payback for her pickin Guido over him.

"So when your father got pinched, there was alotta whisperin around Vinny's about history *repeatin* itself. Goin alltheway back ta Italy, there's always been bad blood between your family and the Carzanos. Some of em are sayin Quantico was a set-up, meant ta put your father outa the picture, without havin ta pay benefits ta your ma. *That's* The Dwarf's payback on her for kickin his ass!"

I didn't know what ta think, especially after I got a call from The Dwarf, orderin me ta come over ta Vinny's right away. He said it was an emergency and that I had ta come alone. I mean, who did he think I was gonna bring? *My ma?*

****

I resisted it, but I had ta figure somethin out before I got there, or else who knows what I woulda been walkin inta? Lolita!—she was my ace in the hole. I knew she had this fixation with me, and she was The Dwarf's niece. If anyone had the inside dope about my father, she'd know how ta get ta it. And all I would hafta do is put out in a big way. I resolved I would do whatever it would take… for my father.

I didn't expect it ta be so awkward, though. When I knocked on the door, Carlito the Ass answered, demandin for me ta tell him what I was doin there. Then when Lolita saw me, she got im his coat and kicked him outa her house. His beggin did no good. It only made her call him "pathetic" as she pushed him out, dragged me in and started takin off her clothes.

"You were just fillin in, Carlito, ya know, pinch-hittin, but *now* I want a real man!"

So Carlito stood outside the window, starin through the slats like a puppy dog, while Lolita put on a provocative show inside. We both watched the black-leather-and-lace strip tease, tan legs in the air, high heels teasin, hips gyratin, breasts quiverin, hypnotizin—sexual, tingly poetry in motion!

She approached me, purred, growled and bit me on the neck before shuttin the slats on Carlito, in tears, forlorn. And when she opened her bedroom door, all I could see was a 360-degree spinnin, fetish, love sex swing, suspended from an eyebolt in the ceilin, just ta the left of the bed.

"I better get my spurs, cuz I'm goin for a *ride*!"

Three hours later, I was bloody and broken, cringin and whimperin over the wounds on my arms, legs and back. I glanced down, relieved that I had survived the ordeal still intact.

"Now, I want you ta tie *me* up, Michael, and *spank* me!"

I didn't think hittin her was a good idea, especially after she set up a camera ta videotape parts of the action here and there. Through it all, I figured I had earned the right ta ask a few questions about my old man.

"Word on the streets is that The Dwarf set my father up, like his father set my father's father up. He's your uncle. What do ya know?"

I wasn't sure she was gonna talk without a little motivation, so I smacked her in the ass real hard, partly outa payback and partly because it just kinda felt good ta do it.

"Ooh, I love it! *Harder* next time, okay? I know my uncle wants ta see ya, and it's supposed ta be a big-time emergency. I dunno if he set your father up, but he ain't worried about that right now. Don't tell im ya was here, cuz I don't want im mad at me. Whatever he has ta tell ya, maybe it has ta do with gettin your father out. Ya need ta get on over ta Vinny's when I'm done with ya."

I hit her again, and harder because what she said was shit for an answer. Three long, gruelin hours with a ragin Succubus for *that* crappy piece of advice? I had ta press the issue, so a smacked her again, this time makin a red imprint of my hand.

"What about my *father*, Lolita? Have you heard anything about Marcelino settin im up?"

Smack! Smack! Smack!—my arm drawn back with rage and passion!

"Ooh, I *love* you, Michael Ponzi! Next time use the leather strap! Oh! I *wouldn't* put it past my uncle. He learned the business from his father. Marco Bello is a damn great-lookin man—even still, but he's one big, selfish, greedy asshole! He's my great uncle, so I'm allowed ta *say* that. Again! Now tie up my wrists and put em over the pole."

Playin on the dominance that was workin up ta that point, I smacked her a few more times, that time with the leather strap because she begeed me to, and I just kinda followed her kinky orders for another thirty minutes. Worn out from the workout, I went for my clothes, kissed her (bitin her lip hard enough ta draw blood), untied her and slipped out the front door.

When I got ta my car, I knew somethin wasn't quite right, but when the windshield of the car behind me shattered after three explosions, I realized someone was shootin at me, and doin his best ta *hit* me! Carlito! That ass! That's also when I realized that all four of the tires on my car were flat, and from the look the liquid that trailed out from under the car, the brake lines were probably cut. If that wasn't bad enough, I noticed what looked like a live wire, rigged inta the ignition—with the other end attached ta a package that was most likely an explosive.

Afraid for my life, I hid behind a dumpster, but I had that meetin with Marcelino loomin. I didn't know what else ta do, especially with bullets flyin, so I called my ma. *Good move!* As soon as she came, the bullets stopped.

Zenobia

It was gettin dark by the time Ma dropped me off at Vinny's, and once I got in, everyone seemed ta be actin like I was in some kinda trouble. I had no idea what I had done wrong. I just happened ta be with my father when he got pinched. It wasn't my fault. Maybe it was part of the set-up, where I would get blamed for incompetence ta help take the guilt and suspicion off The Dwarf, who probably was the main player in the Machiavellian deal.

When I got back ta the booth, four bodyguards were standin by, makin sure no one could enter or wander inta the area where The Dwarf was waitin on me. Ta look at his face, ya'd think he needed ta take a big shit, that it was all backin up inside im, all ninety-two pounds of im. He seemed unusually dark, and angry.

"I call for ya, Michael, and it takes ya six *hours* ta come by and see me?"

"I'm sorry, Marcelino. I had ta deal with my ma first."

He softened.

"Oh! Yeah, yeah. I get that. I can understand that. Sit down."

When I was settled inta the booth, he leaned toward me, lowerin his voice.

"Look, I called you cuz we got an *emergency* goin on here."

I sighed.

"Yeah we do. Have you heard from im? Did ya send a lawyer? When's he gettin out?"

"What the hell are ya *talkin* about, Michael?"

"My *father*. Aren't *you*?"

I paused for a second, confused. Maybe he didn't *know*!

"Ya *do* know he got pinched when we went ta Quantico?"

"Yeah, yeah. Your father'll be fine. I didn't call ya down here for that. We got a real *situation* here."

Real situation? It was obviously somethin more important than my dad gettin nabbed by the feds, somethin more important than him bein held who knows where, or what the FBI, RICO or dirty government operatives had in store for im.

"What is it?"

"I got a special job for ya, Michael" The Dwarf said, his face reddened and angry. "I wish your father was here for this, but he isn't, so it's gotta be *you*."

"What job?"

The Dwarf slammed his fist on the table. I had never seen him so upset.

"I'm so pissed off I can't even *talk*! Brain—*ya* tell im. Ya was there!"

Alphonso the Brain was standin next ta the booth, tryin ta calm The Dwarf down. The whole time, Brain was whisperin under his breath, reasonin with the little boss, tryin ta keep im outa trouble."

"Ya just can't do what ya said, Boss. She's too big a name—worth too much. The Management ain't havin it. You mess around, and you go down, the family goes down, we *all* go down. Do you think there *wouldn't* be an investigation and all kinds of hell ta pay? Not ta mention, her crazy fans would tear ya apart. And the family would disown ya, disavow your actions. They'd *have* ta!"

The message finally began ta resonate.

"They'd send someone after me. They'd hafta shoot me *dead* in the street."

"Now you're *listenin*," Alphonso smiled. "Now you're *finally* makin some sense!"

The Dwarf groaned.

"Aw, I just can't believe the nerve of that bingo-bongo eggplant *broad*! You *heard* what she said ta me! I gotta make her pay! Somehow I gotta make that big-assed moolie black crow-bitch pay for havin the nerve ta disrespect me like that, and in public! I *got* it! I know what I'll do. I want that pampered poochie of hers dead by this time tomorra! That'll teach her."

He looked toward me.

"I want you ta *kill* her spoiled, pampered little rat dog! And I want you ta bring me its head tomorra. Yeah, on a silver platter."

"What, what happened?" I ventured with much trepidation.

"You guys can leave now," The Dwarf said, speakin ta his guards. "Brain—slide on in there next ta Michael. *You* tell im what happened."

Only after the guards had cleared the back area of the restaurant did Alphonso begin.

"Ya see, Michael, we was at the mall, *The Winchester*, on a shoppin trip for Sofia, Marcelino's granddaughter. It was her tenth birthday, so The Dwarf wanted ta take her out ta buy a few things, ya know. Spoil her a little."

"Okay…" I nodded, confused about where he was goin with it—but then again, he was The Brain.

"So we're shoppin, see. Marcelino bought Sofia a new bedroom set at Nordstrom, a wallet and purse at Coach, sunglasses at Gucci, some make-up at Mac, a few outfits at Neiman Marcus and a custom 'terrific ten' pearl necklace at Tiffany and Company."

"Yeah, I get it, Fonso. You guys went shoppin. So what happened?"

Alphonso the Brain was a true genius. He gave alotta detail—usually too *much* detail, so I hadta cut im off. I just wanted ta know what all of it had ta do with a dog's head on a silver platter and why it was so much more important than my dad. He seemed a little offended, but he got ta the point.

"Okay, so we're at the mall, and who comes in? It's Zenobia—*the* Zenobia, with her full posse of hangers-ons and gang-member bodyguards."

"Waitaminute!" I interrupted. "You mean Zenobia, the singer?—the number one R&B/pop singer in the world? This is about *her*?"

"Yeah, it's about her," The Dwarf answered, still seethin. The Brain continued.

"She came inta Tiffany's when we was there—lookin for a ring. So Sofia sees her and goes all apeshit crazy ta meet her. And Zenobia really took a likin ta Sofia too, ya know, like right away. She signed an autograph and all, and she told Sofia she could come backstage if she could make it ta the concert. Said Sofia could bring alla her friends."

"So what was the problem?"

"Everything was goin fine until Sofia notices that Zenobia's got this dog in her purse, a little Yorkie named Mystique. So Sofia asks Zenobia if she could hold the dog and pet it, ta which Zenobia said 'sure.' And then, when Sofia goes ta get little Mystique, the little pooch allofa sudden has this unexpected 'episode'! She's growlin and foamin at the mouth, and just as Sofia goes ta take the dog, Mystique just goes all *Cujo* on her hand and arm—drew blood an all!"

Suddenly, I realized where it was all goin.

"So the dog bit her and Marcelino was pissed?"

"*Pissed* is way an understatement. Marcelino reached over and slapped the dog. Now of course, that didn't go over so well with

Zenobia. Now I don't know if she took the time ta think about it, but then she reached over and slapped Marcelino for slappin her dog, right on the toppa his head!"

Uh-oh!

"The both of ems, they's got egos, ya know. So Marcelino says, 'do you have any idea who I *am*?' ta which she answers, 'Bilbo Baggins—a damn *hobbit*! Do you have any idea who *I* am?'"

He paused ta let the effect of her words penetrate my own brain.

"That's right—Zenobia called Marcelino a *hobbit*. She called im a '*damn* hobbit,' in public—very humiliatin, very devastatin, very rude, cuz hobbits are disproportional for their size, like the dwarfs, and they have big, abnormal, hairy feet, which Marcelino ain't got. He wears shoes—size five, and his wife makes im get pedicures. Hobbits got no class—it was *bad*! But that ain't all.

"Get this—after he threatens her, after he tells her he's a mob boss and she won't live ta see the sunrise, she tells him and the Lollipop Guild ta go back ta the Munchkin city in the Land of Oz! Another insult! Cuz Munchkins, with them high voices, ain't got no balls, and no women want em. So then he says, "Ding Dong, this bitch is dead! And if she ever had any jelly in her fat ghetto ass when she was young and cute, it's now turned inta lumpy marmalade."

"Well, that was kinda weak," I admitted.

Lookin over at The Dwarf, I could tell he was even angrier on hearin The Brain's description of what happened.

"And that was *it*?"

"No," the Brain answered. "They argued back and forth for about ten minutes. And Zenobia, black broad, ya know—she could talk louder, roll her eyes better and snake her neck in rhythm, give that stank-eye. *Shrimp, Smurf, Mini-me!* She kinda got the best of Marcelino and had the people standin around laughin at im—and alla this in fronna his granddaughter, in fronna impressionable little Sofia. And then, when the reporters with cameras started showin up, we realized we had ta get outa there."

"So *that's* how it was left!" Marcelino added. "I can't let that black broad get *away* with that. Maybe I can't have *her* whacked, but I can definitely get that vicious little hyena whacked. I can call *that* shot! The family andeveryone'll understand. That bitch's little bitch dog bit my granddaughter and drew Carzano blood! I need ya ta go ta wherever it is she is and wherever she keeps her dog, and you *cut* that little shit dog's head off! Blood for blood! You got that? *Capiche?*"

I immediately realized I was bein put on the spot. I mean, how was I supposed ta get ta this dog? The Brain already said Zenobia had gang member bodyguards. Maybe the dog had gang member bodyguards too. And I had no idea where Zenobia lived.

"Here's the address, the code for the buildin and a key for the room where she'll be," Marcelino said, pushin me a notepad. "Ya gotta get over there tomorra tonight while she's doin her concert. I went through alotta trouble ta get those. And I paid sixty thou ta get the dog's guards ta be a little less responsible tomorra. You're gonna merk that dog, cut off its head and bring it here ta me, on a silver platter. Tomorra night, Michael, right?"

I had no choice but ta say, "Yeah, yeah," though I wasn't sure if I could do it. I figured he could see it in my face.

"Didn't you sit right there, Michael, in that seat across from me, and tell me two weeks ago you were a killer like your father before you and your grandfather before him? And didn't I tell you once you're in, you're in? I even bought cha a drink."

"Yeah ya *did, Padrino.*"

"Your father isn't here, and that's too bad, so all I got is you. Jake and Carlito lack the finesse and smarts for a job like this. They'd get us all in trouble."

After a lifetime in the mob business, The Dwarf could read a face or a heart like a flashin billboard.

"Come on, Michael, it's just a little shit-for-nothin dog, a big rat. One karate chop, one swift kick in the ass, and it's done. Then *whack!* with a cleaver or an ax—and bring me its little head."

He sensed my hesitation.

"Tell ya what. If you don't give me a little head by tommorra night, it'll be your life for that dog's…"

Alphonso laughed suddenly, haltin Marcelino in the middle of the threat.

"What, Brain? Is somethin funny here? Am I *funny?*"

"No, it was just what you s*aid,* Boss. It just came *out* kinda funny. I'm sorry."

"What I *say?*"

"Well, you told im if he didn't give you a little head by tomorra night... you know. It sounded funny. I was just imaginin—"

"Stop right there, Brain! Stop imaginin!" the midget warned (I can say "midget" in this case cuz he actually *was* a midget), but he continued, "I'll *kill* ya if ya imagin any further. I have a *wife*. We all *know* what I meant!"

And then he looked toward me.

"If you don't bring me that dog's head tomorra, *you're* dead. You're dead, and then I'll send Carlito the Ass over ta where the FBI has your father, and I'll have your *dad* whacked too."

I couldn't believe what The Dwarf had just said ta me. He was threatenin my and my father's life over a little head, a little dog's life.

Freeze the frame—*that* was the moment. *That was the moment I realized The Dwarf was probably gonna have me and my dad whacked anyway.* Our family history went way back all right, but it was *faida*—a family blood feud—probably goin all the way back ta my great uncle, Carlo Ponzi. The Dwarf was gonna end it by takin out the last two remainin Ponzi males in one whop, in one fell swoop, and he would get his revenge on Zenobia at the same time.

"But it doesn't hafta be like that, Michael," he said. "All ya gotta do is your job, and I'll pay ya fifty grand, half of it up front. Ya *gotta* do this, for the family, for me, and for poor little Sofia, who got mauled by that rabid little rat-mutt animal. Do this job, and we'll make sure your father is a free man tomorra night."

The Dwarf disappeared when he went ta stand, and then his tiny head appeared, just above the table top.

"Alphonso will give ya the down payment on the way out, in cash. You bring me that little dog's head. *Capiche?* Or things won't go so well for you... *or* for your father!"

Michael the Vet

I didn't know what ta tell my ma, so I lied. I told her The Dwarf was workin on cuttin a deal with the feds and that dad would be out in a day or so. It didn't take her long ta notice the bulge in the front of my pants.

"What's that? Is that *money*? So The Midget's got ya doin a job when we don't know what the hell's goin on with your father? What's he tryin ta do? Make sure the *both* of you are in jail? How much?"

I placed the bundles of Franklins on the table—two hundred fifty bills in all, separated in five stacks of fifty bills, three bundles from my jacket and two from my pants.

"Twenty-five thousand dollars, Ma. And he said he'd pay me the rest when the job was done."

"No," she protested. "You take that money back ta Marcelino, and you tell him you ain't doin nothing. You ain't doin no jobs at all until he shows you some kinda proof that he's found a way ta free your father. You take that money back ta him now!"

"It doesn't *work* like that, Ma" I sighed, waggin my head. "I don't have a *choice* here."

"Son, I musta told ya this every day when you were growin up, but somehow, ya *missed* it! Ya should go back ta church. Gift from God—you're a free moral agent. You *always* have a choice, Michael. Some of em ya just gotta think your way through. And sometimes you can win even when ya lose."

She eyed the cash on the table.

"Who does he want ya ta take out this time? A federal judge? The governor who shut down that bridge to New York?"

"You're close," I surrendered. "York *is* involved, cuz Marcelino wants me ta take out a Yorkie."

"A Yorkie, as in a *dog* Yorkie?" she sputtered.

"Yeah, but this is no ordinary Yorkie. This is the dog belongin ta Zenobia, who'll be doin a concert at Madison Square Garden tomorra night."

"You mean Zenobia, the *singer*? Marcelino wants you ta kill *her* dog? He's wearin his underwear too small, if that's possible! Why?"

"It's a long story. It's complicated."

"But you're a hitman for the *mob*, Michael. I don't like that you do it, but isn't this job he wants you to do *beneath* you? Isn't it an insult to you for him to ask for you, a hitman, to kill a *dog*?"

Apparently my father had kept her in the dark, so I wasn't about ta be the one ta turn on the light.

"It's a special favor," I explained, understandin why my father always quoted Michael Corleone. "You can't ask me about my business, Ma. You can't ask me about my business. It's a mob rule. We can't share with wives, and especially mothers."

"I saw that little dog on TV. Zenobia carries it *with* her everywhere. She had it when she was on *The View* on Tuesday. He wants you ta kill that poor little dog? What a cruel man that little Marcelino turned out ta be!"

I was silent. I wanted ta think, but my mother was gonna go on all night.

"Why don't you tell Marcelino to put Carlito Soranno on that job? He *likes* killin animals. Remember what he did at your Aunt Rachel's farm? Isn't he a hitman too? That would be a perfect job for Carlito."

"Enough, Ma! I can't *talk* about it. It's against the rules!"

"I raised you better'n that, Michael," she insisted. "Like I said earlier—you take that money back ta The Midget and you *tell* him you don't kill dogs, cats, women, children, grandparents, grandchildren, and most importantly, you don't kill innocents. You *tell* him that!"

****

It was all I could take! I got my computer bag from my room and put the money in there. I went and got my dad's car keys, kissed Ma "goodbye" and drove directly ta the neighborhood liquor store, where I bought a bottle of Bushmills, the whiskey my Irish grandfather and uncles started me out on. Then I drove on up ta Manhattan and rented a room at a seedy dive motel in midtown. There were roaches in the bathtub and there was rat poop along the floorboards, but I didn't care. I just needed ta be somewhere ta think.

Two weeks earlier, I never imagined I woulda been in such a crazy situation, with my father arrested and me bein pushed by the mob ta murder and mutilate a dog belongin ta a celebrity. Ma was right. I shoulda stayed away from the mob, and now I was in over my head. I had twenty-five thousand dollars cash in my computer bag. I thought about rentin a car and just drivin out ta California.

I couldn't do it. That would mean leavin my father in the lurch and gettin in bad with the mob, especially if I took off with their money. Where was my father? I needed his advice. I needed his wisdom. As sons, those of us who are fortunate enough ta have fathers in our lives spend alotta years takin em for granted. The wisdom of fathers is subtle, even in fathers who don't outwardly seem exceptionally wise, like mine. It is wisdom of experience and patience, a deep and abidin confidence, derived from the heightened perspective of time.

It was just a dog, after all—and not even as big as the rat I saw on the way in. I killed a rat once. Ma made me do it when it tried ta take over the kitchen. So I couldn't understand why I was havin such a problem with the thought of snuffin out a tiny dog. I spread the twenty-five thousand dollars out on the bed, its comforter pock-marked with cigarette and pot seed burns. All I had ta do was go in and kill that dog, chop off its head and deliver it ta The Dwarf. Then my father would get out and I would get another twenty-five thousand dollars cash. It was one day's work. I had never made fifty thousand dollars in an entire *year* in all my life!

But how was I supposed ta trust The Dwarf? especially after what I heard about his father, Marco Bello, and after it seemed he cared more about his revenge against a dog than he did my father in FBI custody! And I still couldn't believe he had threatened my father's and my life if I didn't go in there and merk that dog. Where was the loyalty for my father, and for my family?

I did some research on my laptop as I had ta figure out how I was gonna kill the dog. I wanted ta be humane, meanin I didn't want the little dog ta suffer. It had ta be somethin quick and painless. On one site, I read about different anesthetics I could use. It seemed the best bet was the diethyl ether. I saw it was available for purchase on Amazon and other websites, but the delivery would take two ta three days, when I needed ta do the hit within twenty-four hours.

An underground site recommended goin inta an auto supply store and buyin some premium grade startin fluid. If I sprayed enough of it ta drench a face cloth and put it over little Mystique's snout, she would immediately and possibly permanently pass out, meanin she wouldn't feel a thing when I chopped off her head. Of course that meant I would have ta figure out how I was gonna chop it off.

A big meat cleaver seemed like the best bet, if I could make it a clean blow against a solid surface. I thought about a turkey carver, but I was concerned about the dog's wiry hair tanglin up the blade and gettin stalled at the neckbone, and the amount of oozin blood that method would involve. With the cleaver, I could just put the dog out, chop, get the hell outa there, and it would be done. Yeah, that's what I would do.

I found a Pep Boys and an AutoZone in the area for the starter fluid and a Target where I could get a cheap cleaver. The concert was set ta start at 7:30, but Zenobia wasn't supposed ta go on until 9:00. The Dwarf bribed her bodyguards ta get her itinerary. She was leavin the hotel at 6:30 and not set ta get back until after midnight, so I had five and a half hours ta get the job done.

My next Internet search led me ta Zenobia videos. Even before, I knew she was really pretty—no, she was drop-dead gorgeous, but I never realized how truly endowed she was. I mean, she could move her divinely shapely body in ways that were unreal—hypnotic. And what an ass! She was like a combination of porn star fantasy, belly dancers, strippers and a Broadway chorus line, all rolled inta one, only better. She was just so sexy, and talented too, and she had an incredible voice! I never thought in a million years I would have anything ta do with her, and here I was, the one killin her dog. I would be killin somethin she *cared* about. At least we had a connection!

I fell asleep watchin her, fantasizin about her, though I realized she'd hate me when and if she ever found out it was me who merked little Mystique. But what the heck? Bad publicity was better'n no publicity. At least she would know who I was. I wished things coulda been different though. She really *was* a beautiful woman. She was a jaguar, but a different *kind* of jaguar.

****

Only after mornin came did I realize how completely dilapidated the room and the entire buildin was. There were rat holes along the floor, a network connectin all the rooms for them. In the light of day, I saw the irregular stains on the bedspread, on the headboard and on adjacent walls. I could tell they were the results of dried-up slime, or some other gross bodily emission. The carpet probably hadn't been vacuumed in years, the toilet was permanently stained brown and there was no hot water.

Yet in spite of all that, I told the foreigner at the desk I was gonna keep the room for another night. I had no idea what kinda mood I would be in when I finished the job, and I didn't wanna go back ta Ma and hafta answer a bunch of her questions. After the job, I figured I really *could* move ta California, if that's what I wanted. When the dog was dead, the family would get my dad out, I'd have fifty thousand dollars and we could *both* move beyond the mob, but only if we could trust The Dwarf, whom I realized I didn't trust at all!

****

Zenobia was stayin at the Waldorf Astoria, a five-star New York City hotel on Park Avenue near Broadway and Central Park, so it wasn't far away. But all I had for wardrobe was what I was wearin, blue jeans and a hoodie. Maybe I was bein a little overly-cautious, but I was thinkin my outfit would draw a little undue attention and suspicion in that ritzy hotel.

Money back in the bag, I headed for the Fashion District, or Garment District, whatever. It was in Manhattan, in that area between Fifth and Ninth Avenues, from Thirty-Fourth ta Forty-Second Streets. I went there in search for a gay guy who could help me shop, cuz ya know, no one knows how ta dress a man better than a gay guy.

Ironically of course, the quasi random gay guy I found was black, cuz black gay guys, with all their histrionics, the sass, the funny expressions and the finger-poppin—they just seemed *gayer* than the white gay guys. So I met up with a gay black named Stanky Stanley, who agreed ta "make me so sharp, my own *razors* would get jealous."

We shopped for about three hours, and I'll admit, Stanky had his shit together. He got me a suit, shoes, socks, a pocket handkerchief, a shirt, tie, watch, cologne, wallet, sunglasses, a leather shoulder bag and a gold-plated condom carrier. I got everything for under a thousand dollars, so I tipped Stanky three hundred. It was well worth it. When I was droppin im back off, I couldn't help but ask.

"So, Stanky, you got a little money now. You goin ta the concert tonight? What do ya think about Zenobia?"

"Oh Zenobia? *That's* ma girl! Girlfriend got some moves!"

That's when he broke out inta the song and dance. I mean, he was singin and dancin just like her—exact same moves. But we were in a public place, so I was a little embarrassed.

"That's enough. That's fine, Stanky."

"Wanna see me twerk? Work it?"

"Definitely not."

"Did I tell you me and Zenobia are *related*?" he asserted, with a final hip thrust.

"You didn't," I returned, surprised. "How are you related ta her?"

"Well, my brother baby mama did this family tree thang on the Internet—Zenobia cousin is the nephew of ma Uncle Joe father cousin—at least that's what she told me. So I been tryin ta get a family reunion together, cuz I figure Zenobia would *definitely* be there. We could bust our moves together for the talent show."

When he started dancin again, I tipped im another Franklin and asked im ta please stop. I gave im my cell number and told im ta call me when the concert got over—cuz I'd be there, and maybe we could go get breakfast or somethin. Then I gave him a ride ta the Theater District, where the scalpers were standin out there, sellin tickets.

"Thanks for everything, Stanky, and make *sure* you call me when the show's over."

Mystique

I arrived at the Waldorf at about six o'clock, all dressed up, and went ta get a drink ta kill time. They had a couple bars in the place, but I went ta the one with the big cow at the top of everything. Stanky warned me about the prices, and he was right. I coulda *bought* a bottle of Irish whiskey for what they charged me for one drink. I was seated next ta a really pretty blonde who flirted a little, but looked really familiar. When I asked if she was someone special, she told me she owned the place. That was good for a laugh, but she wasn't laughin.

Anyway, when 6:30 came, I thanked her for the second drink and grabbed my leather shoulder bag, containin the whiskey, two cans of premium grade startin fluid, the face cloth, the cleaver and the gallon-sized Ziploc bag for the head—so it wouldn't be bleedin all over the place once I got it. Oh, and I also put the 9mm Glock I got from Jimmy the Weasel in the bag, just in case. I found courage in the whiskey.

Alphonso told me ta go ta the front desk, where a hotel employee who looked like Jay Leno would provide me with a room key, while the private security company would reassign the guards, givin me at least a one-hour window ta get in there, get the head and get out. The Dwarf thought of everything, except for the doggie nanny, who showed up at 6:35 with a doggie companion and a doggie bag containin a steak in it from the restaurant downstairs.

When they told The Dwarf about the nanny, he sent over phony cop ta approach the nanny down at the reservation desk, where she was askin for a key ta the room. After pretendin ta run her ID, the fake cop arrested her, took her phone and drove her somewhere ta keep her away from the hotel for a few hours to give me time ta do the job.

With all the commotion involvin the nanny and a second effort ta shift and reassign guards, I didn't get inta the room until after 9:30, almost 9:45. And just as soon as I got in the door, Mystique started yappin at me and growin at me. I put my shoulder bag down, and when I went ta grab her, she bit my finger, drawin blood, and ran under the bed. The room had a king-sized bed, so every time I tried ta reach under there ta get her, she'd bite me again and scramble ta the other side.

After thirty minutes of the under-bed chase, I decided ta change tactics. Mystique was a dog, after all, so I knew I was smarter than she was. I didn't have anything in my shoulder bag but the things necessary ta the job, so I looked around the room for snacks that Zenobia kept around ta reward or treat the dog. Bingo! She had some kinda bacon-flavored doggie treats.

Takin the bag, I got on my knees, offerin Mystique a treat. I tried ta talk very gently and very nice, so she wouldn't feel threatened. Finally, after about thirty *more* minutes, she took one the treats, but only after I put it down and backed way off. She really liked the treats, but she didn't trust me, so I worked really hard ta earn her trust. I was like a motivational speaker for a dog, *a Yorkie whisperer.*

Over time, she came closer and closer ta me. One time, she even licked the blood off my finger. Another thirty minutes, and she was eatin outa my hand. I didn't even hafta grab er. After a while, she came out and crawled inta my lap, almost purrin while she licked my hand. All I had ta do was spray the startin fluid inta the towel, put it on her face and get the job done.

The problem was she *trusted* me. I had earned her trust, and she had given it. So ta betray her trust like that, ta snuff her out with the startin fluid, seemed a little wrong. In retrospect, I shoulda just took the gun and shot her, but somehow we had kinda bonded in that hotel room that night.

It was a no-brainer. I couldn't leave that room until I had the dog's head in my bag, but my heart was makin a case for some kinda compromise. What if I went out and bought *another* Yorkie— one I *hadn't* bonded with, and what if I cut *that* dog's head off and gave it ta The Dwarf? Only problem there—he'd see Zenobia out with Mystique the next time she made an appearance. Okay, I *had* ta kill the dog, nevermind betrayin the trust. When she was dead, she wouldn't know any different.

So I took out one of the cans of startin fluid and sprayed it inta the towel. It was cold, wet and had a strong petroleum distillate smell. But when I went ta put it on her face, she just kinda looked up at me with pitiful eyes, pitiful because they held so much trust in me. I closed my eyes and went ta apply the cloth anyway, but she then started lickin my hand, meltin my heart again.

Thinkin only of my father, I finally built up the resolve ta do it. I sprayed the cloth one more time and I firmly placed it over

Mystique's nose. Within seconds, she was unconscious. She was breathin, but it was real slow and shallow. As so gently liftin her, I carried her ta the bathroom floor, which was made outa some kinda stone, which I determined was the best surface for choppin off her head. Then I went back ta the bed, where I retrieved the cleaver from my bag.

When I got back ta the bathroom, it hit me. It was a cruel betrayal. How could I chop off that little dog's head when she had trusted me? But ta not chop off her head would mean I would die. So was I willin ta trade her life for mine? And worse, was I *also* willin ta trade my father's life for the life of a dog who acted irresponsibly and viciously, bitin a child?

That's when what my ma said finally sunk in. She had said ta me since I was a kid, "You *always* have a choice, Michael. Some of em ya just gotta think your way through." I didn't wanna kill the dog, and I didn't want me and my father ta die, but there had ta be a way ta think my way outa this thing. So as I headed back ta the bed ta swig the whiskey ta free my thoughts, I heard the sound of someone openin the door.

When it opened, Zenobia was standin there, flanked by two thug bodyguards who looked like twins, while I stood there with the cleaver in my hand. Instinctively, because I had played so many hours of *Call of Duty, Black Ops II*, I tossed the cleaver ta the bed and whipped out the 9mm Glock, pointin it toward the singer.

"Tell your guards ta back out the door and *close* it!"

Her hesitation emboldened me.

"Tell em ta do it now! Or I will definitely *shoot* your ass!"

The guards raised their hands and backed, openin the door.

"I'm a crazy, suicidal fan. You call the cops, and I'll kill her… and me. The way it stands—you go out, she gives me an autograph, and everything's fine. You try ta be gangsta heroes, she dies. Go, now."

When they were out and the door was closed, I lowered the gun.

"I'm sorry, Zenobia. I didn't mean for this to happen."

"You did all this to get an *autograph* from me? You coulda just came to the concert."

Just then, my cell phone rang. It was Stanky.

"It's you. Thanks a lot!"

"Just ta let ya know, Michael, the concert got out *early*."

"Yes, I know that now. What happened?"

"Niggas! Two crazy niggas in the crowd got all excited and threw they beer bottles at the stage, like white folks do, like it was some kinda honky tonk. When Zenobia saw it, when she saw the bottles flyin up there, she ended the concert right then. Are we goin ta breakfast or what?"

"No, I can't. I'm with Zenobia *now*. We got a little business between us."

I had ta hang up the phone and turn it off ta get ridda him, cuz he called back.

"What do you *want* from me?" she demanded.

"Nothin. I didn't expect ya ta come back so soon. I'm not here for you. I came for Mystique, your dog. Do you know she bit the granddaughter of one of the biggest crime bosses in New Jersey?"

"It's not her fault! She's had a bad history," she explained. "She doesn't trust people easily, especially kids. She had cruel kids in her past before I adopted her."

"Yeah, but that don't change things. I gotta kill that dog."

"Mystique?" she panicked. "Where *is* she?"

"In the bathroom. She's unconscious," I answered, pickin up the cleaver. "I gotta chop off her head. It's the price the boss is askin for your dog bitin his granddaughter."

"Oh no you ain't!" she declared, takin a place in front of me. "What the hell is wrong with you? Who *really* sent you? *Who* chops off a dog's head? No, you'll have ta kill *me* first!"

"Look, The Dwarf was pretty pissed off with you, Zenobia, but he's gonna give ya a break. Your dog, however, bit a family member and drew Carzano blood. That dog's gotta die!"

By that time, the singer had rushed into the bathroom, stoopin to kneel by the dog.

"You bastard! What did you do ta her?"

"She's just knocked out. Look, you gotta move. I've got to get her head."

"I told ya, you ain't getting no head. I ain't goin nowhere. What are ya gonna do? Shoot me? Slash me with that knife?"

"Listen Sista Girl, ya slapped a mob boss on the head and ya talked shit ta him in front of his granddaughter. You're lucky he doesn't have someone in here merkin or mutilatin *you*. It's just a dog. You can just go out and get another dog."

I pulled a bundle of bills out of my pocket.

"What's a Yorkie cost? I'll give ya the money ta *buy* a new one. One thousand? Two thousand?"

"No, and when did the mob start puttin out hits on dogs? You must be a real sorry-ass hitman for them ta have you on doggie duty."

Just then, I thought I heard one or maybe two thumps in the hall.

"You must be the little man's retarded son or somethin," she continued. "I take it Bilbo Baggins is your dad?"

"No. I'm not related to him. I don't even wanna kill your dog. He's makin me."

"Makin you?"

"If I don't bring him Mystique's head on a silver platter tonight, he's gonna kill me and my dad. He's the boss. He can order it. I don't have a choice."

"You *always* have a choice," she argued, advancin as I approached the dog. "That's why you're a doggie hitman, and that's why he can threaten you like that—cuz maybe you got balls, but you don't know they're down there."

Just then, I was certain I heard a gunshot in the front room.

"You expectin company?"

"Oh no!

We both jumped when someone kicked in the door.

"Get down!"

I guess instinct took over. I yanked the Glock out of my waistband and hit the wall with my back—just like in the video game. Peekin around the corner, I saw the biggest, ugliest, scariest-lookin black guy I ever saw in my life. It was like his head was almost touchin the ceilin! He was searchin the room, his gun drawn.

"Zenobia—Zenobia, it's just you and me now, Baby! I got a message for you from The Management. I gotta make sure you know who's runnin things here. You walked off the stage again. You can't say they didn't warn ya, girl. Zenobia? Where is your damn *dog?*" Mystique?"

When he tipped past the bathroom to check the curtains by the window, I saw the perfect shot and had ta take it.

Pow! Pow! A direct hit.

I didn't know who he was, so I didn't *kill* im. I just shot im in the ass. He fell to the floor, groanin.

"Zenobia! You *bitch*! You, you shot me in the ass!"

When I went to get my bag, he looked up and glared at me.

"Who the hell are *you*, white boy?"

By that time, Zenobia had scooped up Mystique and was grabbin my arm, pullin me toward the door.

"This is bad! *Very* bad! We gotta get outa here, now! You got a car?"

"Zenobia!" the big guy screamed when he saw her.

"You tell The Management that big hole in yo ass is *my* message ta them! Cuz this white boy here is in the *mob*! I got the Italian *mob* on my side now—that little hobbit guy and *all* his crew! So back *off*, Bubba!"

Out in the hallway, we saw where one of Zenobia's thug bodyguards, who seemed like he was dead, collapsed in the hallway. He was all beat up and slumped across the stairs, so we had ta step over the body. We heard the beginnin of police sirens in the distance, so we hurried down the stairs. By the time we got outside, ran a block or so ta the parkin lot on 48th and found the car, we were frantic.

"Hurry! Someone's coming! They're right behind us!"

Panicked cuz Zenobia was fussin in my ear, I dropped the keys while tryin to put them in the ignition. When I bent down ta get them off the floorboard, the windshield exploded above my head and a bullet tore inta the seatback that, a few seconds earlier, was behind my head. Despite Zenobia's screamin and freakin out in the next seat, I saw im, outa the corner of my eye.

"Jake the Ass! You *bastard*!"

Another bullet! Careful not to sit up, I started the car, threw it inta gear and stepped on the gas. The car lurched forward, crashin inta a Mercedes before I backed and sped toward the parkin lot exit. The police turned the corner seconds after I pulled out onta the street, leavin Jake, who tried ta chase us, unable to follow. I didn't mean ta do it, but I accidentally ran over his feet as I drove past im. I can still see the stunned look in his eyes, lookin at me, when I did it.

On the Lam

It was a good thing I still had that dive motel room in midtown. There was a diner next door, and a coffee shop. Screechin inta a space on the far end of the restaurant parkin lot, I whipped off my jacket and draped it over Zenobia's face and shoulders.

"I've got a room at the motel next door. Don't say a word till we get in!"

It was amazin how good a disguise a man's jacket can be on a woman, even a woman with a bangin body. No one had a clue who she was as we went from the car, across the lot, and inta the room, which smelled like a combination cigarette smoke, cheap beer, rat piss, human sweat and ass. Seein the single queen-sized bed in the room, Zenobia stopped dead in her tracks.

"Now hold on, partna! Nothin personal, but I need ta get my *own* room. We are *not* havin a 'Bodyguard' moment up in here, or anywhere, ever! You know what I mean? You are *not* Kevin Costner."

"And I've heard you sing. You're kinda okay lookin, but *you* are not Whitney. Nothin personal there, either."

I paid cash and got her a room next to mine, joined by a few rat holes and a common door, joined to another door, which could locked separately from either side. With the doors open, we began exchangin information.

"Who was the big guy at the hotel? Some rapper *boyfriend* of yours?"

"The one you *shot*? Please! His name's Bubba, Bubba King. What were you *thinkin*? He's enforcement for The Management."

"The Management?"

"Yes, the Management. They run the entertainment business and everything else. Call it what you want—*Illuminati, New World Order, Skull and Bones, Kappa Beta Phi*—whatever! They run everything."

"They run everything with *everybody*?"

"Everybody and everything, and everywhere—East Coast, Hollywood, London, Hong Kong—*everywhere*! They're there, but then they're *not* there. So long as you go along with the program, you hardly notice them, but step out of line and they'll let you know the deal."

"I take it you stepped outa line?"

"Me?" she laughed. "My own *father* couldn't tell me what to do. I went with the program for as long as I could, but was gettin old, and I was gettin tired."

Tears welled in her eyes.

"They must have had Bubba hurt one of the twins, DeShawn. I *loved* that guy! DeShawn and his wife just had a baby girl."

She looked toward me.

"Bubba's real bad news. Cold-blooded killer—likes torture and mutilation. Get this: he tore out one singer's tongue and left her bleeding in the Green Room with a tissue in her mouth. Another one, he drowned in the tub. And Johnny Love, the singer—people always wonder how he can still hit all those high notes at his age. They say Bubba cut off his nuts and ate them in Sriracha sauce. He's the absolute worst. He's a monster. It's why he works for The Management. So he's probably *real* pissed off at you after you shot im in the ass. He's gonna want payback."

Just great!

"You should probably call your mob boss, Napoleon Littleparts," she warned. "You're going to need all the protection you can get."

"Jake the Ass—" I sighed, "that guy with the metal teeth *shootin* at us in the parkin lot—"

"Yeah?"

"Well, The Dwarf, my boss—he musta sent Jake there to whack me after I finished the job on the dog. They're tryin ta *kill* me. I ain't *got* the mob on my side, so I don't know *why* you were talkin all that shit ta Bubba!"

"*My* bad. Waitaminute, but let me get this straight!" she said, snakin her neck. "You're saying the mob's after *you* because of me, and now, so is The Management, because you shot Bubba? *And* The Management after me because of me, but now so is the mob, because of you? Looks like we got the exact same *people* after the both of us?"

"I guess that about sums it up."

"Well, we gotta figure this thing out. How does it go? *The enemy of my enemies is my friend.* You're all I got. Either we run or we fight this together."

"I don't have a choice," I sighed. "I've gotta help my father. But I've gotta get to im before they do."

She sat on the bed, thinkin for a minute, and she finally stood.

"Now look, Gomer—I'll be honest—you don't seem too bright to me, and it seems you don't mind getting yo ass punked, but I'll help you, as long as you help me."

"That's fine," I nodded, "and while I've always heard black chicks are nothin but trouble, I never believed it. But then I meet *you*, and two minutes later, you force me to shoot a big ugly guy named Bubba, who's gonna eat my balls if he catches me."

"Please!" she said, waggin her head. "I didn't force you to do anything."

"You didn't hafta walk out on the concert early."

"They were throwing beer bottles. *You* didn't have to break in and try to murder my dog!"

"Well, *you* didn't hafta slap The Dwarf on the head!"

"The Dwarf? *You* mean little ol Tyrion Lannister? Well he didn't have to slap my dog!"

"You *started* this whole mess! You didn't hafta tell a little girl it was okay to pet a dog you knew was vicious ta kids! I shoulda just killed er and cut off her head when I had the chance!"

"And your boss would have killed you in the parking lot. You've got some nerve! You should *thank* me for saving your sorry-ass life!"

"Who saved *whose* life? You woulda had your tongue ripped out... and the world woulda been a much more peaceful place, believe me!"

When Mystique stirred on the bed in the other room, Zenobia turned in response, snarlin toward me.

"Yo ass is lucky she woke up! If she has any problems tonight behind what you did, I'm coming back in here and kickin your ass!"

The door slammed behind her. *Black* chicks! *Good riddance!*

****

Fifteen minutes later, she was tappin at our common doors.

"You rented me a room full of rats! They're all around the *bed*, trying to climb up!"

"They probably think Mystique's a female rat," I laughed, a little groggy. "It's *that* time of night, ya know. Can you *blame* em?"

"You're disgusting. I think we should switch *rooms*."

"This room is fulla rats too."

"Then we need to *find* another hotel."

"Not till we get another car," I countered. "I'm sure Jake's already *made* the car we were in. The mob and the cops who work for em will be lookin for me in it."

"Then you need to give me and Mystique *your* bed and you take the couch over there, and *you* need to make sure the rats don't bother us."

I started ta object, but this was Zenobia, and she wanted ta sleep in my room, so I grabbed a blanket and tromped over ta the couch.

"I'll watch ta make sure no rat climbs up there and gets busy with your dog. I'll keep the two of yas safe."

I plopped down.

"I knew it was comin ta this," I said, loud enough for her ta hear. "And *she* said I wasn't Kevin Costner—*now* she wants me ta be her bodyguard."

"You *wish*! Agent Frank Farmer had his shit together—you don't. He didn't have Rachel staying in some roach-infested rathole!"

I ignored the insult. She was still talkin shit! Two could play that game.

"Oh yeah! I can't wait ta tell my friends I *slept* with Zenobia."

"In your dreams. You're sleeping on the *couch*."

"Yeah, in the same room, ten feet away from you, so technically, we're spendin the night together. You'll be sleepin and I'll be sleepin, so we're *sleepin* together. That's my story and I'm stickin to it.

****

The next mornin began with the click of my camera phone.

"Hey! What the hell! Pervert! What the hell do you think you're *doing*?" she screamed, pullin the covers up around her bare shoulders.

"Takin pictures, for my fan club—so they can all see what the glamorous Zenobia *looks* like in the mornin."

She turned her back so I could not see her face.

"Put that thing down! And *erase* that picture! So now the mob's sending out immature *perverts* who kill you by annoying you to death? Put it *down*, Gomer."

I returned the phone to my pocket and sat on the couch.

"By the way, my name's not Gomer. It's Michael. Michael Ponzi."

"You *look* like a Gomer, or Opie, but okay, Michael Ponzi, thanks for *snoring* all night. We barely got any sleep."

"I'm sorry. But I think it was one of your farts that woke *me* up."

"You're gross, and you're lying," she tisked, disgusted.

"I'm not. It musta been buildin up all night. It was so powerful it blew the sheets six inches up in the air."

"Right… If you heard anything, it must have been Mystique. I changed her food recently, and it doesn't agree with her stomach."

"Yeah, blame it on the *dog*. What did *you* have for dinner?"

Her back still to me, she stood, puttin on her jacket, and turned.

"Will you *grow* up? Why does it feel like I've been kidnapped by a juvenile delinquent Brooklyn teenager?"

"Huh? Kidnapped? What do ya mean, kidnapped?" I asked.

"That's what they're saying on the news. It's the big story this morning. Seriously—I saw it on my phone Internet when I was awake with tissue in my ears, trying to sleep through your snoring. Turn on the TV if you don't believe me."

I found the remote device and turned ta the cable news. There it was!

In another late-breaking story, facts are still emerging about the kidnapping of Zenobia, early this morning. Police arrived at the famed Waldorf Astoria in New York City shortly after midnight to find one of Zenobia's personal bodyguards dead in the hall and another bodyguard wounded in her suite. Apparently, Zenobia was kidnapped from the room.

Surveillance camera film is still being analyzed, but police are on the look-out for an unidentified Caucasian male, armed and dangerous, possibly travelling with Zenobia, who is an African American female, under duress. Police believe the kidnapper and the renowned singer— loved by millions of fans the world over, are still somewhere in New York City.

A second Caucasian male, Jake Sorrano, was arrested in a parking lot near the hotel on East 48th. According to a police source who did not want to be identified, Soranno is rumored to be a hitman, a paid assassin who works for the notorious Carzano crime family. Why a paid assassin is involved and the motive for the kidnapping are still unclear, but anyone with information on the whereabouts of the kidnapper and the singer is asked to call the New York City Police Department, Special Victims Unit. A two hundred thousand dollar reward has already been offered by Palmyra, Zenobia's record label.

Another channel featured a mug shot of Jake the Ass as a reporter described the cache of weapons police found in his car, which included two high-power rifles with scopes, a pistol with a silencer, an improvised explosive device, a picture of a dog and a body bag. He was under arrest in the hospital, his feet crushed by my tires. A third news station detailed the history of the Carzano crime family in New Jersey and on the eastern seaboard, along with a sensational litany of the family's brutal misdeeds.

Seconds later, my phone started ringin. When I checked the caller ID, I saw it was The Dwarf, with a missed call from Alphonso the Brain. That's when I realized I had ta get ridda that phone. It was the new Apple, and I had paid a kid two hundred dollars to stand in line all night out in the rain ta get it. But it had the GPS crap in it and I knew The Dwarf called me because he'd be usin its GPS ta find me. He probably already knew where I was.

"Zenobia, we gotta get outa here, now! Get the dog!"

Startled, she grabbed Mystique from the bed. I draped my jacket over her shoulders again.

"We've gotta get movin before they find us! You got a phone?"

She pulled the gold-cased device from her purse.

"Here, let me unlock it, but you have to dial the area code first because it's—"

I threw it on the ground and stomped it hard before she could get another word outa her mouth.

"Hey! Are you crazy? Michael!" she yelled as I stomped again to make sure it was completely destroyed.

"They'll use it ta trace us. I don't know how tech savvy The Management is, but the mob has people who coulda used that to track us down. I'm doin mine as soon as I pull the SD card."

"Well, you coulda taken the phone out of that case first! That case was twenty-four carat gold!"

So after I destroyed *my* phone, we slipped outa the room and then took a mad dash across the parkin lot, duckin and lookin back over our shoulders the whole time.

"Where are we going?" she demanded, outa breath.

"I called a friend last night. He's gonna pick us up at the coffee shop across the street."

"Someone from the *mob?*" she asked.

"No. He's one of you."

"Excuse me? One of *me?*"

"He's *black*, and I hope he's not late. I've heard black people are always late."

Road Trip

Stanky Stanley showed up right on time, but not because I told him to. What I *did* tell im is I had a surprise, and if he didn't show up on time and alone, he was gonna miss out. When he showed up, he was drivin his drug dealer cousin's hooptie, a half-primered, black 1967 Chevy Impala SS Hardtop Sport Coupe on shiny chrome 20s. His little sister, Unique, was in the passenger seat in sunglasses and hoochie wear that could only be Strawberry's.

I was lucky for once. No sooner had Zenobia and I crawled in the back seat did we watch a couple of black SUVs pull up in the parkin lot of the motel. The men who got out were huge, and I could tell they were strapped. Three of the men went to the back of the hotel, while the other four approached the door where we were stayin and kicked it open, guns drawn. Zenobia was watchin over my shoulder.

"Stanky, without makin too much a scene, can you get us outa here?"

He was completely turned around, still starin at Zenobia, transfixed.

"I just can't believe it's you, girl! You look even better in person! You do *know* we cousins? You know you got an uncle name Joe, right? Uncle Joe?"

That didn't mean they were cousins. Everyone had an uncle named Joe!

"Uh, I'm not sure…" Zenobia answered, glancin over at the motel as the men came outa the room and started lookin around outside the buildin. Then she noticed Unique's disappointed expression and thought better.

"What am I thinking? I *do* have an uncle named Joe! Uncle Joe! He's got a *daughter*, right?"

"Yeah!" Stanky exclaimed, noddin, feelin vindicated. "A daughter name Ebai!"

"That's right, EBay! EBay's ma *girl*! But Stanky," Zenobia continued in whisper, duckin in the seat. "We *really* need to get out of here. Can you just drive away somewhere while you're doing all that talking?"

Sensin the urgency, Stanky pulled outa the lot and around the corner, turnin back to look at her every few seconds. *If I didn't know any better, I woulda thought he was in love with her.*

"Ya know, girl, when we get up ta Albany, you gonna hafta watch me do yo dance ta *Didn't I Tell Ya?* I shakes my ass probably better then you do on that one!"

I should have known better, but I thought I heard him mention the place where he was drivin us.

"Yo Stanky, did ya just say Albany? When we get up to *Albany?*"

"Yeah, Michael. You said you and sista-girl had ta get outa the city, said ya couldn't trust anyone either of ya knew. Uncle Joe lives in Albany."

"Uncle Joe?" Zenobia said to me under her breath. "Can we trust *him?*"

Nosey, our eavesdroppin driver answered unprompted.

"Of course ya can trust im! He's yo uncle, girl! Y'all got common *blood.*"

"Did you tell im we were comin?" I asked, growin a little uneasy.

"Naw. I did like ya said," Stanky answered. "I ain't said nothin ta nobody—*not a mouse*—cept this little rodent next ta me here."

As if on cue, Unique turned around, lookin directly at Zenobia.

"There's three of us and *one* of him! *Bust* im in the head! There's a bottle on the floor. You could bust im in the head and we could kick im outa the car!"

"Who?" Zenobia asked, as confused as I was.

"Him!" she indicated, pointin at me. "The *kidnapper!* We three black girls! He don't know who he messin with!"

"I didn't *kidnap* her," I protested.

"You lyin. It's all over the TV. Ya kilt that bodyguard. And you been stalkin ma cousin Zenobia fa three weeks—just like the otha girl you kidnapped. That white girl said you kidnapped and raped her, said ya kept her tied up and tortured her. She said you was a pervert!"

"I am *not* a pervert! *Who* said that?"

"That white girl on the TV—the one you kidnapped and raped before Zenobia!"

I looked toward Zenobia, hopin for a little help, but she just kinda backed away, eyin me with new suspicion.

"I saw just the end of that story this morning. Did you kidnap a *white* girl before me?"

"I didn't kidnap *you*!" I protested, becomin agitated. "We left that room *together*, Zenobia! We ran outa there together! Remember?"

"Bust im in the head with that bottle, girl! He *look* like a pervert."

Stanky, however, proved ta be the voice of reason.

"He don't look like no pervert. Mattera fact, I know he ain't. He's just *white*, that's all."

He turned toward me.

"But nigga, there *was* a white girl on the TV, fa real. I think her name Lolita or somethin like that, and she say you kidnapped er and got all freaky-deaky with er. They got pictures posted online an all."

"And I *saw* em!" Unique interrupted. "He know what he do!"

She held up a smart phone with one of the pictures Lolita took that last time.

"Ain't that you? Same face, same beady little eyes—and you bout ta hit her with that strap! *Bust* im, cuz! We got yo back."

I looked toward Zenobia and sighed.

"I'll explain later. This whole *thing* musta been a set-up from the start! For now, I plead The Fifth."

****

Two hours later, we were still drivin up northbound I-87, just past Kingston. An hour earlier, Stanky put a Zenobia CD in the disk player and he and Unique were annoyin the two of us with the worst sing along I had ever heard in my life. It was aversion therapy. I swear those songs I heard will never be the same, ever again.

They tried ta get Zenobia to sing with em, but she just sat there, clearly annoyed and in pain. And it all kept on until Stanky noticed the red and blue lights behind us—on top of the cop car that was pullin us over!

"Y'all be cool, now," a calm Stanky comforted us. "I *got* this. No problem."

A tall, muscular, white officer showed up at his window two minutes later.

"Well hello, handsome Officer," Stanky said in his most effeminate voice, eyin the state trooper up and down, oglin the weapon at waist level. "Now I *know* I wasn't speedin, and the registration's current, so either I'm drivin while black or you, all white and juicy and tender— you're goin outa your way to meet a sexy someone like me."

"Uh, no," the officer stammered, backing. "Actually, we got a call from another driver on the road who said it sounded like someone was being beaten or murdered in this car. They called in the license plate number. Is everything okay in here?"

"We was just sangin, that's all. Everything's fine, Sir," Stanky answered.

"Was that the new Zenobia CD you were blastin when I walked up?" the trooper inquired, glancin over at Unique.

"Yeah, *Out From Under You,*" she responded, holdin up the CD case.

"It's tight! I gotta get that one," he smiled, doin a little Zenobia move. Then saw me in the back seat, behind the driver.

"Sir, I'm gonna have to ask you to step outa the car."

"Who? Me?" I asked. "Why?"

"Just step outa the vehicle, Sir, and keep your hands in full view at all times."

When I complied, he told me to keep my hands up while he took me ta the back of the car. Then he told me to place my hands on the trunk while he patted me down, whisperin.

"Don't look up. Pretent I'm not talkin. I couldn't help but notice, partner. Three of *them* and one of you. Is everything here on the up-and-up? What are they *up* to? Drugs? Pirating feature films? They kinda look like marijuana salespersons to me?"

He eased up to me, uncomfortably close, whisperin in my ear.

"They *got* something on you? Are they holdin you against your will? I've had SWAT team trainin and my cousin's a Navy SEAL. I can *help* you."

"No. No, I'm fine," I assured him, floored about what he asked me. "I'm *married* ta one of em—the female one in the back. We were just goin to our family reunion in Albany."

"Oh! Okay, *I* understand," he smiled, embarrassed. "Just checkin. We gotta look out for each other, ya know. Can't be too careful."

"Yeah, good lookin out," I whispered in reply. "Hey, I think the one in the front really *digs* ya. I can set ya up if ya want. We could end up bein family—*us two* against the three of them."

"Uh, that's okay. I've got someone I'm kinda seein."

By the time I returned to my seat and got strapped in, Stanky and Unique were singin again: *Break the Chains*.

"You all enjoy your family reunion in Albany," the officer muttered, while lookin almost directly at Zenobia as the little dog barked. "And too bad about Zenobia! I hope they catch that pervert!"

"Baby be *fine*!" Stanky reassured him.

"Hey, you *know*..." he said, lookin at me in the back. "Your wife almost *looks* like Zenobia. Almost—if she lost some *weight*, maybe ten, fifteen pounds. Kinda *chubbier* in the cheeks, ya know."

He grinned at her.

"Hey, that's a *compliment*. So lose a little weight already?"

While she forced herself to smile, she had a look on her face like she was holdin a mouthful of Mystique's excrement.

"Thank you, officer."

Givin me a thumbs-up and a wink, he turned and went back to his car, and it took no time for Zenobia to turn on me.

"You told him I was your *wife*?"

"I had ta make somethin up, ya know. He was askin alotta questions."

"Why would anyone in their right mind *marry* you? What *else* did you tell him about me? I saw that little *wink* he gave you."

Unique answered for me.

"That's cuz he told that cop he had *sex* with you last night. Y'all spent the night in a room all by y'allselves. So even I wanna know. *Did* y'all have sex last night?"

"No!" Zenobia retorted.

"How *old* are you, Unique?" I asked. "Why would you even ask a question like that? How *old* is she, Stanky?"

"She thirteen."

"Thirteen goin on thirty-nine. You said you were comin alone. Why'd ya bring her?"

"Cuz she thirteen and too nosey for her own good. She was listenin when you called me. And then when that stuff come on the news, she was like, 'I'm *goin*! and if you don't take me with you, I'm *goin* ta the news—CNN, so then *you'll* be in jail for aidin and abettin kidnappin and I'll be famous and a millionaire."

"She's shakin ya down at thirteen?" I sighed, unable ta believe the girl's balls! "Ya oughta be workin for the mob!" I told her."

Sittin nexta me, Zenobia was clearly outa her element. She was used to rollin around in the back of luxury limousines, with drivers in suits, but there she was, in a ghetto hooptie, reekin of green bud, cheap gin and Unique's rancid perfume. She was used ta sittin back, sippin champagne and givin orders, but there she was sittin in the back seat of a rattlin car, relegated to a lumpy seat in the corner, under a torn headliner hangin down.

She was outa danger for the moment, but I could tell she was thinkin. She didn't like Stanky, she rolled her eyes whenever Unique said anything, and she definitely didn't care much for me, especially after she saw the *YouTube* video on Unique's phone—it was a thirty-second clip of me spankin Lolita after tyin her up. But Zenobia didn't have a phone. She couldn't call anyone, and she wouldn't be safe if she did. She was just hatin her life right then.

What was funny was the big, fat cockroach that crawled outa her purse. I saw it first, but when she saw it, her eyes opened so wide I thought they'd roll out and fall ta the floor. Then her mouth opened in a silent scream of horror as she pulled Mystique onto her lap, away from the bug, who sat there on her Coach, gawkin like a crazed fan, wrigglin its antennae. I could tell she wanted to smack it, but she was too afraid ta touch it. So in instinct, I slapped my hand down on top of it, splashin its guts all over her purse and a little on her shirt. She almost hurled as she swept the purse ta the floor and pulled her feet onto the seat, rollin her eyes.

"This was the *best* you could do?" she snarled under her voice.

"*That's* the thanks I get for savin your life? Those people back at the motel we just left. They *weren't* the mob, if you didn't notice."

"That was The Management," she answered, almost to herself. "They must be really pissed this time. They told me if I ever walked off the stage again, it would be my ass, but I think Bubba was goin ta kill Mystique to make a point. That's just *men* for you!"

"Men?"

"Don't you watch Steve Harvey?"

"What *man* watches Steve Harvey?"

"*That's* the problem. That's what he's always *talkin* about. So I walked off the stage, big deal! They could have just found a calm moment, sat me down and tried ta talk to me about it. They could have asked what might have happened that *made* me walk off the stage, you know—they could have tried to see things from my point-of-view. Maybe I had a *reason!* We could have worked it out. But no—they're men. They've just got somethin to prove."

"What about all the people who paid out their hard-earned money for tickets?" I asked.

"What about *me* and my safety? One of those beer bottles could have *killed* me! But of course you'd take *their* side, cuz you're a man. Woman 'disobeys,' and *The Man*'s gotta make sure she knows who's boss. So they want to punish me by hurtin my sweet little dog who ain't done shit to nobody!"

"That dog *vicious!*" Unique, ear hustlin, interjected. "She been growlin at me every chance she get. Let er try and *bite* me. I'll throw ha little ass out the window."

"You *too*, Unique?" Zenobia scolded. "I thought you were my *cousin?*"

"I am, and I *still* don't like yo dog. I ain't *gotta* like yo dog!"

"Now y'all need ta leave Zenobia alone," Stanky pleaded. "Ain't nothin wrong with that dog. She a little vicious, but that's cuz she's spoilt. She don't know she a dog."

"She gonna know it when we get ta Uncle Joe's, cuz he don't play that," Unique countered. "He say 'people who treat dogs like people is exactly the same folks who treat people like dogs.'"

The rest of the ride to Albany was mostly uneventful. Thirty minutes outside town, Zenobia insisted that we stop so Mystique could have a potty break and stretch her legs—all four inches of em. Stanky and Unique went in the food mart to get orange soda pops, givin me a chance ta talk ta Zenobia in private. I could tell by her face she was miffed.

"I don't know why I was *stupid* enough to follow you?" she exploded, and then she spoke in an undertone. "Rats, roaches, and I had to ride in that *ghetto*-ass car with that annoying singing and that gangsta girl. Do you even have a *plan?*"

"Yeah, I have a plan."

"What is it?"

"It's an unfinished plan, and I'm gonna need you ta help me finish it. We'll talk when we get ta Uncle Joe's. And just a word of advice: stop bein such a diva. I don't know Uncle Joe and I ain't black, but somethin tells me he doesn't put up with spoiled dogs, or spoiled *singers. Capiche,* Chubby Cheeks?"

****

I had been ta Albany four or five times in my life, all those times visitin Ma's relatives. She had two older brothers and a younger sister there. So I was a little alarmed when Stanky passed up all the I-87 Albany exits and was headed more toward in the direction Schenectady.

"Yo Stanky, ya just blew through Albany. I thought ya said your uncle lived there. Where are we goin?"

"We almost there. Ma uncle has a farm next ta a creek outside of Schenectady. Eighty Acres and *Two* Mules—that's what my Uncle Joe calls it. It's a *workin* farm. Isolated—ain't nobody gonna be lookin fa y'all up there."

"I hope that doesn't mean we'll be sleeping in a *barn!*" Zenobia interjected.

"Naw. He gotta big ol house, but like I said, it's a workin farm. You don't work, you don't eat. And just so y'all know up front—y'all won't be sleepin in the same room tanight. Ma uncle religious. He a Mennonite."

"Why would I want to sleep in the same room as *him?* He's a *pervert,*" she tisked again. "But what does that mean, your uncle's a Mennonite?"

"He's Amish?" I asked.

"Almost kinda like Amish, but *not*. Amish is all-*white*, and they like it that way, but there's alotta black Quakers and Mennonites like my Uncle Joe, in Pennsylvania, Illinois and New York. You'll see. Unique know she gotta come up outa them hoochie clothes, and Zenobia can't be showin all that ass she put out there."

"So your uncle wears a straw hat, has a long goatee and drives around in a horse and buggy?" I queried.

"All that. He got the horse and buggy, but he got a Cadillac too—brand new model every year. He be ballin."

"Just when I thought it couldn't get any worse!" Zenobia whispered to me. "I know who they are now. They're *weirdoes—Children of the Corn*. They probably still practice live *sacrifice*."

"Just little dogs name Mystique," Stanky joked. "But fa real though, ma uncle's farm—it ain't no place fa little dogs!"

Uncle Joe's

The paved surface gave way to a dirt road as we made our way up a hill and around a bend, and there, nestled in the corner of a glen, sat three structures. On the right was a large, two-story house with a basement, painted tan with white trim. The roof was steep with an attic window near the top of the home. There was a broad porch area in the front and a carport to the right.

Two hundred or so feet to the left was a big red barn with tall double doors, and next to it was a long, wide structure, made of plastic or glass. I figured it was some kinda greenhouse. A white picket fence separated the home area from the rest of the property.

Stanky opened the gate and drove the car on paved road around to the back of the barn. Without sayin anything, he and Unique got out the car, retrieved bags from the trunk and went in through a back door.

"Okay," Zenobia sighed, "we're outa danger for the moment, but this is whack. Things are just going to get worse unless we figure something out. You said you had a plan."

"I'm figurin it out," I said. "I've got family in Albany—FBI and other Feds. They don't trust me and I don't trust them, but I know there's an answer to all this out there somewhere. We just gotta find it."

"I need to get to a phone, but I'm not sure who I can trust," she countered. "The Management is so big. Like I told you—they control everything—probably even the mob and the FBI. If they really want us dead, we don't stand a chance."

"We can survive this if we can get them ta understand that we're more valuable ta them alive than dead, or if we can get somethin on em, some kinda leverage. Or maybe if we can give them somethin they want."

"And what are you proposing?"

"Nothin yet. I just hope we can trust this Uncle Joe character. I'm sure that lie about the kidnappin is all over the news."

When Stanky and Unique got back ta the car, we hardly recognized em. He had changed inta slacks, a white shirt and a tie—and he was wearin a belt, so his pants were pulled all the way up past his waist. He also had on glasses. Unique had on a blue modest day dress that reached down, way below her knees. She wore plain, black tie-up shoes and a bonnet on her head.

"*Excuse* me?" Zenobia blurted, "but what happened ta y'all?"

"Like I told you," Stanky explained. "My uncle is a Mennonite, so when we come here, we dress appropriately. He doesn't have a phone or a television—by choice. So he didn't know we were coming."

"And you *speak* appropriate too! I'm figurin," I said. "Right, Unique?"

"It's no big deal. It's just what we do when we're here," she answered. "You can say whatever you want to say about my Uncle Joe, but he's a good man. You might not be able to tell by looking at him, but you'll see. He'll be the wisest man you ever met, and real."

Zenobia and I were stunned by such an utter transformation! It was like two completely different people had gotten back in the car. Stanky drove it around the barn to the front of the house, where we saw an older, grayin man with a beard and goatee, seated in the swing on the porch. He wore a straw hat and sipped from a glass of iced tea. On seein the car, he stood and came down the steps.

Engine off, Stanky opened the door and got out, followed by Unique.

"Come on out and meet Uncle Joe."

The older man removed his glasses so he could see us better.

"Stanley? Margaret? My, my! Well it certainly is a pleasure to see you! And you've brought guests? Come on up!"

Reluctant at first, Zenobia and I got outa the car.

"You all must be thirsty after such a long ride. Let me get Mary and we'll get you some cool lemonade and some snacks. Have a seat out here. I'll have someone get the rooms ready."

Stanky, Unique and I sat, but Zenobia lingered by the car.

"It *was* a long ride, so Mystique's got to stretch her legs and go potty. I'll be back."

She took the dog outa her jacket, and walkin a few paces, she put her down in the yard.

"Uh, Zenobia!" Unique called out. "I wouldn't *do* that if I were you!"

Too late! No sooner had Zenobia put Mystique down and Mystique ran a little distance to do that squattin thing that female dogs do, then there was this big *Woosh!* and Mystique was gone! It happened so fast I thought my eyes were playin tricks on me and then I tracked up to see a very large bird, some kinda owl or eagle, with little Mystique in it's talons. Mystique was barkin and growlin as the bird disappeared over the trees.

I looked ta Zenobia, who had ta be in shock cuz it happened so fast. She just stood there with her mouth open and no sound comin out. Then her hands flew to the sides of her head, where she musta squeezed hard enough to produce the loudest scream I ever heard. It was like she did in some of her songs, only louder.

Stanky ran down to where she was, and then he ran toward the trees where the bird and dog disappeared, but he stopped, realizin they were both long gone.

"I'm sorry, Zenobia. Margaret tried to warn you, and I told you the place wasn't safe for little dogs."

"I wanna go *home*!" she shrieked. "I wanna go home! I don't care what they do to me. I wanna go home now!"

Still sobbin, she wiped the tears with her sleeve.

"Take me home, Stanky. I'll pay you whatever you ask. Ten thousand, twenty thousand dollars! Just take me home now."

By that time, Stanky's Uncle Joe had come back out onto the porch.

"What was all that screaming about? What happened?"

Margaret was quick to answer.

"Zenobia had her dog out there, and some big bird just swooped down and ate it."

The older man just laughed to himself.

"It's dusk. It's when they hunt. Why didn't the two of you warn her?" he scolded. "Tiger Owls—Bubo and his wife. They've been a breeding pair over there for six years. It was probably the wife if it took a dog, but they hunt around that barn all the time."

"Is there any chance Mystique's still alive?" Zenobia asked in a plaintive voice.

"I'd like to tell you otherwise, young lady, but between the two of them, she's already gone. We'll check the pellets under their tree in the next few days. We'll find her."

She turned toward Stanky, who was returnin to the porch.

"Are you going to take me home?"

"You all just *got* here," Uncle Joe protested. "And we gotta find what's left of your dog."

He went down the steps and guided Zenobia back toward the house.

"I know you're upset, young lady, and I'm sorry. Come on up and sit a spell. Have some lemonade. Sometimes things happen where you got no control. You mustn't worry yourself about it. You just have to trust that God knows what he's doing."

****

The rest of us ate, while Zenobia went to one of the bedrooms and cried for hours. Every hour or so, she'd go back outside to the spot where Mystique experienced the unexpected Rapture, just starin at the grass, like the owl was gonna bring her back or somethin. After starin and an occasional tantrum out there, she'd come back in, head for the room and cry some more.

Mary, Uncle Joe's wiry wife, seemed concerned for her.

"Them there owls—that's ol Bubo and his wife. I'm sorry they got your dog, Jezebel, but that just how it goes out here. This is natural country living. Everything has to eat."

Arm over Zenobia's shoulder, Mary guided her down the hallway.

"You've cried enough, girl. Now dry up those tears. I don't know where you come from with all that nail polish, hair all fallin out, pagan gold and rings on fingers and hands that obviously have never worked, but I got you some towels for your bath, nail clippers and some decent clothes to cover up your woman parts."

By that time, Zenobia had cried so much that her eyes were almost puffed shut, her head ached and she was barely able to walk.

"Come on. You take a bath and get presentable. We're having fricasseed rabbit for supper. Go on now. Tomorrow we work."

Zenobia was upstairs in the bathroom for three hours, missin dinner. She had to share her room on the north side of the house with Unique, or Margaret, as they called her, while they had me in a room with Stanky, or Stanley, as he insisted I call him there.

Sittin at the table, rabbit, gravy, biscuits, greens, beets and cornbread on our plates, we could hear sobs and wails comin from the bathroom. If Zenobia was hatin life before, she was up there chokin it ta death.

"Your friend—is she all *right?*" Uncle Joe asked, makin a circlin gesture with his finger at his temple. "You know? Did someone drop her on her head when she was a baby? It was just a *dog!*"

"Be nice, Uncle. She's your *neice*," Stanley insisted.

"Naw. I really think she's your *Aunt Mary's* niece."

"Good Lord, no!" Aunt Mary protested. "My sister's *husband* died last month, and she didn't cry nearly that much! Was there something, you know—something *improper* going on between that girl and that dog? All that crying is in no way natural."

"That dog meant a lot to her," I answered. "You gotta understand she saw Mystique kinda as a family member."

"A *dog* as a family member? Do you hear what you're saying? King Solomon, the wisest man ever, said a dog will return to its own vomit, but I've seen them do worse. I don't know about you, but I don't have *any* family member that would do that."

"Waitaminute!" I interrupted, suddenly realizin why they didn't get it. "You don't have television. Do you know who she is?"

"Jezebel, and she came here because she's your so-called friend," Aunt Mary answered. "But she dresses like fornication has been her lifestyle, poor girl."

"No, her name is Zenobia, and she's a famous singer all over the world. She's sold millions of records and made millions of dollars."

"How many records she's sold and how much money she's got means nothing to us," Margaret countered. "We lay up our treasures in heaven. We have no part in this world. Just stop already. They have no idea who Zenobia is."

Who was this girl? Just hours before, Unique was makin crip signs at cars out the window with her fingers!

"They have *no* idea who she is," Stanky, or Stanley, assured me. "They just think she's a little 'troubled,' to put it nicely. She is making a pretty big deal over that dog. They're not used to such behavior."

It was like an alternate universe! The two slang-talkin, urban hipsters I rode down with had, once we got inside the gate, turned inta the *Stepford Negros*.

"They *really* don't know who she is?"

"That's right," Margaret answered. "They've never watched a TV, ever. They don't listen to the radio and they don't go to the movies or buy music. How would they *know* about her?"

"And all Mennonites are like that? So isolated?" I asked.

"I don't know about the rest of them, Micahel, but my Uncle Joe's that way," Stanley answered.

"So if I stood up here and recited the *I Have a Dream* speech by Dr. King, and I told em I made it up, just off the top of my head—they would think I was a genius and just a brilliant speaker?"

"They've never heard of Dr. King. They're not political"

"And *Barack Obama*?"

"Nope."

"Well then, *that* can't be all good!"

****

Her "diva-ness" aside, I kinda felt sorry for Zenobia. After all, this was a woman who slapped a mob boss on toppa the head for slappin her dog, a woman who had stood between her dog and me, when I had a meat cleaver and a gun, ta save the dog's life, and just like that, and literally outa the blue, a big bird swoops down, snatches and eats her pet!

She was really broke up about it and never came down for dinner—claimin she wasn't eatin rabbit cuz they're also pets. She had ta be hungry, cuz she, like me, hadn't eaten all day. Stanley, Uncle Joe and I sat on the swing on the front porch, while Margaret and Mary did the dishes.

On one end sat the old man, puffin on a pipe. Stanley and I had cigars that he retrieved from the hand-crafted humidor on a mahogany wood credenza against the wall and across from the dinin room table. As we all puffed away, Uncle Joe spoke in a low voice.

"We're harvesting the cabbage and collards tomorrow for market, and maybe the carrots over by the creek. The women folk will be hoeing on one of the parcels we rested last year."

He glanced sidelong toward me.

"You ever work on a farm, Michael?"

"Yes. My Aunt Rachel's farm, but that was a long time ago, when I was twelve."

"It's hard work, maybe a little too hard for spoiled city boys like you and my nephew here. But you mustn't worry. We will have Shadrach working with us tomorrow."

"Shadrach?" I asked.

"That's his son, my cousin," Stanley answered, briefly fallin outa character. "Ma *fine* cousin! He lives with my grandmother Ollie, about a mile from here."

"The troubled girl you're courting—" Uncle Joe nodded toward me. "Does she know this is a working farm?"

He thought Zenobia and I were datin? I guess, in a way, we were—by default, by the most generous interpretation of the word toward me. Even half-crazy, Zenobia was hot, but we *were* kinda stuck with each other.

"What do ya mean when you say 'workin farm'?"

"It means we make a strict application of Saint Paul's command, *that if any would not work, neither should he eat.* Exact same rule applies to the women folk, ever since my great grandfather owned this farm. He was a Quaker."

"A Quaker?"

"A Quaker and an abolitionist, who was best friends with a family of Quakers, who were white. This property and the old barn were one of the last stops on the Underground Railroad. Here and all the way up to Schenectady."

He puffed on the pipe, blowin smoke from the sides of puffed cheeks before he continued in a gravelly voice.

"That was then. Now the farm is part of Community Supported Agriculture, where our customers pay for shares of what we produce up front, and then, during the harvest, they come and pick up fresh produce, eggs, milk and meat once a week. Some even come a few days to share in the labor. Times change."

"It's hard work," Stanley added, blowin at the cherry of his cigar. "But at the end of the day, you feel like you've made a difference... about something. Sure beats *home!*"

Stanley and I continued the dialogue in our room, lights out.

"So who *are* you? Stanley or Stanky? And are you... are you gay, or was that just an act?"

"That's... that's who I am in the city. I'm a different person when I'm here. I ain't long found my family. Two years. I've known my Uncle Joe two years only. I met him at my father's funeral—the father I never *met.* The funeral was right here, on the farm, and ever since, I've just sorta been in between the two worlds. It's a good place for Margaret too."

"So which guy *are* you?"

"Both. I see no burnin need ta choose one over the other just now."

"I know a few people who might argue that."

"Then that's a problem they got with themselves. Me, I'm fine with it."

"But there's such a difference between the guy I met in the city and the person you are here. I wonder how many people *live* like that?"

"Probably more than you *know*, Michael," Stanley sighed. "Now go ta sleep. We hit the fields at butt-crack of dawn."

****

It was still dark outside when Stanley's Uncle Joe turned the lights on.

"Let's beat the sun out of bed, boys. Days and women don't get younger, and neither's promised."

Was he really serious about that "workin farm" business? I thought. I was a guest in his home! Did he really expect me to get out of bed ta go and slave in a field in order ta eat? Apparently, Stanley knew the routine. He went right to the chest of drawers and started gettin dressed. When I looked around, my clothes were gone.

"You'll get them back when it's time for you to go. Aunt Mary put together an outfit for you—sewed it herself, next drawer down. Better hurry up. If you don't make it downstairs in time for breakfast, you don't eat, and that means for a very long day."

When I got downstairs, the entire crew was seated at the table, almost done with breakfast. They had eggs, sausages, potatoes, biscuits and gravy, fish, grits, apples, peaches and cantelope melon. Uncle Joe and his sons, Shadrach and Joab, who lived down the way with Miss Ollie, their grandmother, had on black denim overalls, with long-sleeved plaid work shirts.

The boys, like their father, sported goatees, threadbare in places, and each had intricately-woven straw hats with black bands, which they would have never thought to wear in the house.

I couldn't help but notice that Shadrach, the oldest, was very handsome. Okay, so I'm not gay. I'm no Tommy Rotten, but a straight guy can admit when another guy was good-lookin, and this guy had it all. He had ta be about six-four, nice face, square jaw, perfect white teeth, and he was built like Superman. *God ain't fair!* I thought, till Shadrach opened his mouth.

His actual voice was okay, but I got the sense that his elevator stopped one or two floors shy of the penthouse, and yet he was a cool guy, just humble and fair-minded. His brother, Joab, looked more like Aunt Mary's side of the family. He wasn't as big or good-lookin, but he was married ta an Asian woman. His wife, Rahab, who musta been eight months pregnant, would be stayin at the house ta prepare lunch.

Right across from me sat the boys' sister, Ebai, who seemed shy and wouldn't even look at me. Had ta be about twenty, twenty-one. Pretty, but like Margaret, next ta her, she was dressed modestly—a long dress, not an inch of flesh showin, zero make-up and a bonnet.

The two of them flanked and attended Aunt Mary, who with spindly arms and legs and a black head coverin, literally looked like a queen bee. She was dark, wore glasses and was the undisputed Bible manners maven of the hive.

Everyone was downstairs, except for Zenobia. I was hopin she was okay, and I knew she shared the room with Margaret, so I asked about her.

"Where's Zenobia? Wasn't she with you?"

Margaret's answer seemed more like an announcement.

"She said all we *field* niggas need to do what we do out there. She said she was grieving and not getting up, that she was going to be a *house* Negro today."

The table erupted in horror for the degree of disrespect in the statement, but Aunt Mary just wagged her head and half-sighed, half-laughed out the words.

"Leave her be, children. Leave that poor girl be. The Lord works in mysterious ways."

Talk about white servitude! Mennonite Joe Green worked me like a Hebrew slave. From six a.m., he had me non-stop pullin weeds, hoein fields and haulin baskets of potatoes, and then cabbage, from the field ta the barn. I swear I never worked so hard in my life. I wasn't the only white guy, though. There were a few of us out there, but none Italian. When lunch came at noon, I was curious about Zenobia and about why she insisted on stayin at the house, so I went over there. Turns out she was up ta somethin.

From behind a tree, I watched her walk along the property in the Mennonite clothin that Aunt Mary apparently made for her. I spied on her as she sneaked out of the house and into the woods. I followed, makin sure she didn't know I was there, as she walked through the forest, peerin up into the trees. Then I saw her throw a few rocks at somethin up there. After thirty minutes, she went to the top of a hill, where I was sure she had a cell phone in her hand, where I was sure she made a call. She musta stayed on maybe five minutes.

Perplexed, I hurried back to the workers' lunch camp, where I managed to get a piece of lamb and ear of corn from the barbeque. As I ate, I was convinced that Zenobia was up to something for sure. There was somethin *else* ta her relationship with Mystique. It really didn't make any sense ta me that this so-called *Management*, as powerful as she said they were, would come after her like that just for walkin out on a concert where beer bottles were flyin. And the show of force at the motel the next morning? There had ta be somethin *else* goin on with her.

And since her dog was gone, *why* wasn't she still insistin on goin back home? If they were threatenin Mystique ta pressure her, well then, that leverage was out the window, or up in the air. I thought back. It seemed that I had heard mention of *The Management* before. Sometimes when my father had his guard down, he mentioned that name. And sometimes, when certain mob figures was talkin, they whispered it, even The Dwarf.

That's when I started ta wonder if the story about Zenobia's encounter with The Dwarf was even *true*. Maybe they were *all* in on it. Maybe it was part of some bigger overall scheme, and I was just the patsy who would take the fall or die! At that point, I trusted no one. I really needed ta talk ta my dad.

I worked the rest of the day harvestin a field of radish and beets. I swear I had ta stoop over for so long I thought my back was gonna break. I mean, who did this kinda labor for a livin? Then I saw Uncle Joe, one lot over, fillin twice as many baskets, barely breakin a sweat. But the real beast was Juan Pedro from Mexico or South America or somewhere else Latin. Whatever that guy put his hands to got done in a hurry. He was good at everything.

For the men, our day ended at about four in the afternoon. We walked back to the house, where the women were preparin dinner. I tried ta play it off, but I was lookin out for Zenobia, hopin to pull her aside for a talk. I was in the main room, waitin for my turn ta get washed up in the bathroom when she walked past, ignorin me on the way ta the kitchen.

"Is that fried chicken?" she exclaimed. "Oooh, that smells good! And turnip greens? Sweet potatoes! Aunt Mary, you sho can cook! Need me ta do anything? Set the table? Put out the silverware?"

"You can do that if you want, Jezebel, but you can't set a place for yourself, cuz you are not eating any of this dinner tonight."

"What?" Zenobia laughed. "You can't be serious. I haven't eaten anything all day!"

"That's because you haven't done any *work* all day. Look out there—"

She led Zenobia to the back door, facin the fields, and opened it.

"Now, I'm not saying you can't eat, but *your* dinner's out there. You just got ta find it, and fix it up yourself. All *kinds* of fruits and vegetables out there."

"But I'm your guest!" Zenobia protested. "Here you've got more than enough food and you won't let me *eat*?"

"You see that out there?" Aunt Mary persisted. That's where the *house negroes* go to find their dinner. Maybe you'll think to be a *field nigga* tomorrow."

The Mystery

I caught up with Zenobia after dinner. She was sittin on a tractor tire swing under a big oak tree, a tomato in one hand, a cucumber in another, bitin alternately from each. When she saw me comin, she swung around, givin me her back.

"How's your dinner?"

"That Aunt Mary is an evil woman! I can't believe she would do that! And she calls herself a Christian! I swear—if that old hag calls me Jezebel *one* more time!"

"Zenobia, they tried ta tell ya—"

"You were right in the other room when she said that—I *saw* you. Why didn't you stand *up* for me? We're supposed to be some kinda *couple* comin here! What kinda man *are* you?"

"A man who brought you two pieces of chicken and a biscuit."

She swung around instantly.

"Where?"

"Right here," I answered, handin her the paper towel-wrapped meal. "I smuggled em out when no one was lookin. You learn ta be clever when ya grow up in the mob."

"More like shady. Did you wash your hands? And you didn't *do* anything to this chicken, did you?"

"No. But if you don't want it, you don't have to eat it."

She was already scarfin it down, her mouth too full ta reply, so I responded ta what she had just said.

"We're supposed ta be some kinda *couple*? You and me?"

"That lie you told that cop—Margaret repeated it when Aunt Mary asked how we knew each other. The girl said we were engaged."

"Engaged, but not married?"

"She *said* married, but I corrected it to 'engaged.' If we were married, we'd be sleepin in the same room, and that just wasn't going to happen by me. Aunt Mary insisted there would be no fornicating in her house, so she put me with Margaret—told her to keep an eye on us, to make sure our private parts stay private."

It was as if I was lookin at Zenobia for the first time. She didn't have a lick of make-up on her face and she was wearin a plain but pretty blue dress and tie-up loafers. Her hair was pulled back, in a bonnet. There I was, in awe of her natural beauty, without all the glitz and glamor. She was just a very pretty woman. I also noticed then that Ebai kinda looked like her. They shared some of the same facial features. I smiled as Zenobia finished the chicken leg.

"That dress looks, I mean the whole look—" I stammered. "I just think you look nice today."

"In this?" she returned, her face incredulous. "Margaret told me that old woman *burned* all my real clothes! My leather slacks! Those Christian Louboutin heels! They were seventeen hundred dollars! Wrinkled witch had the nerve to say they made me *an abomination unto the Lord!*' An *abomination*, she said!"

"She *burned* all your stuff?" I laughed.

"It's not funny. I'm going to burn something of hers before I leave here."

"I'm glad you mentioned it. Leavin, that is, ya know. I came back ta the house and *saw* ya this afternoon. You have a *cell phone?*"

"What? Are you *spying* on me?" she answered, ignoring the question.

"Like my father always says, 'somethin ain't *smellin* right here.' There's somethin else goin on that you're not tellin me about."

She glared at me for a moment and sighed.

"I got the phone from Margaret. She had left it in the car because cell phones aren't allowed here. I traded her my gold necklace, a diamond earrings and my tennis bracelet for it."

"I figured as much. So who'd you call?"

"No one yet. I had to go up on a hill just to get a signal, but I was on the Internet, watching the news."

"And?"

"Well, *we're* all over the Internet, you and me, and in the tabloids and magazines. They're all on the tip that you kidnapped me and the mob's in on it. I mean the rumor mill is just going crazy out there! And that Lolita chick, the ex-girlfriend you tied and beat up—she's saying she's pregnant with your child."

"No way!"

"And your boss, The Midget—he's saying your dad went rogue and you were never really in the mob, that you're delusional. He was saying he never even met *me*, until they found some YouTube video of me slapping him on the head. His credibility was shot."

"Anything else about my father?"

"Your father issued a statement. Said he needed to talk to you."

"So he's still *alive?* That was it?"

"Yep. Oh yeah, and your *girlfriend baby mama* Lolita wants you to call her too."

"What a mess!" I sighed. "None of this was ever supposed ta happen."

"It's what you get for bein such a pervert, but I'm not judging you for the S&M thing. Different streaks for different freaks, I guess."

"Lolita *made* me do that! Besides, it *wasn't* what it looked like. Just nevermind! Are you plannin on callin someone with that phone?"

"I need to find my dog."

"Your dog was last night's *dinner* for a couple of owls! What are you talkin about?"

That's when it hit me. That's when I knew for a fact that Mystique was a bigger part of the story than Zenobia told me earlier. I thought back. The Dwarf was very specific. He wanted me ta bring him Mystique's *head*. Then, when Bubba King broke inta the Waldorf suite, he wasn't after Zenobia—he was after Mystique. And Zenobia, even after she watched the owl snatch up the dog and carry her off, she was still obsessed with findin Mystique. Maybe there was somethin in her collar? Some kinda leverage.

"Zenobia—when ya talk about The Management and them bein after you—what do they *want* with you? So ya walked off the stage—so what! This whole business with you and them has nothin to do with you walkin off that stage, does it?"

She paused a moment and wagged her head.

"At least you're smarter than you *look*. Do you know anything about The Management, Michael?"

"I've heard the name."

"Of *course* you've heard the name. We've all heard the name. When people talk about 'The Man,' when they say *Don't let The Man get you down*, or *You up against The Man*, or *He The Man*, most people don't get it. 'The Man' is short for 'The Management.' And who's The Man? *The Man* is the the one person who runs everything, including the government, banks, the mob, FBI and CIA, military, judges, politicians and everything else!"

She sighed and laughed to herself, sarcastic.

"And this is *all* whack, because I'm sitting here with you, having this discussion, but for all I know, *you* could be part of The Management, and you coulda set this whole thing up!"

"Right," I groaned. "If I was with The Management, I woulda never shot Bubba in the ass."

"Maybe, maybe not. I just don't know if I *trust* you."

"And I should trust *you*? You *lied* about why they came after you. You're sneakin around with a secret cell phone. And you got me involved in some crazy shit involvin men in black, drivin SUVs. I'm not sure if I even believe this whole conspiracy theory about *The Man* and about how powerful these people are. So what are we gonna do?"

"Do you have someone you can call? Someone *you* can trust?" she asked.

"Well, my dad. But the FBI's got im. I could call my cousin, Patrick. He has access to my father."

"Is he FBI?"

"Yes."

"Then we can't trust him. They're all in on it. We got to find Mystique, *wherever* she is now."

"Why? What is it?"

"I spotted the owls' nest today," she said. "We'll pretend we're taking a nature walk tomorrow, you know, as a couple—and we'll see if there is anything left of her around the tree. And if that doesn't work, you can just *climb* up to the nest."

A Day on the Farm

Zenobia was up bright and early the next mornin for breakfast in preparation for a workday, and everything seemed ta be goin fine—until Zenobia feasted her eyes on Shadrach. I could see it on her face, and then she started doin that thing that women did when they, allofa sudden, were lookin at a guy they wanted. She started primpin her hair and checkin her face, and sittin up a little straighter and pullin in the sharp claws and fangs.

But what was funny—he had no idea who she was. All her fame and money were wasted on him. Well, she was a pretty woman anyway, so I noticed im checkin her out when she wasn't lookin. All along, she was tryin ta get his eye. She just couldn't see when he was actually eyeballin her.

"Shadrach," I asked, clearin my throat, "can you pass the biscuits and eggs over to my fiancée, Zenobia, please?"

Her claws and fangs came back out and she gave me a squintin, hissy look before smilin and fake-laughin.

"*Fiancée?* We're actually just very good *friends*, right Michael?"

"*Friends?* Okay, whatever you *say*, darling."

Zenobia was sittin next ta Ebai that mornin, and lookin at the two of em, you'd *swear* they were sisters—coulda been Irish twins. I wondered if I was the only one thinkin that. Maybe there was somethin to Stanky's claim, after all.

****

From the plot I was workin on, I could see buffed Shadrach in the alfalfa field. He was standin on a flatbed platform, drawn by a horse and buggy. His shirt was off and he had a grapplin hook in his hand. And every so often, he leaned off to the side, effortlessly grabbed a huge hay bale and hand-stacked it on the platform.

He looked like a professional athelete. His ripplin muscles glistenin with sweat in the sunlight as he worked—somethin that was not lost on Zenobia, who had stopped her hoein ta watch the show. When we were at lunch, she managed to get a place next to him, where she feigned interest in Margaret, tryin ta seem all motherly and sweet. She smiled up at Shadrach and laughed at his comments, even when they were just plain idiotic, and not funny.

When I could take no more of it, I got up and approached her, whisperin in her ear.

"You're *embarrassin* yourself, darling," I said between my teeth.

"Get *away* from me, honey," she said between hers.

And just like that, we went from bein married, ta bein engaged, ta bein just friends. The disloyalty was disturbin ta me. She was all smiley with me the night before. If I didn't know any better, I woulda thought she was *flirtin* with me, and then *this* guy comes along! She had ta know I was kinda pissed, but she didn't care.

"So Shadrach," she asked, "do you like music? Do you *sing?*"

"I guess so," he answered, shy and embarrassed. "So Jezebel, do you like music? Do *you* sing?"

"My name's not Jezebel. It's Zenobia. And yes, Shadrach, I *do* sing."

"It's *not* Jezebel? Well then that's *good.* Jezebel was a bad,mean lady. I read about it in the Bible. What do you sing? Church music?"

"I *can* sing church music."

"Well, will you sing for the family tonight? After dinner? I have a favorite song you can sing if you know it, but I can't tell you until dinner. It's kinda my secret."

"I *like* a man of mystery!" she laughed. "That's fine. I'll sing for you tonight, Shadrach."

Just sickenin! The only consolation was Ebai, who actually *spoke* ta me.

"I just thought it was improper before to talk or make friendly with you," she blurted, "being you were engaged and all. But since you and Zenobia are just friends, I suppose *we* could be friends too. I don't meet too many new people around here," she smiled. "I am pleased to make your acquaintance, sir."

"Please—it's Michael."

"Well then, I am pleased to make your acquaintance, Michael."

"That's better. And I am pleased to make *your* acquaintance, Ebai."

The rest of the workday was more bearable than the previous day. They had me on strawberries and cucumbers. As I toiled, I still felt *bothered* by the way Zenobia had treated me. I spent my breaks kinda spyin on her, watchin her work her magic, drawin all the attention ta herself. She was good at that, bein an entertainer and all.

Well, I figured, if it wasn't Shadrach, it woulda been some rapper guy or actor or athelete. The only way she woulda been interested in me is if we were away from everybody and everything, and if there was no other elegible black guy around. But in my case, Shadrach, Mr. Perfect, was the spoiler. Zenobia had actually been warmin up to me, but just like that—she put me in the *friend keep*, or the genie's lamp.

Women should *know* better. No guy ever—and I mean *ever*—willingly goes into the *friend lamp*, no matter what he tells ya, unless he's gay of course. Ta "put im in the lamp," ta bottle all that raw lust up, ya gotta maybe beat im about the head, beat im down a little (or a lot) and then stuff im in there, shove his head between his knees, slam and lock the lid and throw the damn thing away. Doin that, ya make im a desperate genie, trapped against his will in that lamp. If he can ever escape (because believe me, he'll try at every opportunity), like when you're drunk, vuneralble or distracted, he will, and it *won't* be *magic*, believe that! Better off just gettin a dog or a cat!

But that wasn't the point. Eighty Acres and Two Mules wasn't our life. Zenobia was a multi-millionaire pop star with over a hundred million dollars and millions of fans who wanted her back. After the news stories, she was probably gonna be even more rich and famous than before. She had ta get back ta that. And I had ta save my father and restore my family's name.

I was beat after we finished the day and we got back ta the house, but Zenobia had somethin else on her mind.

"Okay Michael, you and me agreed yesterday that we were going to take a nature walk to look for Mystique. I think we have about an hour and a half before dinner to do that."

"You said we were gonna do it as a *couple*! But now we're just friends."

"Then we'll do it as *friends*. You want to get off this farm just like I do."

"Yeah, you're right."

"But then again, if I get with Shadrach, maybe I might stick *around* here for awhile. I could use a break from performing. I got enough money now."

"My ma always said: *ya can hide from everyone but yourself*. Are we lookin for the dog, or what?"

****

So we walked inta the forest, toward the trees where Uncle Joe and Zenobia indicated the owls lived.

"Did you bring your gun like I said?" she asked.

"Yeah, I did. But why?"

"You're an animal hitman, aren't you? I'm going to *pay* you to kill those damn owls! When they got my Mystique, I swore to her I would avenge her death. When we get back, I'll pay you five hundred thousand dollars for each owl."

"No," I sighed. "I can't do that. I thought we were out here lookin for Mystique's collar or somethin. I'm not killin any owls."

"You're an animal hitman, aren't you," she persisted. "You kill animals for a living?"

"Well yeah, I guess."

"And I'm offering you a *job*! And payin good money! Are you trying to negotiate here? All right, I'll pay a million dollars apiece and not a dollar more. Deal?"

"Ehh," I answered, hesitant. "I'm not really feelin that."

"I don't *get* it! You'd refuse two million dollars to shoot up in that tree and kill two stupid owls? What the hell is *wrong* with you? Little boys shoot birds all the time, for fun and for free!"

She was even more intuitive than I imagined, or maybe I was just that easy ta read.

"Hold on, Michael! Don't tell me. I already know. You're an *animal* hitman, which is already lame, but you've never even *killed* an animal, have you? Is that it? Am I *right*?"

I was embarrassed, because it really was kinda lame, but I wasn't shootin up a tree at some owls!

"Well yeah, I guess. That's pretty much it."

"And *Lolita* was your girlfriend? I saw what she looked like. Guys are drooling over her pictures."

All I could do was shake my head.

"There *is* something about you, though," she whispered, softening. "I can't put my finger on it, but you've got something going on, or maybe *we* do."

She placed her palm on my face, strokin.

"There is something I *like* about you, Michael Ponzi. Just *maybe* we coulda, you know, explored something if—if Shadrach hadn't come along."

And just like that, she went back ta bein the diva.

"I'll point out where I found pellets and *you* break them up. I'm not digging in owl vomit."

We found dozens of owl pellets under the tree. Then I had ta break em up and search through the fur and bones.

"What are we lookin for? A collar? They wouldn't eat that."

"We're in this together, right? It's not a collar—it's a microchip."

"A microchip? What's *on* it?"

"It's a long story," she explained, "but now's as good a time as any. Do you remember the guy from a few years back who was a computer genius working as a contractor for the National Security Agency? He leaked like 2.4 million classified U.S. documents to the international media?"

"*That* crazy guy? The one that went to Russia and then Venezuela? Yeah, the story was all over the news."

"Well, that 'crazy' guy actually *was* my cousin—a little geeky, but we were close when we were young. So we got into this conversation about five years ago when he was working for the CIA or some other agency, and I was telling him about The Management and how they ran everything. I told him no one believed me because *The Man* could control everything and everyone. He listened and said he was working on something similar. Then he *floored* me when he told me I was right."

"Okay…" I urged.

"Three days before he split the country, my cousin gave me a microchip, and he told me that microchip had my proof that *The Man* was real. He said if *The Man* ever had any suspicion that I had it, they'd come after me."

"Let me guess. You put that microchip somewhere on Mystique's head?"

"In one of her teeth. In the filling."

"Your *dog* has fillins? Wait! I'm not surprised."

"There's no trace of her in any of these pellets. You're going to have to climb that tree."

I figured she was gonna say that. The only problem—the *owls* were up there, and they were pretty big, too. A five-foot wingspan!

"I can't *climb* that tree!"

"Of course you can! Our only bit of hope is up there. Don't you want to save your father?"

"Those are birds of *prey* up there," I protested. "Two of em, both with sets of—like five-inch claws."

"You have a gun. *Shoot* them! My two million dollar offer is still good."

"Tomorrow," I countered. "I'm gonna have to come up with some basic protective gear. I'll go up and check that tree tomorrow, same time, same channel. I promise!"

Courtin

It had been a long day, so I was ready for dinner, until I heard what was on the menu: Possum Pot Pie, in a long pan. Apparently, Uncle Joe spotted an entire family of the critters in a tree earlier that day, and a turtle in the creek. My only relief was gonna be the look on Zenobia's face when she heard that were eatin the little family, and she did not disappoint.

"I worked hard labor all day for some Possum Pot Pie! That's not even *people* food! A *dog* wouldn't eat that!"

But then she looked toward Shadrach, whose mother had spent two hours skinnin seven possums, crackin open a terrapin and slavin over the stove.

"But I'm adventurous and always ready to try new things. So, Shadrach, *serve* me up!"

The meal actually wasn't bad. If I hadn't already known it was possum, I woulda thought I was eatin somethin that was a cross between dark meat chicken and pork, sprinkled with a little forest dirt. The terrapin was chewy, but Aunt Mary also heated up some baked turkey from three nights before. Bellies full, we all seemed to sigh in unison, a final punctuation for a long day.

"Mom, family, guests—the song I would like to hear Zenobia sing is *Farther Along*, because everyone *knows* it was Granddad's favorite, and Dad plays it so good on the guitar."

He smoothed a piece of crumpled paper against his chest before handin it ta Zenobia.

"I, I got the words right here. I copied these down all by myself. Can you sing it?

"This song was *my* grandfather's favorite too," she smiled. "We sang it for years when I was young. I don't *need* the words, Shadrach, if it's what you want me to sing."

"You are *so* pretty, Zenobia. Yes, I do. Very much!"

Uncle Joe began the tune on a worn acoustic guitar, the plastic pick in his wrinkled fingers bringin the metal strings and hollowed-out wooden body to life. A folksy, bluesy, church-like melody resonated, transformin the room to a simpler place in time. It all felt real. The magical moment came when everyone at the table, besides me, began the refrain.

Farther along we'll, know more about it
Farther along we'll, understand why
Cheer up my brother, live in the sunshine
We'll understand it, all by and by

Zenobia cleared her thoat quietly, awaitin her musical cue to begin the verse.

Tempted and tried will, oft' me to wonder
Why it should be thus, all the day long
While there are others, living about us
Never molested, though in the wrong

Her voice was clear and angelic, though vulnerable in a sad, hauntin way. I looked at her, and I felt more love than I had ever felt in my life before, though not necessarily for her, but for love itself, and for what love made possible. Ebai, Margaret, Rahab and Aunt Mary sang the second refrain with her.

Farther along we'll, know more about it
Farther along we'll, understand why
Cheer up my brother, live in the sunshine
We'll understand it, all by and by

I felt a tear escape the corner of my eye and, self-concious, I brushed it away. I had never understood what they meant by 'soul' music, but *that* was it! Zenobia sang again.

Sometimes I wonder, why I must suffer,
Go in the rain, the cold, and the snow,
When there are many, living in comfort,
Giving no heed to, all I can do.

She looked at me. She actually *looked* at me, like she was singin that last verse ta me, but I knew better. It was all for Shadrach. The final refrain:

Farther along we'll, know more about it
Farther along we'll, understand why
Cheer up my brother, live in the sunshine

We'll understand it, all by and by

By the time the song was over, Shadrach was cryin in sadness and joy, and ta my surprise, his mother, Aunt Mary, was cryin too.

"An angel has visited this house tonight," she sobbed, truly touched. "Zenobia, you have the most beautiful voice I have ever heard in my life. *Thank* you for that!"

Zenobia's singin was incredible, and she was good at what she did. She had finally won over Aunt Mary. It was a done deal. Shadrach, big, bone-headed, simple, good-lookin guy that he was— he beamed as he took a seat next to Zenobia. Takin her hand in his, he bowed his head.

"Zenobia, I really *like* you. Out here, we don't get many opportunities to meet eligible, you know, eligible other *people* of the opposite gender, so we take advantage when the Lord provides."

"I completely understand," she agreed, noddin vigorously.

Ebai looked at me, smilin, all of us knowin what was comin next.

"I would like to propose… I'd like to propose a question," he stammered.

All eyes on the new couple, Zenobia shifted in her seat, anxious.

"You don't have to be nervous, Shadrach. *Ask* me."

"Zenobia?"

"Yes, Shadrach? I'm listening."

"Zenobia—I'm sorry. Zenobia, are you a *virgin*?"

It was clearly not the question she was expectin. It was the first time I ever saw a black person blush. She was at a loss—from elation to horror in two seconds, which ta her probably seemed like two hours.

"We, we barely know each other, Shadrach," she stuttered. "Why would you ask me a *question* like that in front of all these people?"

"Because I need to *know*. I've saved myself all my life for the woman one who would be my wife, and so I need a woman who has saved herself in the same way for me that I have saved myself for her. So I have to ask. *Are* you, Zenobia? Are you a virgin?"

Again with the question that hit her like a wreckin ball!

"I, I don't believe that is an appropriate question in public, Shadrach. I think it's disrespectful. We can talk about it in private."

"My mom told me if that you said yes, then that it would be a *lie*. But I told her she was wrong. *Am* I, Zenobia?"

"Oh *snap!*" Stanley interjected, breakin character.

Half of me felt amused, but the other half felt sorry for her. It was rude of Shadrach, after all, ta call her out like that, about whether or not she was a virgin. I mean, she coulda lied, because I've heard there is no true way of tellin. Coulda been a bicycle accident or a fall—legitametely. Besides, these people were the black Waltons, who never watched TV or looked at a supermarket rag.

"Zenobia *is* a virgin," I announced. "I know it for a fact. She's been ta a doctor an all. I can *vouch* for that!"

Feelin relieved and a bit vindicated, she smiled at me and nodded, her angry glare fallin on Aunt Mary.

"So there you've *heard* it. Any more embarrassing personal questions? Ma'am?"

"If he *says* you're a virgin, then maybe you are, and maybe not. And I never said you were a harlot. I just said you were wearing the *garments* of a harlot when you came here."

Zenobia stood.

"I'm not feeling well. If you all will excuse me, I'm going to bed."

"Uh, Zenobia, can I speak with you on the porch for a minute?" Shadrach asked.

"No," she interrupted. "You had your chance. I'll see you all in the morning."

Ebai filled the charisma vacuum that persisted after Zenobia left with a warm smile. She cleared her throat and spoke to her father, Uncle Joe, though the request was for everyone in the room.

"Daddy, I would like your permission to begin courting Michael Ponzi. He has proven himself a hard worker and an upright, honest individual. And since he and Zenobia are only *friends*, then he is an eligible candidate for marriage."

The only commentary was Margaret's cough, which sounded an awful lot like the word, "Bullshit!" causin Joab and Rahab ta snicker.

Whoa! I thought. Ebai wanted ta marry *me? Just like that?*

"Michael Ponzi," her father said, "Are you asking permission to begin courting my daughter, Ebai?"

If Zenobia was in an uncomfortable spot minutes before, I had taken her place, front and center. I thought sayin "no" would embarrass Ebai, who really was an incredibly beautiful young woman, even covered up the way she was. But ta say "yes" would mean we were officially datin for the purpose of gettin married. I looked around for help that never came.

"Yes," I replied, trying hard to disguise my reluctance.

"Let me get this straight. *Yes*, you are asking permission to begin courting my daughter, Ebai?"

Somehow, it sounded more severe the way he said it.

"Yes," I nodded, dizzy as I considered the repercussions.

I figured I'd talk ta her the next day and tell her I wanted ta take things real slow for a while, and then I'd let her down easy—just before Zenobia and I split the place. Ebai was a sweetie. The last thing I wanted ta do was embarrass her, hurt her or break her heart.

"Then it's official!" Ebai declared as she reached over and placed her hand on mine, strokin, smilin. "The good Lord has *sent* me a man!"

Ebai

Breakfast the next mornin was uncharacteristically quiet. I didn't know exactly who was mad at whom, but there was a definite feelin of animosity in the air. I could tell Zenobia was really pissed at Shadrach from the night before. As much as he worked to get her attention, she wouldn't even look in his direction. It was also clear she had it out for Aunt Mary, who was equally irritable.

Uncle Joe tried ta lighten the mood by complimentin the ladies' hard work the day before, about their appearance and about the size of the grapefruit and melons he saw from them earlier in the week. I hadda agree with the latter, cuz I remembered gawkin at the size of the melons Ebai had from the day before.

I was waitin my turn to get my breakfast when Ebai placed a perfectly-prepared, generous plate of food in front of me. I was shocked, cuz I wasn't used to even bein considered, let alone served. She had fixed my plate—the same way Aunt Mary always fixed Unlce Joe's plate, and while I was surprised, Zenobia seemed offended. She leaned toward me, whisperin between clenched teeth.

"What's *up* with that simple, country girl fixin your plate?"

Ebai, a house cat with keen hearin and the beginnins of her claws bared, was quick with a response.

"Didn't Margaret tell you? Michael and I are *courting* now, and I made his plate as a sign of respect."

Eyebrows raised, Zenobia looked at me.

"So now you're *courting* Ebai, honey? When did *this* happen?"

"Last night, I guess," I half-shrugged, half-affirmed.

"But I thought *I* was your fiancée?" Zenobia insisted.

"Friends!" contested Ebai. "You're just *friends*! You told all of us that just yesterday. *That's* how I knew he was available for courting. Everyone heard you say it."

The fangs were showin.

"It's all good," Zenobia replied. "I just had no idea how *desperate* you were!"

"And just yesterday," Ebai countered, "you were all giddy about courting Shadrach, *Virgin!*"

Zenobia gave Ebai her hand as she leaned toward me.

"*You're* way out of line, Michael! You're as *foul* as tofurky! We'll talk later."

****

The sun was hot and the air was still as most of us spent the day in the pear orchard. When Uncle Joe asked for two volunteers ta harvest a few peaches in the adjacent lot, I went over. Ebai tried to be reassigned with me, but Zenobia beat her to it. And so, with baskets in the rows between trees, Zenobia and I began pickin the peaches.

"How *dare* you!"

"How *dare* me? What did I do?"

"Just stop! You know what you're doing. Weren't we supposed to be *married*?"

"We were, but you bumped it down ta 'engaged' and then down ta 'just friends'—remember? You did that!" I hissed between my teeth.

We did not look at each other as we spoke ta hide the fact we were havin a heated conversation. I continued.

"I thought I had a chance, but ya threw me under the bus for… for that Shadrach!"

While a few of the peaches were still green, most were orange and purple. Uncle Joe said to take em all. A ladder stood in one of the rows for the high fruit.

"I don't get it. Why aren't ya still all gaga for Shadrach?"

"Listen Micheal, don't get me wrong. Shadrach's handsome and all, a big, wonderful country boy, but even you can recognize he's not too bright. He'll be on this farm his whole life, and he'll never know what it's like out there. On the other hand, I'm the *embodiment* of everything out there. I'd date him, but I couldn't live here like this, and he and I would never make it out there."

She handed the peaches down, one at a time.

"The same goes for you and Ebai."

"Well, maybe," I countered. "I suppose that'd be as silly as thinkin ya can restore a girl's virginity by simply sayin so, and *vouchin* for it."

"By the way, *thanks* for that. The look on Aunt Mary's face when you stood up for me was priceless! Old bat!"

Zenobia came down from the ladder and stood aside as I moved it ta the next row.

"We could tell em all we're now *re-engaged?*" she suggested. "Come on—you and me, back together again!"

"Naw, Zenobia. Naw, we couldn't do *that*. It would hurt Ebai. She's got a heart of gold, and I don't wanna break it. She's gotta be about the sweetest girl I've ever met."

"That's because you've never seen her mad or territorial. She's no different than the rest of us. It's a *trap*. If I were you, I would be very careful with that one."

Zenobia sighed, waggin her head in disgust.

"You know, the whole world is whack for women, even out here on the farm!"

"Why do you say that?"

"Well, when Ebai announced her intentions last night, did anyone bother to ask if *you* were a virgin?"

We worked the next thirty minutes sayin little, except for dialogue necessary ta pick the peaches. Then, right before we were done, Zenobia stopped and turned toward me.

"So, is your new little girlfriend going to have a problem with you and me going to the owl tree today after we finish?"

"Oh, that," I stuttered. "I've been thinkin about it, and I really don't think it's a good idea."

"Oh, *no!* You gave me your word. You said you'd do it today. Besides, we can't stay here forever, and you've got to work on saving your father."

"You're right. I'll just have ta get some protection from the barn. I'm climbin that tree taday!"

****

When I told Ebai that I had promised to help my 'friend' Zenobia find what was left of her dog, she pretended to be okay with it, but I could tell the whole idea of me spendin time with another woman vexed her.

"It's just that it's our first day courting, and you're going off with her, *alone*. Please tell me the truth: is it really true that you're just friends? Do you have feelings for her?"

"No. Not at all. She's just my friend. It's just that I promised yesterday, even before you and I were courtin, that I would help her find what was left of her dog. I just wanna keep my word."

"Well, you *are* a decent man, Michael Ponzi. Please don't think ill of me, but I don't trust her. Between you and me, somehow she doesn't *look* like a virgin."

"I'm not sure what you mean. What does a virgin look like?"

She shook her head and smiled.

"Me, and that's all you need to know."

I kept my distance from Zenobia as we walked along the trail into the woods. All along the way, she kept tryin ta hold my hand, just ta increase the suspicion in Ebai's mind. It was hard ta resist her flirtin, but I couldn't tell if she wasn't just playin with me.

A day before, I woulda done anything ta be near her, but I could feel Ebai's eyes burnin inta my back. Imagine that! What millions of guys *wouldn't* have done just ta even have a single minute with Zenobia! And there she was, kinda inta me as far as I could tell, playin seductive, wantin ta tell em all we were re-engaged, and I just walked along there, hesitatin, keepin my distance!

Bubo and his Wife

It took us about fifteen minutes to reach the tree, a giant sycamore, I think. I was wearin my regular work clothes, but I also had on Stanley's oversized, meant-ta-sag jeans from the back of the car, his ghetto jacket and his New York Knicks baseball cap. Before meetin up ta leave, I tucked the 9mm Glock in the waistband of my first pair of pants.

"You can climb in all that?"

"Yeah. You worried?"

"More about you getting Mystique's head. After you get that, you can *fall* to your damn death for all I care."

"Nice. The Dwarf was right about you."

"If The Dwarf was here, I'd have *his* little ass climbin that damn tree! It's his fault we're in this whole situation in the first place."

She looked toward the nest.

"The owls are gone. You need to get up there."

And so I started climbin the tree, fifteen feet, twenty feet— the nest had maybe forty feet up there. Uncle Joe said it was an old hawk's nest that the owls took over and added to, but it had to be about eight feet across and made of thousands of criss-crossed sticks, most of em about two feet long and an inch thick. I could smell the stench before I got to it. *Uggh!*

I had ta get positioned on an adjacent branch ta look over into the nest, and when I did, I understood why everything that walked or crawled out there feared the owls. There were skulls, spines, pelts and limbs from hundreds of animals, wedged in here and there, across the tangled, owl poop-stained latticework of sticks and branches. From what I could see, there were remains from skunks, crows, bats, weasels, porcupines, rabbits, foxes, cats, turtle shells, lizards and what looked like last night's wild turkey dinner.

Scannin back and forth, I didn't see any trace of Mystique. I guess I got a little nervous, lookin at all the carnage, and realizin the owls had viciously torn all those animals apart. It was like bein at the bloody crime scene of a serial killer who had stepped out, without backup. What if one of em, or what if both of em came back when I was up there?

So just as I was about ta leave and get back down the tree, I saw it—it was Mystique's shriveled little head, teeth still bared in a snarl, wedged between two sticks near the top of the nest on the other side. I leaned across, but it was just out of reach. *Oh screw me!*

Gettin the head meant gettin up ta the next branch and reachin alltheway across that disgustin collection of body parts. Anxious ta get it over with, I held my breath and lunged, breakin part of the left side of the nest as I reached in and tugged at the head. I took a good look at it ta make sure it was her, shoved it in my pocket and scrambled out the nest, but I guess the sound of me tusslin up there woke im up.

"*Ho-ho-hoo hoo hoo!*"

Bubo was on a branch in the next tree, starin straight at me, claws clenched. He had this look on his face like he was sayin: *Sorry, but I gotta kick your ass. My wife's in the next tree, and she ain't havin it no other way.* When I spotted her, she seemed still asleep, so I slid down the trunk of the tree to the next branch, my eyes pleadin with him ta give me a break. She was a lot bigger than he was, so when one of her eyes opened, I knew I was in trouble.

She didn't move. She only looked at him the same way my ma did at my dad before sayin: *Handle it, Asshole!* With a start, he was in the air, circlin the tree and me as I slid down to the next large tree limb and scuttled to the other side of the trunk, away from him. His wingspan had to be at least five feet wide! Zeroin in on me, he wove through branches and leaves so fast I hardly saw im comin, and when I knew anything, there was this sharp pain in my shoulder and I was bleedin. *Sonofa!*—

I was in no position ta defend myself in that tree, but I did have a gun, and so takin it out and releasin the safety, as I had done so many times in video games, I leaned ta the left and took aim. A little cocky because I was such an easy mark, Bubo got a little bold and careless, maybe showin off for his wife, so he came at me full on in the next attack. It was so easy. I just squeezed the trigger.

Pop! And Bubo, his body nearly torn in two, trailed down to the forest floor. His wife, obviously wantin no part of me and the gun, took off, never lookin back. Good thing too—cuz I wasn't prepared for when the gun recoiled, so I dropped it, thirty feet down. If she came back, my ass was out there, vunerable. Panicked, I hurried down the tree trunk, leapin ta the ground when I was still twenty feet up. I sprained my ankle as I landed, but Zenobia was right there ta help me up.

"Did you *get* it?"

'Yeah, and I almost got myself *killed* in the process!"

"No, no! You don't *understand.* I promised you a million dollars apiece ta kill those owls. You're a *millionaire* now, Michael! Where's the head? I want it!"

"Ooh!" she complained, when I pulled it outa my pants. "It's so shriveled!"

"As my college roommate used ta say," I groaned. *"A little head is better than no head at all.* What do we do now?"

"I know exactly where it's at—bottom left, second molar. We'll pull the tooth, and then we'll save the head for a burial when we get back to civilization."

So takin the pliers from the jacket pocket, we pulled the tooth and I gave it to Zenobia for safekeepin.

"Whatever's on it," I insisted, "we can't access that chip until we can get to a computer, and there ain't one for at least thirty miles around."

"Then we have to go somewhere where we can get to one. We can use Stanley's car."

"Right!" I laughed. "We probably have ta be the most two sought after people in the *world* by now! So we're gonna just *drive* inta civilization and use a computer?"

"I thought about that. They already have it in their mind what they're lookin for: a goofy, perverted white boy, and me. That's why you have to disguise yourself as a hot white girl, if possible, and I have to dress up as a thug-lookin black guy. I have a few hundred dollars. Stanley could pick up the things we need. No one will ever know it's us."

"Okay, so we access the chip, and then what are we gonna *find?* How is that gonna *help* us?"

"We'll find *some* way to leverage it—the information on the chip for our lives back. No, wait—you didn't *have* a life before you met me. Maybe you could get yourself even *more* money and save your father at the same time."

Before we left, we searched the forest and found Bubo, body all ripped apart, feathers everywhere, tongue hangin out and talons on his right foot still twitchin. *Poor bird!* I felt bad. I had never killed anything or anyone before in my life. At that moment, I thought about his wife and about how *she* musta felt. They were *family*, after all. Uncle Joe said they had been livin there for seven years. That must've been like *fifty* together in people years!

****

I had a hard time eatin dinner, thinkin about it. We were all around the table, sharin a catfish dinner, like a family, while Bubo lied near the base of the tree he lived in for seven years, providin a meal for worms, or maybe an oppossum. I *did* that ta him. Stanley said he thought he heard what sounded like a gunshot earlier, but no one else did. I though I should have buried Bubo, if only ta hide my shame. Glancin out the window, I knew his angry wife was out there, and if she got the chance, she'd make me pay for what I had done.

I never even had to get up from the table. Ebai made my plate and drink and served them to me, all the while intimatin that Zenobia should do the same for Shadrach, as a symbol of respect. But Zenobia, kitty that she was, had lost all interest in Shadrach, causin me to remember the words my grandfather always quoted—*learn a lesson from the rat: what's cunnin in the kitten may be cruel in the cat.* She was sarcastic with him, and condescendin, though he wasn't smart enough to notice.

Divorced of interest, amused at her own power, she cruely toyed with him, twirlin him between exposed claws, stabbin him on occasion, nippin him and lettin im go, only to pin im down again, exertin complete mastery over him, especially after it was established that she was chaste.

"I don't see why you can't make *my* plate, Shadrach. *This* virgin is feeling a bit light-headed, especially after the *long, hard, passionate* day she experienced during and *after* the workday."

Ebai's reaction was peculiar to me. If she was as pure as she led us all to believe, she would have never caught the innuendo in Zenobia's comment. Instead, she exposed razor-sharp claws, warnin Zenobia against triflin.

"A virgin knows when and when *not* to open her mouth, that is, if she wants to *remain* a virgin. You mind *your* man, and I'll mind mine. If your man doesn't have the mind to know better, who am *I* to mind for mine?"

Zenobia was quick to parry, between bared fangs.

"Virgins who open their mouths can *call* themselves virgins, but every man knows, a ho's a ho."

The exchange was lost on Shadrach, Uncle Joe and Aunt Mary, who had no idea that the two cats were sparrin. A jaguar versus a house cat? I could tell Zenobia was holdin back, awaitin a better opportunity to sieze the jugular and shake Ebai to death. In the meantime, Shadrach verged on bein embarrassin in the suck-up department. He made Zenobia's plate and doted on her the whole night long.

"On Monday, I need you to leave your shirt at home when you go to work, Shadrach, and if I get tired, you can *carry* me."

After the family prayer and the old folks went to bed, after Shadrach and Ebai went back home to where they lived with their grandmother, Zenobia, Stanley, Margaret and I sat alone at the table.

"Here's four hundred dollars," Zenobia whispered to Stanley, "and there's plenty more where that came from. We need to get outfitted. Michael needs to become a hot white girl, and I need to be a teenage gangbanger. You know—*hard!*"

Margaret rolled her eyes.

"He'll need a wig and you're gonna need to cut off all your hair."

Reluctant, Zenobia nodded.

"Yeah, I guess so."

"*Give* it to me. Or give me a million dollars like you gave him and I can *help* you."

"Yeah, right," Zenobia laughed. "As Margaret, you're alright. I like you a lot better than that damn Unique, but what are *you* gonna do?"

"I know where you can go to use a computer, one they can't trace. Sarah, my friend from church—her father left the religion and he's like a crazy computer hacker. I spent the weekend with her over there two or three times. He's got everything you need. I don't have to tell him who you are, but he can help."

"Better than nothin," I concluded, "though I can't promise you a million dollars."

"You can give me the money *she* promised you."

"I don't have that money yet. Besides, *who* told you she was givin it to me?"

"*She* did, and I told her if *I* had a gun, I woulda kilt *both* them owls for the money. They ate her dog!"

"No," Zenobia interrupted. "If you can help us and it works out, Margaret, *I'll* give you the money. A million dollars."

"Okay!" the girl beamed, "When we go to church tomorrow, you can meet him. He still goes on Sundays on accounta his parents are there and he has to pick up Sarah."

Stanley just sat there, waggin his head.

"So I get four hundred dollars, and Unique get one *million?* What's up with *that?*"

"You're just driving," Zenobia returned. "She's *thinking.* Besides, she's had my back since I been here."

"She ain't had your back. She just don't like Ebai, that's all. Suckin on that big ol *hate-sickle!*"

The Plan

When we got to the church the next mornin, I finally understood why Ebai may have been so desperate, why she was havin such a hard time findin a suitable husband. It was like Forest Gump had fathered all the boys in the congregation—not Tom Hanks, but Forest Gump. They all looked and talked just like Forest, even the black one. It was actually kinda funny, until you realized that's all she had to choose from. And the girls—think Mel Gibson, permanently dressed in drag. No surprise *they* were all virgins.

Besides Ebai, maybe one of the twenty-five or so single young women in the church was even doable, and that would be like after a six-pack of malt liquor. But they were all savin it for Shadrach, who had decided he was savin it for Zenobia, who was an international pop star, out of his league and out ta punish him for embarrassin her in front of the family,

And there I was, sittin between Zenobia and Ebai, in church, yes, but in heaven at the same time. It didn't hurt that as cats, they were competitive and territorial. It wasn't that Zenobia had any real interest in me. It was, rather, that Zenobia knew Ebai thought she was *takin* somethin away for Zenobia, somethin she *thought* Zenobia wanted, ya know, as a *taker*, as the winner.

Always the top cat, Zenobia had to either make sure Ebai and everyone knew she never *wanted* me in the first place, or she had ta defend her territory and her kill, until *she* decided she was through with it, or me. No one was gonna take anything from Zenobia, real or imagined. In that sense, I was the prize, though it was possible that neither of the women actually *wanted* me. Once again, I was just a piece of meat, yet deep down inside, I got the feelin that Ebai actually *liked* me.

Sarah's father was this dweeb named Clark, though he wanted us ta call him *Kal-El*, which he said was Superman's real name. *Kal-El* was one of those guys who would do anything for you and ask no questions, as long as you were flatterin im and makin im feel important. So when Zenobia did that thing she does, just charmin the entire room, and kinda flirtin with *Kal-El*, which she was a pro at, she coulda told him ta slap his ma and he woulda clean knocked er out.

"Margaret said you almost got arrested for being part of *Anonymous*. I can tell you're a computer genius, *Kal-El*, and I trust you. You left the church a few years ago and you're on the web. Do you know who I *am*?"

"You're Ebai's cousin, who looks just like her," he answered in his best flirtin Gump voice, "only a little *prettier*."

"*Much* prettier. Anyway, my real name is Lois and I'm a reporter. I need your help on a super secret story I'm working on."

"Okay…"

She nodded toward me.

"This is Jimmy. He'll pretty much be your flunkey, you know, your *sidekick* through all this. You get to tell him what to do, and he'll do it."

"*Okay!* Hi, Jimmy."

"You're going to give us your address and directions, and we'll come to your house tomorrow morning. But when we come, we'll be in our super secret disguises. You might recognize us, and you might not."

"Okay, we'll see about that. I'll be ready. What time?"

"Ten in the morning. And *Kal-El*, you can't breathe a word about this to anyone, you understand?"

"Never! in the name of Truth, Justice and the American Way!"

Women and Hens

I rode back to the farm with Uncle Joe, while the rest of the family and Zenobia walked over to the home belongin ta Miss Ollie, Uncle Joe's mother. I was a little nervous about bein alone with him, expecially since Ebai and I were "courtin," and I knew how protective fathers could be about their daughters. And sure enough, he didn't head directly home. Instead, he pulled up the reins, stoppin the horse and buggy in front of the henhouse.

"They *all* look like hens to you, don't they?"

"Well, yes. They *are* hens, I think, all except the rooster."

"But they're *not* the same. You just have to know how to look at them. Come on."

Applyin the brake, he opened the door and got out the buggy, summonin me. Although the henhouse had been cleaned the night before, it still smelled like, well, like a henhouse. By the way, chickens poop a lot!

As the hens scattered and clucked before us, Uncle Joe reached down and picked up a stocky white bird that had ta be about at least five pounds. He cradled her in his arms as she rested there, blinkin her wide open eyes.

"Fried chicken you ate the other night—it was probably one of her sisters. This here is a Cornish X—best chicken in the world for meat, a fryer. Wonderful legs, thick thighs, lush, juicy breasts— what more could a man *want?*"

It was then that I realized the diversion wasn't specificaly to educate me about chickens.

"Most desired chicken in the world… for meat, for flesh, to satisfy fleshly hunger. That's all the good she is for most people, a product to be sold or consumed."

He gently placed the hen back on the straw-covered wooden floor and zeroed in on another bird, a reddish-brown chicken with a red comb and golden eyes. She relaxed as he lifted her and stroked her throat.

"Now this one is a Buff Orpington—okay for eating, but her real value lies in what she has inside. Oh, she won't give you her treasure all at once. It's the genius of God. Nature won't let you take everything all at once. She limits you to one a day, but she's dependable and consistent. She's one of the best egg-layers I got."

He reached toward me and placed the chicken in my arms.

"A man will consume the Cornish in one night, or he'll sell her and he'll be done with her. But that one there—he *keeps* her, because while he feeds and takes care of her, she gives back to *him*—a lifetime of return that he can eat or sell, and babies. Of all the hens in the yard, the Orpingtons are the best brooders and mothers."

He took the bird from my arms and guided me out the henhouse.

"Of course you're not stupid, Son. You know the point I'm making. It is not lost on me that, while you are courting Ebai, you have a secret yearning for Zenobia. I understand. Zenobia is a good-looking young woman, but she's a Cornish. She's superficial, fleshly, worldly—not the kind you keep, if she would even keep *you* around for long."

He placed a hand on my shoulder as we walked back to the buggy.

"Now Ebai is a little more plain, and maybe she's not as provocative or charming, but she's a very pretty girl, and she's an Orpington, a keeper. You can count on what she has inside. She's giving, unselfish, loyal, faithful and supportive—maybe not the qualities a man lusts after, but qualities that make her valuable over a lifetime. And she'll give you beautiful little children, Michael, a wonderful family."

He stopped and turned me toward him, starin directly into my eyes.

"The fact is you've got to decide what you *really* want: the works of the flesh, or the works of the spirit. But let me make my *real* point here. I've been hunting my whole life, killing what needs to be killed. My daughter, Ebai, is at a vulenerable age and at a vulnerable stage. So whatever you do, take care not to, in your own selfishness or lust, hurt my daughter or tarnish her chastness in any way, because if you do, I'll hunt you down and put a bullet in your careless heart."

Okay... so what did I say to *that?* A potential death threat from a man who wanted me ta marry his daughter? *Maybe I had already lost my taste for chicken!*

"I promise to respect your daughter, sir."

It was as if the threat never happened. He embraced me, huggin me hard and offered me one of his best cigars on the way over to Miss Ollie's, where there was a big Sunday barbecue and picnic planned by the lake. It was actually more of a homecomin reunion, with many estranged and disaffected children returnin ta visit parents and grandparents.

Naughty Kitty!

Of course, Zenobia and I grew a little nervous about the outsiders returnin, where if someone recognized her, they'd go back to civilization and start up a media frenzy, alertin The Management and the mob about where we had been hidin out. She pulled all her hair under the bonnet, kept her head down, and when Shadrach invited her for a nature walk along the creek over to the old well, she accepted.

Ebai introduced me as "the man she was courting" to all her friends and relatives, who seemed excited to meet me and welcomed me into the community. They asked when we were gettin married and where we were gonna live. It was awkward, until Ebai explained that her father had promised to build us a house on the property and start us out with our own farm.

Ebai was a nice girl and I found myself really likin her, but I could still hear Zenobia's words warnin me ta watch out, warnin me about a trap, about bein careful with Ebai, especially after her father threatened to put a bullet in my heart. Ebai wanted me to go with her on a nature walk around the lake, which was in the opposite direction from Zenobia and Shadrach, so I agreed.

We had walked for maybe forty-five minutes when we came to a clearin where a huge tree had obviously fallen a long time ago. The portion that remained was about twenty feet long and was a nearly symmetrical log bench that time had sanded, stained and glazed. Takin my hand, Ebai led me to a cloistered corner and sat me next to her.

"Do you want to marry me?"

I didn't know how to answer. I wasn't used to a woman bein so direct... except Lolita, who was *too* direct. I hadta admit, Ebai was a woman I coulda married, but I had just met her a few days earlier, and it coulda been a trap. I hadta tell her the truth.

"I do, but we hardly know each other."

"Michael Ponzi, for two people pure of heart who want to do the right thing, it does not matter. How long you date is nothin compared to what is in your heart."

She was right, and she seemed so sincere. I thought about it. I coulda married her and stayed right there. She was everything I ever wanted, and though the farm life would take a little more gettin used to, it wasn't so bad. It was a decent livin, a simple, happy life where family was just a part of everyday livin. But my father! I had so much unfinished business at home.

"Ebai, when I came here, I had no idea I would meet you. I would marry you right now, but I just can't right now. I have things I have to do back where I come from first. It's family business. I will come back here when I finish it. I promise."

"Are you telling me the truth, Michael? Why are you so uncertain? Is it Zenobia?"

"Zenobia?"

"On the way over, Zenobia told me that she was definitely *not* a virgin, that she and you had lied down together. She said she spent all night with you on the day before you came."

Naughty kitty!

"She *told* you that?"

"Yes. Is it the *truth*?"

"Lie? That I *lied down* with her? No."

"Did you spend the *night* with her, in the same room? She said she slept in your bed."

"Yes, but I did not *lie* with her. I lied on the couch, while she and the dog lied in the bed."

Ebai sighed, relieved.

"Well, it was inappropriate for you to spend the night with her, unmarried, and I want to believe you, but why would she tell me you were intimate if it were not the truth?"

"I have no idea. Maybe to get her *claws* inta you? You're *women*, for godsakes!"

"Are you telling me it was her *purpose* to deceive me?"

"I'm sayin what she told you isn't the whole truth."

Ebai seemed confused, and then angry.

"And she told me a lie because, because she wants you for *herself*!"

I hadn't really thought about it that way, cuz I knew it was more of a *top cat* thing.

"Ebai, you should consider it as a compliment. Zenobia said it because she feels *threatened* by you."

Like a woman, Ebai was already headed toward the bottom line.

"And when you leave to go take care of family business, will *Zenobia* leave with you? Will you be spending more time alone with her?"

She removed her bonnet, exposin long, loose braids of wavy jet-black hair.

"Lie *down* with me!"

I was stunned, cuz I went to Sunday School and I knew what she meant by that. I mean I couldn't believe my eyes when she started takin off her dress.

"No, no, no, Ebai! Please don't *do* that!"

"You don't find me *attractive?*" she asked, her face tremblin in fear and desperation.

"Of, of course I do! *Extremely* attractive!"

"Are you coming back for me?"

"Yes, I *told* you that."

"Then why don't you lie down with me. You're a decent man. If you lie down with me, I *know* you'll come back."

She slipped her shoulder out of her dress and began peelin the garment down her body, which I had no idea was as firm and as shapely as it was—her flawless, unblemished shoulders and arms exposed in the sun for perhaps the first time ever! I felt embarrassed, being perhaps the only man who ever eyed the cleavage at the top of her bra, traced down her waist and flat stomach to fix on her sexy navel. I could not even imagine what her butt and thighs would be like! For the love of hens!

"Stop!" I demanded. "You can't do this. *We* can't do this!"

"Over *course* we can. There is no one around for miles. It will be our little secret."

"No, we can't," I said, turnin my head before the dress got any lower. "You have to save yourself for marriage, for your husband."

"Well, are *you* not going to come back for me and be my *husband?*"

"Yes!" I insisted. "As soon as I take care of my family business, I'll be back to finish courtin you."

"Then what difference does it make? If you are *really* coming back to marry me, then we can *do* this deed. I will be giving myself to my *husband.*"

Glancin back over my shoulder, I was tempted ta just go for it. She looked like a bronze goddess standin there, confident, without a hint of shame, but she had nothin to be ashamed of—a toned, well-shaped athletic, body, a beautiful face. At that moment I thought I coulda just done it and then I coulda come back, but marriage? Plus, I was thinkin about her stern father. I did not want a bullet in my heart. I think she read inta my hesitation.

"Unless the *truth* is that you are really *not* coming back, Michael Ponzi," she sighed as she began to pull the dress back up her body. "You said I had to save myself for my *husband*, but you didn't say that husband would be *you!*"

She seemed genuinely crushed, embarrassed and humiliated for the seemin rejection of her desperate offer. When I saw a tear trail down her face, I was overwhelmed.

"No, no," I protested. "I *promise* I'll come back for you, if I can. You have ta understand: this family business of mine is very dangerous, but if I'm lucky, I might survive it. I can't be with—*lie with you* unless I know I'm gonna survive this, which I *don't* know. I will not tarnish your chasteness."

What was this new, crazy language I was speakin? But at the time, it made sense. And readin Ebai's face, it had worked like magic. Tears gone, she rearranged her dress and bonnet and rushed to embrace me.

"I have never met a man like you. You are so principled. I love you!"

I had no idea how to respond, so I kinda winged it.

"Ebai, Love is a rose that develops, buds and blossoms over time. I care about you, but let's enjoy and savor the entire process. When I come back, we will have all the time in the world to let our delicate flower bloom."

A little cheesy, but it worked. On the way back to Miss Ollie's, Ebai admitted that she felt jealous and resentful toward Zenobia, who had probably *fooled* me about her bein a virgin. She told me to be careful in "that woman's" company.

"Stay away from her! Don't even go near her after you leave here. You will lose your self-respect and end up in debt to some cruel person for the rest of your life. Strangers will get your money and everything else you have worked for. Come back to *me!*"

Dinner at Miss Ollie's was fabulous. We had barbequed spareribs, turnip greens, potato salad, fresh-squeezed lemonade and sweet potato pie! We were gone before sundown, as Monday was a workin day. I said my goodbye to Ebai, while Zenobia joked with Shadrach that if he ever got man enough to release his mama's apron strings and come ta the city, she'd show him a whole new world.

Pretty Hot in Drag!

We ate the next mornin, but we didn't go ta the fields, as we were preparin ta leave. With everyone gone, Zenobia and I put on the clothes Stanley got for us. He had me in a St. John's knit dress, which I thought was totally inappropriate for that time of year, ya know, with the heat. The worst part wasI hadda shave my legs. Otherwise I woulda looked absolutely gross in that dress, ya know, with all the hair. And my toes—I hadda shave them too.

First the first time in my life, I was a blonde, with long wavy hair that I found it fun to flick, wag and shake. Stanley stuffed my bra with large heirloom tomatoes, while Margaret did my face and explained ta me how ta walk in stilettos. I was wobbly, but I was gettin the hang of it.

Zenobia didn't end up cuttin her hair. She braided it, pinned it up under a wig with dreads, covered by a baseball cap. Then she used ace bandages ta strap her breasts flat against her chest. I offered ta help, but she only threatened ta give me a knee-blast ta the macademias. Stanley got her a fake diamond grill, ta give her a kinda Lil Wayne look.

Kal-El's place was located maybe twenty miles away. Stanley dropped us there and said he'd be back in three hours. As we looked around his "war room," we realized that Margaret was right. If anyone could help us, it would be the superman-obsessed geek, former Mennonite, dressed up as Clark Kent.

"*Who* exactly are you?"

"It's me, Lois, *Ebai's* cousin," Zenobia answered. "This is a disguise. I'm really a woman."

"Who's the hot chick?"

"Hey!" I protested, sensin what seemed ta be the beginnins of nerdy, lusty thoughts, though I was a little flattered that he thought I was hot. I mean, especially after the work I put in ta look nice and all.

"That's not a chick! It's a dude. That's *Jimmy* in disguise."

Kal-El barely heard her. He was still checkin me out.

"Well, she's a MILF anyway!"

I blushed, until I worked up in my head what words made up that acronym, especially after I caught im starin at my tomatoes. Zenobia though, seemed a little offended that I was gettin all the play. I figured it was probably because she was used ta comin in a room and suckin up all the attention, from men in particular. And here this man was ignorin *her* and droolin all over me. She was jealous!

"You're a pervert, Kal-El," she sighed. "Can we get started?"

"Okay. What do you have?" he asked.

"This," she answered, holdin the chip toward the overhead light.

"Let me *see* that."

"Um, you might wanna use an offline computer for starts, Kal-El," I suggested. "Just in case there's somethin embedded that'll let em detect when the chip is accessed.

"Good idea, but I already thought of it," he nodded, as he studied the tiny chip in his hand. "It's IBM, and no doubt about it, experimental. Where did you get it? This technology does not exist yet, at least not outside the government..."

He placed it on a white card and went over to a microscope at his desk.

"Maybe not on this planet. Maybe it's *alien* technology? Definitely atomic scale, quantum computer phenomena."

"Let's just say from somewhere on Earth for now," Zenobia insisted. "Can you access what's *on* it?"

He seemed offended.

"Everything in this room is beyond state-of-the-art. I worked specialized R&D at IBM doing this exact same thing! If *I* can't read what's on it, you'll never be able to find anyone else who can!"

After two hours, he was still unable to access the chip.

"Can you call your cousin in Russia who gave it to you?" I asked Zenobia.

"Are you crazy? He's in Venezuala now, hiding from the American government, who wants to *kill* him!"

"Uh, how much longer?" I queried Kal-El in my most feminine voice. "We were hopin ta see what's on it and get outa here by now."

"Blasted!" he groaned. "It's heavily-encrypted. I know I can break into it, but it's going to take time, like until tomorrow. You'll have to come back tomorrow."

"Then copy it, and give it back to us," a thug-like Zenobia concluded. "We're comin back tomorra. And lissen, Al, ya betta not share nothin about this with no one, cuz that'll be yo ass!"

Almost…

Stanley picked us up and took us to a motel in Albany off the I-90. Now, I still had all *my* money, so I was gonna spring for separate rooms, but Zenobia contended we had to remain in our "cover," which was as a "couple," so we got a room with two queen-sized beds.

"Here's an extra two hundred dollars, Stanley. Just don't tell Ebai that Zenobia and I are stayin in the same room, with one bed. Believe me, nothin's gonna happen."

I may have been a little paranoid, but I could swear I saw Stanley sneak a peek at my tomatoes, and then at my legs.

"Out here it's Stanky. But I ain't seen nothing, ain't heard nothin. Y'all do what y'all gonna do."

"Um, Stanky—here's an extra three hundred. Can you get me a new dress and some heels? We've gotta see Kal-El again tomorrow, and ya know, I don't wanna go back there wearin the same dress. Oh, and get me a purse too!"

After we took our showers, put on our regular clothes, ordered pizza and got two bottles of wine, Zenobia and I sat, each on separate beds, formulatin the plan.

"On the night that my father got pinched, my cousin, Patrick—well, he pulled me aside before he let me go, and he was sayin these kinda *weird* things ta me, things that didn't make sense that night. So all that time at the farm I was thinkin about what he said ta me."

"What did he *say?*"

"Said things aren't always the way they seem. Said he was doin me and my dad a big-time favor, that this whole thing was bigger than I could imagine. He also said, 'trust *no one!*'"

We both kinda thought about it for a while.

"Well," Zenobia said, "your mob godfather *did* try to kill you—maybe they were going to kill you and your father that same night at the hotel?"

"I thought about that. If my cousin and uncles knew the mob was gonna take out my dad, maybe they busted im ta save his life? He woulda *never* believed em. And you—I have a feelin your argument with The Dwarf wasn't about Mystique bitin his granddaughter. That whole thing was a set-up. He probably caught wind of the microchip you put in Mystique's mouth, so they went over there ta take your dog from you that day?"

"The mob?" she wondered. "How would the mob know about that? And what would *they* want with the microchip?"

"Look," I said, leanin closer, "some wiseguy probably heard about it from the doggie dentist who put it there. People talk. You said it had information on it about The Management, and you also said the Management ran everything, includin the mob. So maybe The Dwarf wanted that chip and what's on it so he would have some leverage in dealin with them?"

"I don't know how the mob works, so I never thought about that," she muttered. "Come to think of it, I thought it *was* a little odd when Bilbo Baggins and his entourage came walking up on us at the mall. And they seemed a little *too* interested in Mystique."

"That's because they were after the dog in the first place, and they woulda tried ta dognap her when the granddaughter was holdin her, but Mystique bit the little girl and started up a big commotion."

"That makes so much *sense* now! Mystique knew!"

"But The Dwarf wasn't givin up so easy, see. So he pays off the guards and sends *me* over ta your hotel room to kill the dog and bring him her head. Figured there was probably somethin on that microchip he could use ta blackmail The Management."

"He was trying to take on The Management?" she sighed. "No one could say that little man ain't got gigantic balls!"

After our chat, Zenobia did what she called her "beauty routine," along with a glass of wine, in the bathroom, while I watched television and went over things in my head. She came out the bathroom for the local eleven o'clock news, because we both wanted ta know what had happened in the world in the time we were away.

The President and Congress were still at odds—no real work was gettin done. Rush Limbaugh said somethin else controversial about women and the Pope. Farmers were complainin about what the weather was doin ta their crops. There was a fad goin around where kids were tattooin their left earlobes purple—The Purple Lobes. All that crap.

But then a Zenobia story! Apparently, someone had spotted Zenobia in close proximity of a white or Hispanic male in a *San Francisco* nightclub! There were even three pictures of Zenobia and one of me. An FBI investigator commented that the photos were real and it was not clear if Zenobia was there under duress or of her own free will. One of the experts zeroed in on a bulge in my pants that "coulda been a gun."

Next came *The Tonight Show* with Jimmy Fallon. The monologue wasn't Leno, but it was funny enough. And then came the big surprise: one of Fallon's guests was Lolita Cardullo, who was goin by the new name of Lola Fox. It was amazin how fast things could happen in the media. In a matter of one week, she had somehow become this national or maybe international celebrity.

She came out in a sleeveless shirt with a plungin neckline and a super-short mini-dress and sat with a deliberate Sharon Stone-like crossin of her legs. Jimmy and the audience were wowed, transfixed, as she smiled, flirtin with the camera.

"So Lola, this is the first late night show you've been on, under duress? Please excuse my reaction and that of my audience. It's just that, you know, after the video, we're not used to seeing you with your clothes *on*."

After a few additional comments about her appearance and references to the video, the host began the interview in earnest.

"I take it you heard the news that Zenobia and your ex were spotted in a San Francisco nightclub? We've all heard a lot of stories. Did he kidnap her? Is she with him because she wants to be? We've even heard a story from a casino owner that they got married in a Las Vegas chapel. What's your take on all this?"

"Well, Jimmy, it may have *started* as a kidnappin, but if Zoey somehow discovered what an incredible *lover* Michael is, it's probably the other way around—she's holdin *him* in contradiction of his will."

"*Right…*" Zenobia groaned in disgust from where she sat.

"And the stories about him raping you and kidnapping you? Those weren't true?"

"All lies! He actually freed me! Michael Ponzi *liberated* me! All you women out there, tired of the same-o-same-o sex in the bedroom, right down ta the same spot on the sheets—ya gotta understand. Ya can have it *better* than that, but ya gotta learn how ta take it. Michael taught me that. He is the most adventurous, most wonderful lover in the whole wide world! Zoey, you give him back now! Michael, call me, baby, please."

If I thought Lolita was hot before, she was sizzlin on TV. Hair perfectly-styled, face made-up, designer clothes and shoes—all that bare, smooth tan skin and her dazzling smile! I could see why she had become an instant sex symbol. But her incredible looks didn't show Jimmy and the world what I saw, which was a hungry cat, ready ta take on all comers.

"But as you know, the *FBI* is still treating the matter as a kidnapping, with the mob involved. Michael Ponzi? Was he or was he *not* involved in the mob? We know his father, who's been missing for almost two weeks, was involved. So was Michael involved?"

"How would I know? *I'm* not a mobster."

"You're from Hoboken, you and Michael. But isn't your uncle Marcelino Carzano? Isn't your uncle the leader of the Carzano crime family?"

"My uncle is a *businessman*," she bristled, "CEO of Carzano Enterprises. So since when is it a crime ta be an Italian and in business? And tell me, Mr. late night Barbara Walters, did ya bring me on ta talk about my uncle, or about me?"

Backing from the razor-sharp barb, accompanied by a hungry glare, Jimmy smiled and moved on.

"Well, it's been a mercurial rise to celebrity for you, Lola! Talk shows, cable news interviews, book publishing offers and even the beginnings of a deal to get your own reality show! Anything else?"

"This is just the beginnin. I got offered a cameo in a movie they're shootin next week to be some rapper's girlfriend, who gets killed. We'll see. I ain't really inta rappers, cuz most of em are little boys. Anyway, the whole *world's* my oyster now!"

"Whatever Lola *wants!*"

Zenobia finished watchin the interview and shrugged.

"Wow, you dated *her?*"

"Yeah. Why do ya seem so surprised?"

"Because she's hot! That girl's out of your league. And all that talk about you being such a great lover—*that* was only to get you to call her so the mob could get their hands on you."

"No, *that* was the real deal," I nodded, refillin our wine glasses.

"Right… *You?* Some kind of incredible *lover?*"

"Yeah, *me!*" I smiled as I sat directly across from her, starin into her eyes. I could tell she was a little tipsy after three glasses of wine, but so was I. "I'm right here, so ya don't have ta take *her* word for it."

When I leaned in, she did too, so I just kinda went for it. Our lips touched for a quick kiss the first time, and then it was on—lips locked, tongues entangled, heads tilted this way and then that way, her hands claspin my face, my neck, my shoulders. The perpendicular was definitely headed perpendicular. My fingers ran through her hair, massagin her neck, her back, her butt, and— Whoa! *Big* mistake!

"*Excuse* me!" she yelled, pushin me away. "What the hell was *that*?"

"What was *what*?"

"You grabbed my ass!"

"No, I just kinda *massaged* it cuz it seemed like your ass was just so there, like it *needed* attention. Ya know, we were kissin and…"

"Did I *tell* you my ass needed massaging? Kissing is kissing, but ass-grabbing is on the way to something else! You got me twisted! What do you think this is? In your drunken mind, did you think you were going to *hit* this tonight?"

"Hit? Oh, no, no! My *hand* slipped! I didn't mean it like that!"

"Like I'm some cheap thrill? You spring for an economy motel room, a cardboard-tasting pizza and a bottle of nasty-ass wine from *Texas*, and you think you're gonna get somma me? This is *Zenobia* here—Queen Bee—not some Lola!"

"I'm sorry. I'm sorry—*that's* not what I wanted," I pleaded, "but there was some kinda electricity between us. I *felt* somethin. Didn't you?"

Her eyes dropped to my crotch, where my pants were still slightly distended.

"I felt you bumpin up *against* me. *That's* what I felt. Sorry to burst your bubble, but it ain't happening. No way!"

"*No way*, like you mean *never*? There *is* somethin between us!"

"I'll tell you what. If you find a way to get us out of this mess and back to our normal lives, you will prove to me that you're the man. And after that, I just *might* let you take me out on a *real* date where you're spending real money and putting in some real effort. I can't promise anything, but we'll see how it goes."

Well, at least it gave me a reason ta stay alive!

Plottin and Plannin

The next mornin, I was frantic as I shaved my face. The dress Stanky brought over was a full size too small—*a nine/ten!*—meanin it was tight in a few places, especially on my butt. The shoes were cute, though. And then, when I went ta get the tomatoes, I realized someone had taken a big bite outa one of em.

"Why would she wanna bite one of my tomatoes?" I said out loud, and then to Zenobia, "Jealous bitch! Oh no you *didn't!*"

"Oh *yes* I did! They've got drugs and procedures for wannabes like you. If you want boobs so bad, go grow or buy some *real* ones!"

It made me look a little lopsided, but I fixed the damaged tomato with a wad of tissue paper. Then we took Stanky ta breakfast with us ta hear all about the phone call.

"So," I asked, "ya called my cousin, Patrick, on the disposable cell phone we bought yesterday, from somewhere between here and the farm? And ya told im I wanted to meet im or talk to im? What he say?"

"He said he was glad to hear from you and that the FBI arrested your father to keep him safe after they learned the Carzano family had a hit out on him. He said he did it for your mother."

"Anything else?"

"He said Zenobia had some dangerous information that didn't belong to her, and the longer she kept it, the more danger you would both be facin. He said you'd never be able to get to what's on that microchip anyway, and even if you did, you would have no idea what it meant. Said if you turn it over to him, he'll make all the craziness go away and both of you can get back to your lives."

"And did you tell im like I told ya? That a big owl caught and ate the dog with the chip inside? And we've seen no trace of the dog since?"

"I did, but he said that was a lie. He said someone tried to access the chip just *yesterday* afternoon, that there's a record of it. He said if you're as smart as he knows you are, you'll meet with him taday so you can turn it over ta the FBI. Then he'll fix everything with the mob, and you can be reunited with your father."

"Anything else?"

"No."

I sat back in the booth, crossin my smooth legs, which I had shaved just that mornin.

"Zenobia—you said the microchip had somethin on it that The Management didn't want out there. Why do you think the *FBI* would want it?"

"I don't know. Why *would* they want it?"

"For the same reason the *mob* wants it. They want leverage when dealin with The Management. Your cousin musta put some very damagin information ta The Management on that chip!"

"That's what he *said!*" she chimed in with a rapper's twang in her voice. "He said he had proof on it that '*The Man*' was real, and he said the chip had proof to identify exactly who '*The Man*' was."

For the second time, we noticed a group of three tattooed-up bald guys, probably skinheads, sittin across from us, starin over at our table. They were throwin hard looks, and we figured it was because they were lookin at a cute white girl in a short dress, sittin between two black dudes, with one that looked like a rapper. One of the baldies in particular couldn't stop glancin over, and he blew me a kiss or two or three. Zenobia was amused, so when I got up to use the restroom, she reached over and smacked me hard on the ass.

First of all, it was embarrassin, and second, it was demeanin ta slap my ass in fronta those other guys. I whinnied, fakin it, and when I looked over at the skinheads, the one who was flirtin was so mad he was hyperventilatin, like his head was ready ta explode. Then when I got back ta the table, Zenobia grabbed me by the ass to guide me into the seat, all the while tauntin the skinheads, darin em ta say somethin.

"They're doin all that staring. Might as well give em something to complain about!"

That's when Zenobia started rubbin my thighs, on the insides, which made me very uncomfortable, because the other guys could clearly see what her hand was doin under the table. It was inappropriate. I tried not ta let all the rubbin affect me, but it did, so when we got up to pay, one of the guy's noticed the slight tent at the front of my dress. After a spasmic double-take, I watched his smile morph into a sneer as his friends laughed at him.

"Look, for the record, I wasn't flirtin with the likes of her...
or him! I just felt sorry for her, sittin over there between those two
thugs..."

And then he turned toward me, infuriated by the betrayal.

"But you—you are one sick asshole! Go back ta New York
City, damn liberal *freak*!"

****

Stanky dropped us off at Kal-El's at 9:30 that mornin, with
specific instructions ta come back for us in two hours. In the
meantime, he was gonna set up a tentative meetin between me and
my cousin, Patrick, at a location ta be determined by me after we
got the lowdown on the microchip. Patrick told Stanky that no one
would be able ta crack inta the chip and even it someone did, we
wouldn't know what ta do with what's on it. I knew from
experience. My cousin was a weak poker player.

My odds were on the Superman geek. After all, it did seem
like Kal-El had this sorta crush on me when I was wearin a dress,
and I must admit, I *was* lookin pretty sexy that day. I was thinkin—
maybe a little flirtin, a wink here and there, if I told him to, he
woulda cracked the *Kryptos* cipher over at Langley for me.

And much ta Zenobia's dismay, his eyes were all over me
when he saw me, so she didn't benefit from hatin, from bitin me.
When we walked inta the war room, Kal-El swore he was on the
verge of a breakthrough. He said that after workin all night, he had
opened the files on the microchip, and he was just waitin on one of
his own custom-designed programs ta decipher the code.

"Exactly how much information is *on* that chip?" Zenobia
asked, suspicious.

"Well, just for starts, this atomic scale magnet memory is at
least 200 times denser than conventional memory and solid state
memory chips, and that's a low estimate."

"And that means what?" I asked.

"You know the public library on Fifth in Manhattan and how
many books are down there?"

"Yeah?"

"Good for you. Completely useless information! I didn't make
this chip, so I don't exactly know its capacity, but with atomic scale
magnet memory, they've got storage down to twelve magnetic

atoms per bit, when it used to be one million. Technology from another world, I swear!"

"We don't care about all that," Zenobia interjected. "How long before you break the code?"

Kal-El went back to his desk and sat, peerin at the screen.

"I'm seeing part of what's on it now, mostly folders making up some sort of labyrinth with risky black holes and dead ends. Lot of data you'll have to go through, and then you'll have to find out what it means and what to do with it."

"Can't you do that for us, Kal-El?" she insisted. "Can't you go through the main stuff that's on it there, give us an idea and let us tell you what might be important to us? I'll pay you money, whatever you ask?"

"You're just a black kid," he countered, glaring at her saggin jeans. "You can't *afford* me. But you could give me this *microchip* when you've got everything you want off it..."

"You don't understand, Kal-El" I said. "There are some very powerful and dangerous people who want that little baby, and there's just no negotiatin unless they can get it back."

"Then you can just give them *another* chip—one that looks exactly *like* this one. During the time I worked at IBM, I managed to acquire five chips just like it—exact same IBM-owned design, but I have never had the technology to write on them."

He watched as his system assimilated the chip's programin in unbroken lines of numbers that scrolled down his screen.

"I'll tell you what. I can copy *some* of the data from the chip you have to one of my blank chips, compromise a few files here and there, and you can give *my* microchip to them. Believe me, this stuff is so new and cryptic that they'll just have to assume that whatever was written on it somehow got corrupted. They would never imagine you could get your hands on another chip."

It sounded too good to be true, which made me think it coulda been a set-up. Either this mook was a very good actor, or he was the biggest geek I'd ever met. If nothin else, I was pretty good at readin people.

"You ever work for the government, Kal-El? I mean, why did you leave the church, and your family?"

"Digital divide, I guess. My parents and the elders had no idea about what I do—some were calling it divination, and fooling around with the propriety of God. They branded me an apostate."

"And the government?"

"Corrupt, morally bankrupt—every last one of them, every agency, every department. I told you before: the government has suspected all along I am one of the key figures in *Anonymous*, something I've never confirmed nor denied."

"So why do *you* want my microchip?" Zenobia asked.

"To advance my cause—which has nothing to do with you. I am going to prove that we are not alone in the universe and the government's been lying to us all along."

"You're a very smart dude," she smiled, "but a word of advice: keep all that crazy talk about aliens on the down-low, or not only your church and family, but the rest of the world will think you're a kook!"

Reachin down, she reclaimed the microchip, which she had never let leave her sight.

"I'll let you copy it, but I think I'll keep the original. You just never know."

When Stanky returned, he had a package of thirty high-density CD-Rom discs and a terabyte external hard-drive, which Kal-El used for downloadin files he identified as "relating to The Management," involvin, configuration, personnel, operations, documentation and codin.

After a lengthy explanation to us about how to access information, Kal-El copied the files downloaded from Zenobia's microchip to a separate external drive and created a protocol and directory on one of his newly formatted chips. That way, Kal-El and I could divvy up the folders and go through them faster. Finally, he created two microchips with corrupted files that I could use in negotiations with the FBI and the mob.

"And you're sure this will work? It'll fool the FBI and everyone else?" I wondered aloud.

"Come on, Cutie—that chip was embedded in a filling in a little dog's *tooth* for over six months! I was very surprised it *wasn't* completely useless!"

Cousin Patrick and Uncle Liam

"Michael! You cagey rascal, you! If you had just *listened* to me that night we had you and your dad and quit the business, it would have saved us *all* a lot of trouble."

My cousin Patrick pretented that he was alone, but he worked for the government. We were sittin at a corner booth table in a coffee shop/diner off the I-90, fifteen miles outa Schenectady. Despite all the stipulations and changes we went through ta finally be sittin face ta face, I knew he and everyone at the FBI knew exactly where I was and everything I was sayin. But Irish liberal/politically-correct Democrat that he was, Patrick was a little put-off by the heels and, ya know, my shapely legs.

"So what's with the *dress*, Michael? You explorin your, uhm, feminine side?"

"It's a disguise. My lovely face has been plastered all over the newspapers and TVs. People either love me or hate me. I might as well be *your* boss, the President."

"And let me guess," Patrick interrupted, ignorin me, extendin his hand, "this must be the world-famous Zenobia, in the flesh? *Somewhere* behind that grill?"

She extended her hand, kinda mockin me because he was payin more attention ta her.

"It is. Patrick? So I hear you're the playa who's going to help us *solve* this mess?"

"Can't take credit for that. I'm working for you as a representative of the agency, of course," he nodded. "The way I see it, Zenobia, your cousin did you more harm than good. He's a traitior to our country, and now he's put your life in danger."

"You don't know my cousin, man, and you don't know what was on that microchip he gave me, so I don't know how *you* can call him a traitor!"

"On the contrary," Patrick contended. "I probably know more about what's on that chip than either of you do. I was assigned to investigate your cousin over a year before he breached protocol and downloaded 2.4 million top secret government documents, compromising our national security. I know he's your cousin, but so *not* cool!"

"I wouldn't be so sure about that," she countered, "because I know what's on it, and I know you're not *allowed* to know. It's above your pay grade."

"Well, maybe so, but you have to realize I'm the only one who can help you at this point, so whether you like it or not, you're going to have to *trust* me."

"We don't hafta *trust* ya, Patrick," I cut in, "but I guess we'll have to *work* with ya, or through ya, but *you're* gonna hafta trust *us* when we tell ya we had that chip checked out, and whatever was on it got all jacked up while it was jammed up in that little dog's dental work, or when it went through the guts of that owl, ya know."

"You've *got* the microchip with you?" Patrick asked. "I told your little friend, Stanky, that you would never be able to access it. I don't know why you even tried. I'm sure there's nothing wrong with it. You just had no idea what you were working with. Let's see it."

"Why do *you* want it?" I asked.

"It's got classified NSA files on it, information that just doesn't need to be out there… and could fall into the wrong hands. The government called my bosses this morning. They want their files back."

"Okay, so they get their files back," I nodded, "but I got the mob after me. I got a big black guy named Bubba after me, and you guys still got my dad. If I go home without im, Ma'll kill me."

I paused to let it all sink in, and then I continued.

"Zenobia here, is on the run from The Management. Not her management, but 'The Management'—the somebodys who run everything—even the FBI, which is why we really can't *trust* you."

Sensin he would get no where with me, he appealed to Zenobia.

"Your label's been in touch with us. They're spinning this whole thing as a big publicity stunt in advance of the album you were secretly recording. They expect it to break all kinds of records for sales, your biggest release ever. The world wants you back!"

He sighed, softening his voice.

"Zenobia, I know you're tired of all this running and hiding… and *him*! All this just isn't you. As far as I'm concerned, this whole matter is *your* call. It was *your* dog, and so it's your *microchip*. If you want your life back, don't listen to Michael."

He glanced toward me, reactin to the look I used ta give just before I kicked his ass.

"Come on. I'm just *sayin*, Michael! I got a job to do! And I'm trying to save your dad."

He paused, bowed his head and took her hand.

"Look Zenobia, I would be interested in knowing what you thought you might need the government to do for *you* in order for you to turn that microchip over to me."

"It don't work like that, Patrick," I argued, "you *know* that. The people you work for can't be trusted. They're in power cuz they're more sleazy, bloodthirsty and more give-a-shit-less than anyone else out there. Zenobia was right. This whole deal is above your pay grade. We ain't dumb."

"Who are you working for, Patrick?" she asked, "and what do they want from us?"

"Simple. I work for my bosses, who are getting their orders from somewhere *else* up the line. What do they want? That microchip you've got. They have authorized me to basically give you whatever you want if you turn it over to me and forget you ever had it."

"Well, what if I want *The Man* off my back?" she asked. "What if I don't want someone telling me what songs I can record, what I can wear, what I can say, who I can hang out with, who I can marry and when? Dictating *if* I can have kids, how many and what gender? What if *that's* what I want?"

"If you put what you just said in writing, I'm sure we can work out something you'll like. But more important than that, I want you to have you life back, and the government just wants to secure that chip."

"Why?" I asked. "We all know the government secrets are already *out* there, in China or Russia, or Venezuala. But we know that Zenobia's cousin—he pulled secret data from *global* sources, and what he worked up on that chip he gave her specifically relates to information he dug up on *The Man*. So tell me: why are the FBI and the government so anxious ta get *their* hands on it?"

"Please!" Patrick laughed, "You're not telling me you believe *The Man* is an actual person? You think there's some literal *man* out there, running things?"

"I *know* there is!" Zenobia interrupted, "I know from experience, and I saw proof! Are you trying to tell us you work for the FBI and you believe *The Man* isn't real?"

"Urban legend. Great story, though it would be *cool* if there *was* an actual man on top of everything. Listen, both of you: we live in the age of conspiracy theories. You just can't believe every story they put out here. *The Man?* Might as well be the Man in the Moon!"

"Okay," I postured. "There's no man because you have spoken. So who where those goons in suits in the black SUVs who rolled up the mornin after Zenobia and I left the Waldorf? Was that the *FBI?*"

Patrick seemed confused, but he tried ta play it off.

"Yeah, that was us. When we heard the mob was making a play for the dog, we figured it was time for us to move in."

"So, where *were* we, me and Zenobia, that mornin you came after us?" I asked. "Do you even *know?*"

"What do you mean, where *were* you?"

"I mean when you claim the FBI came after us that next morning. At what location did they come *lookin* for us?"

Patrick made the face he always made before he told a lie, and then he did that other thing he always did—he rubbed his nose.

"I wasn't on that detail, but I could find out the location with a simple phone call."

"But accordin ta what you just said, you were on that case for a year. Whadaya mean you *weren't* part of that detail? You didn't *know* about it? Your own agency comin after the dog to get the chip *you* were after for a year?"

His eyes studied me for a moment, and then he decided to call my bluff.

"Oh, I get it now, Michael," he groaned. ""You're making this whole story up. You're trying to trick me into lying about us being there to ruin my credibility with Zenobia. Well, I was playing along, but I know for a fact the FBI did not send a detail out for the dog the morning after she disappeared."

"You *know* that?" I asked.

"Yes, I know that," he asserted, doublin down. "I know for a *fact* we didn't send anyone out."

"Oh really?" Zenobia interjected. "Well, Michael isn't lyin this time, Patrick. Someone *did* come after us that morning. If it wasn't the FBI, then who *was* it?"

"Ask Michael. He said the mob was after him. Maybe it was the mob?"

"Naw," I sighed, "it wasn't the mob, unless they got some equal opportunity program goin on I don't know about. One of the guys was Chinese or somethin, and another was a black dude."

"Sorry, Patrick," Zenobia concluded. "You obviously have no idea what's going on. Either you don't *know* about The Management or you're clueless about what your own agency is up to on a case you're *working* on. We need to move it up a level. Who is *your* boss?"

"Aw, come on, Zenobia!" he groaned. "Cuz! Cousin Micahel! You wouldn't *do* that to me, go over my head! That's embarrassing, and it's not right! Michael, come on! I can handle this!"

"What did you tell *her*? The whole matter is her call? Bein it's her microchip an all? What do you *say*, Zenobia?"

"I say we talk to someone higher up. Who's *his* boss?"

"Guys, you can't *do* that!" Patrick pleaded.

"It's his dad, my ma's brother, my Uncle Liam," I answered. "He's been with the FBI for over forty years. He's got all kinda juice over there."

After five minutes of back and forth about the matter, Patrick finally conceded and dialed his father's number, sulkin, resignin himself to a corner of the booth. Ten minutes later, my Uncle Liam showed up, and glancin over at Patrick, he shook his head, sighed and sat.

"Michael, my favorite nephew! No, my favorite *Ivy League* college-boy nephew! In a *dress*? And this is obviously the one and only Zenobia. Ya know, from the beginning I told Patrick it would be best if I handled this matter, but he insisted. So here I am."

"And here *we* are," I responded. "We're tryin ta come to some sorta deal here, one that gets the mob off my back and *The Man* off hers."

"*The Man?*" he retorted, half-laughin. "You oughta know *better* than that, Mikee. Everyone knows *The Man* ain't real. That's all make-believe tabloid shit."

"I already *told* them that, Dad," Patrick added. "They wouldn't listen."

Sensing our resolve, Uncle Liam turned toward his son.

"Patrick, I'm sorry, but I'm going to have to ask you to leave us for a few minutes. I *got* it! Your ma wants one of us to pick up the brisket for after the baptism on Sunday. You might as well run over ta Gabriel's ta grab that now. I'll fill you in when you get back."

"Aww! Not this again! You're sending me *away*?" Patrick whined as he stood. "If there really *is* no such thing as *The Man*, then why can't I stay for this?"

"The agency has rules, Son, and I don't make em. Be sure you get the coupon in the front of the store. You'll save two dollars per pound off the regular price."

With Patrick gone, Unlcle Liam was all business.

"Tell me you have the microchip, Michael. Tell me you're ready to turn it over, and say what you want."

"You already know what we want, Uncle. I'm dealin with the mob and she's dealin with *The Man*. We have the microchip. Why don't you tell us what you can *do* for us?"

"Well, if you turn over that chip, which you shoulda never got in the first place—not so smart on your part—turn that over and I'll be able to make a deal for the two of you."

"Make a deal for us?" Zenobia asked. "Did you *hear* him? *We* have the chip—*us*, me and Michael! If *that's* what it takes, what makes you think we can't just use it to make a deal for ourselves?"

"Because you'll never be able to know what's on it, that's why," Uncle Liam, interrupted. "The two of you'll never be able to *read* that damn thing! It requires highly-specialized equipment and the services of a computer expert who can decipher millions of lines of complex codes. My guess? You're not up to it, but then, neither am I. We've got a lab in Virginia where it can be done."

"What if I told you, Uncle, that we've already *deciphered* the chip?"

"I'd say that's impossible, unbelievable... for you two. No offense."

"As unbelievable as the idea of *The Man* being a real person?" Zenobia asked. "You're underestimating us, Agent O'Brien. We have the smarts and the resources, and we've got my millions at our desposal. So if you want to sit here and tell us how dumb we

are and that *The Man* ain't real, then you need to head over to the
store to get some side dishes to go along with that brisket you sent
Patrick for. I guess we're all through here."

When Zenobia slid outa the booth and stood, I kinda studied
my uncle sittin there. He had unbuttoned his jacket, tuggin it near
the waist so we could both see the holster on his chest with the
butt of his semi-automatic pistol exposed. Lookin from the gun
and back into his eyes, I got up.

"I hope you don't think were so dumb that we brought that
chip *with* us, Uncle. The Ponzis still have a few loyal friends in the
mob and elsewere. So after we deciphered it and copied the files we
wanted, I got a family friend ta hold onto it for us, just in case
things got a little rough."

"Where are ya goin, Mikee?" he protested. "Zenobia, why are
ya standin up? Where are ya goin? Sit back down, please."

Since we really had no where ta go, we pretended ta hesitate,
and then we sat.

"You say you two *deciphered* the chip?" Uncle Liam shrugged.
"Tell ya what—if ya can produce maybe an authentic file or two, ya
know, from what we happen ta *know* is on that device, that'll be
enough for the right people at the bureau ta start listenin."

"You already *know* what I want," Zenobia began. "Are you
now willing to admit you know *The Man* is real?"

"I know all *about* The Management," he nodded. "And I'll tell
you right now, young lady—there's no way in hell the two of ya are
gonna cut a deal there. Not with them. You might be smart and
have millions, but they're The Management—they run everything
and everybody. You're a flea on an elephant's ass, on a whale's
ass."

"So if The Management is so powerful, Uncle Liam," I cut in,
"why is the FBI tryin ta get their hands on the microchip? If we
give it to ya, what are ya gonna do with it? Use it for leverage?"

"I got two years till I retire. Are ya crazy?" he sighed. "No. My
bosses happen ta know there's some very damagin information on
that microchip that'll expose The Management ta international
scorn and resentment, create a public hysteria, and that'll make it
much, much harder for em ta do what they've been doin for years,
which is managin things."

We were both listenin with rapt attention.

"My bosses also happen ta know The Management will be very appreciative, if ya know what I mean, to whoever is able ta find that chip and turn it over. The want it so they'll finally be able ta assess exactly how much damage was done, ya know, ta determine the extent of how much was compromised by that thief and traitor. Ya can't hedge against what ya don't know."

"Okay," I concluded, "if we can provide a couple of files from that microchip, files that prove we were able ta access what's on it, are you gonna take it ta The Management and negotiate on our behalf?"

"Until we turn it over, we'll have the leverage ta get just about anything."

"And what would you do for us?"

"Well, for Zenobia," he stammered, "I think we could get The Management ta back off a little, ta maybe be not so controllin."

He looked toward her.

"You don't want em ta tell ya who ta marry, and you wanna be able ta have a kid without their approval. I'm pretty sure I could get ya that. And they'll be so glad about containment that I'm sure they'll forgive you for not turnin it over in the first place."

"I want to sing my own music," she insisted.

"They've probably made enough money off you. Sure, we could make that part of the deal. I have a feelin they might go for that."

"What about me, Uncle?"

"Well, you shot their muscle. You shot him in the *ass*! What is the big guy's name?"

"Bubba King," Zenobia answered.

"Yeah, Mikee, you shot that huge, scary black man in the ass and he's still very pissed off. Hell, I don't even want im ta know I'm your uncle," he sighed. "But I guess if they get the chip and can see what's on it, they'll make im back off."

"You keep saying 'they,'" Zenobia complained, "when you know there is a single *person* at the top: *The Man*. Yeah, it's a big organization, but there is one person at the top, callin the shots. The *proof* of that is on the microchip!"

"I'll believe that when I see it!"

"What can you do about my dad, Uncle Liam? And what about The Dwarf, Marcelino Carzano, and the mob, who's after me?"

"Your dad, Mikee—your dad says he needs ta talk to you, and I can make that happen. As for the mob, The Management can take care of Carzano. Either he'll have ta back off or they'll dress up another thug and make *him* the boss."

He reached over, patted my hand and winked.

"But you're gonna hafta provide the *proof*, young lady."

Slingin my purse onto the table, I reached in and pulled out two of the HD CD-Roms with some of The Management files on it.

"Right here, Uncle."

"I don't *believe* it!" he groaned, eyes wide and mouth open. "How *did* you...?"

"It's like Zenobia said. We've got resources. So you can take that to whoever you need to take it to. I wanna see my father tomorrow and I'll need some kinda guarantee that the mob will be off my ass, at least till I can make my case before the big bosses. When ya pick us up tomorrow morning—cuz we know you already know where we're stayin—Zenobia will have her list and I'll have mine."

Uncle Liam picked up one of the plastic CD cases, tappin it on the table.

"So we got some of the actual files on here? From that microchip?"

"Files that could come from nowhere else. So take *that* to your computer expert with all that highly-specialized equipment and see what he can make of it. Our ride's waitin outside."

The Set-Up

Our plan was workin out so far. My uncle was gonna have his agency carefully examine the files on that CD, and it was gonna blow em all away. They'd have to see their doctors for erections lastin much longer than four hours! It'd be a snack, but they'd wanna come back for the full meal. Only, we were gonna give them the microchip with the *corrupted* files and keep the real deal for ourselves, as insurance for me and Zenobia.

Ambition is a strange and dangerous thing, a deceivin hunger that causes a man to bite off more then he can chew. It's what made the snake think it could swallow an elephant—and we know how that turned out—*hungry ta boot*. And what do those with power want? They want more power. The temptation was irresistible. It was a rare opportunity for the FBI ta stick it ta The Man, though the agency did not outwardly acknowledge *The Man* even existed.

Zenobia and I knew the FBI wasn't keen on helpin us. They woulda just as soon thrown us under the bus and paid the driver ta make it look like an accident, if they coulda got away with it. But we had that microchip they wanted, and we didn't need *them* to decipher it. That bein the case, the FBI also knew that we had the option of cuttin a deal with the mob or someone else who mighta saw value in the microchip. Go figure! Maybe even with *The Man*!

Earlier in the day, I asked Stanky to go to a courier service and mail a package ta Tommy Rotten, who was always close ta my father, and who was also very loyal to my grandfather and the Ponzi family over the years—not that any of my family was known ta be gay.

Anyway, I included a note warnin Tommy not ta say anything ta anyone about the package and that I'd be comin back ta Vinny's pretty soon ta have a showdown with The Dwarf. The last thing— I asked him ta deliver a note from me ta my grandfather's old friend, big boss Don Aldoberto Toscano, with a list of the things I wanted in exchange for the information on that chip.

In the meantime, Zenobia used a disposable cell phone ta call the CEO over at her label, some guy who probably pissed all over himself on hearin her voice. She said she had a message for Bubba King, *The Man*'s big black enforcer. So when Bubba calls back, the first thing he tells her is he's gonna kick my white ass and then kill me. And he's talkin real harsh ta her, see, until she tells im she's got the chip and she's deciphered all the files. *Game changer.*

When she called Bubba back thirty minutes later, he was much nicer ta her, but while I couldn't figure *everything* he said on his end, I knew he was tryin ta plant little seeds of doubt and distrust. He was tellin her she didn't know who I was, that I coulda been workin with the FBI, the CIA or the KGB. Then he was suggestin that this whole "bullshit drama" was a set-up by Carzano and the mob, who wanted the chip all along, in order ta renegotiate terms and percentages with *The Man.*

When he told her he wanted ta meet with her, she told him that I would hafta come along, and he was not allowed ta kill me or kick my ass, to which he cursed for about twenty seconds and finally agreed. He said she would hafta provide some kinda proof that she still had the microchip and the deciphered files—somethin we were ready for.

"We emailed them to you fifteen minutes ago, from a 'Lois Lane' email account. We'll let you know when we're ready to meet. And Bubba?"

"What, Bitch?"

"How's that *hole* in your ass?"

Zenobia and I actually had a real sit-down dinner that night, as ourselves, though we had ta do it in the motel room. On the way back, we stopped at the most authentic Italian restaurant we could find and ordered take-out. It was one of those "television commercial Italian chains" that got the food right zero percent of the time, and though it didn't taste like real Italian food, it kinda *looked* like it. Drink enough Chianti beforehand, and *anything* is edible!

"I guess I do have to admit, Michael," she sighed, meatball on her fork, "you're a lot smarter than I gave you credit for."

"You thought I was *dumb?*"

"Not exactly dumb, but a bumbler, a dweeb, you know, a Daman."

"A *Daman?*" I asked. "What's that?"

"*Da man ain't got no brains,*" she answered, affectin her best Jamacian accent. "*Da man got no game. Da man ain't goin nowhere wit tat sorry attitude* or *Daman still live with him mom!*—like that. *Daman.*"

"How about *Da man like da woman?*" I attempted, closin the distance.

"Naw! It's more like *Da man gonna draw back a nub if he grab my abss again.* Now just back off!" she demanded. "I still don't know if you're on the up-and-up. Bubba got me thinking. What if this all *is* a mob set-up and you've been playin me all along?"

"Awww, come on!" I groaned. *"Really?* After all we've been through?"

"I don't know *who* or *what* to believe. I mean, what's your background, Michael? You went to an Ivy League college? And from what I'm hearing, if you were in the mob, you couldn't have been in for long. Maybe the Mennonite farm thing was just another part of some big set-up. I don't *know* anymore!"

She stood, walked to the window, turned her back to me, crossin her arms, and continued.

"I only know people have been going to great lengths to get the information on the microchip, which was supposedly impossible to decode, and then *we,* just by some kinda dumb luck, we just so happened to stumble across a nerdy genius who could decipher it? I don't know what it is, but *something* doesn't add up."

"Come on, Zenobia. You're smarter than I am, but even *I* could hear what Bubba King was tryin ta do. He's tryin ta turn you against me, ya know, *divide and conquer?* I just didn't think you'd fall for it so easy. He's the muscle for *The Man* for cryin out loud! Ya think *he's* got your best interests in mind? Ya trust him more than you trust me?"

"I'm not saying that," she answered. "But tell me the truth: did you really go to some kinda Ivy League school?"

"Uh yeah, I did. I went to Cornell up in Ithaca. Not a big school—private, humble philosophy. From the beginnin of the college, anyone could go there, regardless of race, religion or money. My mobster grandfather, Guido, he always wanted me ta go there, so he paid my way. Alotta people go ta college."

"Did you finish?"

"Well, yeah," I shrugged.

"That's it! Then you're *obviously* up to something," she sighed, waggin her head. "You have an Ivy League college degree, and the best you could do after college is flunkey around for a midget who ordered a hit on my dog? There's no way I could believe that! Would *you?*"

"It's… it's just a little complicated," I answered. "It's not the way it seems, but if you sit back down, I'll tell ya everything you wanna know."

She was unresponsive, just shakin her head and talkin ta herself.

"Come on, Zenobia! We were gettin along so well earlier! You gotta admit we make a great team. I've had your back all along! Please, sit down."

Reluctant, she looked over at me, strugglin ta maintain her serious demeanor, but she yielded to curiousity and returned to the table.

"I'm listening."

"So what do you want to know about me?"

"Why didn't you get a regular job?" she asked. "Why did you join the mob to murder people's pets?"

"Well, I was an English major in college, which meant I coulda either became a teacher or I coulda tried ta be a writer. Teachin wasn't for me, so I tried ta write a book. Of course, book writin ain't as easy as it seems. Ya know, I couldn't figure what ta write about that hadn't already been written. It seemed like for all my best ideas, someone already wrote the story before I got around to it."

I slammed the table.

"*Fifty Shades of Grey!* That was my shit… till that James woman beat me to it!"

"So you sucked at being a writer? *Failure to perform?*"

"More like 'failure to finish.' Thought I'd be the next Mario Puzo—instead of *The Godfather*, I'd write *The Dispatcher*, about my family business, about a family where the tradition was ta be hitmen. Never finished it."

"And was it the tradition in your book that they were all hitmen, preying on helpless family pets? Dogs, cats and parakeets?"

"The hitmen part, yeah, but as for the animal thing—I didn't know about that until recently, until I actually went out on a job with my dad. I thought we'd be, ya know, whackin a real person. But no, when it was all over, I realized the target was a dog, a black dog, named Ziggy."

I continued after realizin how lame what I just said sounded like.

"But my family—we don't kill just family pets, ya know. There've been chimps and kangaroos and beetles and snakes, and my dad told me my grandfather took out an elephant belongin to the Sultan of Brunei for insultin one family Don when he went ta visit Borneo. And of course, my dad was asked ta whack a killer whale over at Sea World over some family beef, but that was after that particular killer whale whacked the niece of a family friend."

"And so after all that, The Midget sent *you* out after a three-pound Yorkie, with orders for someone to whack *you* when the job was done?"

"I guess so," I nodded. "But Marcelino—he's a very powerful little man. When we meet em, if you're there, you probably don't wanna call im a midget, though ya gotta know he *is* a midget, so ya gotta recognize that. You wanna call im The Dwarf. Not 'a' dwarf, but 'The' Dwarf."

"Marcelino? Marcelino the Midget sounds much better than Marcelino the Dwarf."

"Yeah, that what my ma always says, but it's kind of a short man's thing. Believe me, ya wouldn't understand."

"Whatever!"

"And definitely don't call him an elf or troll or a Hobbit, which I heard ya did. We're tryin ta negotiate a deal here."

"I'll remember that," she nodded. "So when did you go back to Hoboken?"

"About a month and a half ago. I couldn't find a job upstate and I had a goddaughter ta pay support for, so I decided ta pack it in, move back with my parents and go inta the family business."

"Wait! You pay for your goddaughter?"

"Goddaughter, yeah, but I call her my daughter. She's actually my 'married' cousin Tony's daughter, by my ex-girlfriend, so it's kinda complicated."

"The family business? A daughter? Wow! Okay, but tell me, Michael, why do you *talk* like that?"

"Like what?"

"In that exaggerated, stupid 1970s Brooklyn movie gangster lingo, like you never finished high school. I mean, can't you speak like a normal person? Like the college graduate you are?

"Oh," I retorted, "you mean like *you* do with all that mumbo-jumbo, gold-teeth wearin, *ghetto* language you use in your songs?"

"That's art. It's a *Blatino* thang, you know, Black-Latino, but that's all about persona. I speak differently off-camera/off-stage, as you already *know*. But you finished at an Ivy League school. Can you say something to me in Standard English?"

"I could, but never on a first date. I just don't think I know ya well enough for that yet."

****

Strange thing! When I went out ta a local restaurant ta use the bathroom cuz that motel room was small (and there was no *way* I was takin a number two with her in the next room!)—when I was out there, I got the feelin that someone was *watchin* me, or followin me. I could feel his eyes on my back, and more disturbin, it was like someone had me in a scope, finger on the trigger, followin my every move.

Then when I got back ta the office, the manager told me some guy with a husky voice had called earlier, askin about me and Zenobia. I knew we were runnin outa time. It hadda be someone The Dwarf had sent. Maybe it was Carlito the Ass.

Suffice it ta say, there were no sparks that night when I got back ta the room—no flirtin, no fantacizin—just more questions and more convincin. In all the time since we cracked the microchip outa Mystique's tooth, Zenobia had never let it outa her sight or possession. Even when she gave it over ta Kal-El, she had her eyes on it at all times. A shell-game operator couldn't have switched it on her. And after Kal-El copied it, she took it from him and hid it somewhere, where I never saw it again.

I had asked Kal-El for an extra copy chip, so I could switch it out for the actual microchip if I got the chance, for safekeeping. But I had no idea where she had stashed it. I wanted ta search for it, but I knew if she caught me searchin, she'd be more suspicious than she already was.

When I looked over at her in the next bed, I could tell she was only *pretendin* ta be asleep—the same way I was pretendin ta be asleep in mine. I was thinkin maybe she was gonna search my things for proof about what I was really up to. Anyway, we pretended for most of the night, but I think I dozed off at about five and woke up to the sight of her riflin through my wallet.

"Zenobia? What the hell are you doin?"

"I was going to run out to the store for breakfast. I needed some money."

Embarrassed for bein caught in the act, she handed the wallet over.

"Took a Franklin. I didn't know your middle name was Marco."

"Yeah," I answered, adjustin my position and the covers so my mornin stiffie was out of sight, "My dad named me that in honor of Marco Bello, The Dwarf's father."

"So, it's *Marco* the Dwarf?"

"No, he's a regular-sized man, close ta six feet. He's gotta be in his late seventies by now, I think seventy-eight, seventy-nine. You'll probably meet him if ya go ta Vinny's for the meetin. We've got a few scores ta settle, goin alltheway back to grandfathers and great uncles."

After she left, I knew the chip had ta be on her body, cuz everything else of hers was left out in the open. I did notice that she furtively grabbed the cell phone on the way out, which meant she was probably gonna call someone, though I had no idea who she might wanna call. Thinkin about it, there was a lot I didn't know about Zenobia. Maybe *she* was up ta somethin? Maybe she was in on a set-up?

She probably didn't think I noticed, but just before we left Uncle Liam at the coffee shop—while we were outside waitin for Stanky—Zenobia claimed she left her notepad on the table and went back in ta get it. Only, when I went ta the door and peeked in, I saw her talkin ta my uncle, and I saw him handin her somethin. Maybe it was a buggin device or maybe a card or note with his number. I dunno, but it was *somethin*. Maybe she was callin him ta cut a deal with the FBI, or callin the government ta get *The Man* off her back.

Zenobia came back ta the motel twenty minutes later with some kinda chicken and waffles concoction, which apparently *some* black people saw as *goin* together, like some kinda *integrated* meal. And then I started eatin, and wow! I swear, white people have no idea! Chicken and waffles! It's an *incredible* combination, but who woulda figured? One day, some famous white person is gonna "discover" chicken and waffles, and then it's gonna be a global phenomenon, like twerkin. Anyway, for some reason, Zenobia was in a really good mood—smilin, jokin, flirtin with me, though I always felt the piranha-filled moat that she kept up around herself.

"So who'd ya call?"

"Why would you ask me that? I went out and got *breakfast* for you, and now you're acting all suspicious? No 'thank you.'"

"Well, ya took the phone."

"I took it so you couldn't use it to cut a deal behind my back."

"Or maybe ya took it to cut a deal behind *my* back," I retorted. "You've got the chip, after all, and it's deciphered. Maybe you were thinkin you don't *need* me?"

"But *you've* got the deciphered files, and you've got connections to the FBI and the mob. Maybe you're thinking you don't need *me?*"

"What were you talkin to my uncle about yesterday?"

"What are *you* talking about? You were there the whole time."

"Naw, I mean when you went back *in*. You went back ta the table and you talked ta him for about two, three minutes, he gave you something and you gave im somethin. What was that about?"

"Oh, *that*," she admitted, clearly uncomfortable. "Well, *that* was between me and your uncle."

The FBI

Okay, so later that morning, we began our series of meetins. Uncle Liam's crew showed up at the motel in two black SUVs at a little after ten o'clock. True ta my suspicion, they tried ta separate us, with Zenobia in one car and me in the other, but we were ready for that. We weren't splittin up, and we decided we were gonna do all the meetins together, no matter what—the FBI, *The Man*, the mob, all of em!

My uncle drove us ta the airport in D.C. where we rented another couple of black SUVs ta take us down ta Quantico in Virginia, which is where the FBI has their crime lab, which is also the place me and my father were when he got pinched. Uncle Liam said they were holdin my dad somewhere else, but they were drivin im up ta meet with us after we met with FBI interrogators.

By one in the afternoon, we were all sittin in a room at Quantico, with me and Zenobia on one side of the table and the agents on the other. No one ever said the FBI wasn't a smart outfit. Apparently, they guessed that puttin up the older, white authority figure was as equally ineffective as the straight-laced, goody-two-shoes, All-American redheaded white boy. When we got ta the table, we were greeted by a tall, handsome, muscular, Dwayne Johnson-esque agent in a clean suit, standin next ta a woman who looked so much like Lolita Cardullo that I almost ran out the room.

"Zenobia, it's very nice to meet you! I'm Agent Looker, and this is Agent Di Stefano," he said. "Before we get started, would you be kind enough to sign your last CD for my daughter, who's your greatest fan. I'm a single dad and I work a lot. Come on, you'll make me a hero in her eyes."

She was flattered, but she was street enough ta know what he was up to. She cooed, flippin the script, and ended up workin him before signin the CD and flashin a big, phony smile ya coulda seen from space. Apparently, the agent chick at the table had taken the time ta study Lolita's speech and behavior patterns, completely unaware the mere sight of her had me ready ta crap my pants.

"Let's get started," the muscle-bound, pretty-boy announced. "Agent O'Brien has informed us on all foundational issues involving the creation of the microchip, the nature of acquisition by Zenobia and subsequent efforts at deciphering encoded data contained therein. I don't know how you two did it. It's something that should have been impossible by everything we know, but the two of you apparently mastered an extremely sophisticated, ultra high level encryption. Congratulations! What my bosses want to know is *how*."

"With our *brains*. What else?" I answered.

"Everything with Zenobia checks out," Di Stefano interrupted, takin over, "but you, Mr. Ponzi, are a different story all together. Your great uncle was *the* Carlo Ponzi—extremely well connected in all realms. Your grandfather, Guido—he had a second and much more illustrious career *after* he went to prison, while your father for most of his life has seemed humble and unremarkable, *except* for the fact that he's a hitman who takes contracts for sokokes and great danes. We've known about the quiet blood feud between the Ponzis and the Carzanos going back for years, and we know about the unsettled business and revenge that your grandfather Guido never forgot about."

"Before he died," Looker, continued, "Guido Ponzi told his roommate, Sal the Wop, that *you* were his greatest hope for settling up family business, Michael. He said he put everything he had into you and taught you everything he knew."

"By all accounts," Agent Di Stefano picked up, "you were very close to your grandfather, Guido, weren't you, Michael? You visited him every Thursday, right up until the day he died?"

"My grandfather was a great and wise man," I shrugged. "So I was *close* ta him. What does any of that have to do with why we're sittin here taday?"

"Was your grandfather grooming you to be a boss? To take over the family?"

"You know and I know that is not possible, Agent Di Stefano," I answered. I'm not full-blooded Sicilian, and I'm only half-Italian."

"Marcelino Carzano, aka The Dwarf and boss of the Carzano crime family," she continued, "He took a *contract* out on you. He meant for Jake the Ass to put a bullet through your head on the same night he ordered you to kidnap and decapitate Zenobia's dog for the microchip inside the tooth."

"*That* I know," I nodded. "Midget *bastard*!"

"*Hobbit* bastard!" Zenobia added, "Munchkin bastard! Smurf bastard!"

"The assassination attempt didn't work out so well for Jake," Di Stefano said, readin from a report. "Turns out that when you ran over his feet with your car, you hobbled him for life. Oh, he'll never walk again, but he *is* able to shuffle along, feet together, at no more than ten feet a minute, and that's if he doesn't fall down. He paid for the betrayal. You effectively *retired* him that night."

"Carlito the Ass," Looker added, waggin his head about the name, 'The Assassin.' "He swears he's going to kill you on sight… that he's going to torture you and feed you Ponzi *polpetti* before you die."

"Hey, are you two really a *couple*? You know, officially," Di Stefano asked outa the blue, totally changing the subject.

"No!" Zenobia blurted out, perhaps a little offended, but not so offended as she was on the first occasion someone suggested it. "But we're definitely down for each other. We're in this together. No daylight between us."

"Even at *night*?" the agent countered, nudging her partner. "Well, I just asked because *I'm* the one who was puttin all those stories out there. The wedding chapel sightin in Las Vegas and the phony marriage papers, the jealous spat at the San Francisco nightclub, the death threat Michael made ta the TMZ reporter, the photoshopped baby bump—we wanted to keep the mob and everyone else confused until we found you and secured the chip. Of course, you brought it *with* you, didn't you?"

"Let's see, how should I put this?" I answered. "We opened up somethin of an *escrow* with a neutral party, and that's where the chip is right now. So we've already provided a list in your emails, detailin what we want, terms we've already given to this neutral third party. In the meantime, this party will verify for you the information on the chip is the real chip and safely stowed. In the end, when this third neutral party determines our list of conditions is wholly met, he or she will give ya what you want in exchange for ya givin us what we want."

"And how do we know we can *trust* this neutral third party?" Looker asked. "I mean, can this person really be a neutral party when *you're* the one who picked him? Is he part of the mob?"

"You mean my Uncle Liam didn't *tell* you, Agent Looker?" I said, sittin back, feignin surprise. "This is a take-it-or-leave-it offer. After we meet with my dad later taday, we've got a meeting with The Dwarf, who wants the information that chip maybe more than you do. Then after that, we'll be meetin with someone who works for The Management, so who knows *what* we'll be able ta work out before this is all over?"

I stood, signalin ta Zenobia that she should do the same, which she did.

"On accounta family, we're givin the FBI first crack at it. You meet the conditions on our list, and you'll have that chip in your hands taday. But just ta be fair, we're givin conditions ta the mob and ta *The Man*, along with contact information for our neutral third party. So it's just that simple: whoever meets the conditions first, wins—and the winner gets what's on the microchip. You'll have something like a two ta three-hour headstart... beginnin now."

****

My dad didn't look any worse for the wear. In fact, I think he *gained* a few pounds! But he sat there, across the table from us, starin at Zenobia.

"The pictures, the television don't do you any justice, Zenobia. You are one beautiful woman!"

"Oh, thank you!" she gushed, acutally blushin.

"So you're *married* now, Michael? To this Zenobia here!"

"It's not exactly like that, Dad. Ya know, the FBI did a little embellishin ta give us cover."

"But you're datin?"

"Well, we've been spendin alotta time..."

"*Sleepin* together! I saw pictures of the two of yas comin outa that motel room. I *know* how a man *walks* when he's been sleepin/*not* sleepin, ya know," he concluded with a wink. "I say *not* sleepin. Hell, *I* wouldn't be sleepin!"

"Dad," I advised, "ya gotta know the FBI's listenin in and tapin everything we're sayin in here, right?"

"And what so wrong with them knowin my son's gotta be one of the luckiest guys in the world? Look at her—she's absolutely ravishin, talented and she's rich, all of which you ain't!"

"I talked ta Ma. She's really been missin ya."

He became somber at once, bowin his head.

"I miss your ma too, but I *don't* miss her meatballs on Fridays. I'll have meatballs one last Friday when I get outa here, but never again!"

"But she doesn't make meatballs on Fridays. Meatballs are on *Tuesdays!*" I sighed, perhaps a little embarrassed by his behavior. "*Zuppi di Pesce* is on Fridays."

That's when he gave me that look that made me realize *he* was bein clever and I was bein dumb. I *got* it. He was lettin me know that the showdown with The Dwarf was gonna be on the *Friday* right after he got out, which woulda been the next night.

"So Michael, are you two here ta break me outa this place?"

"You'll be goin home tomorrow, in the mornin. They're flyin ya inta JFK, where Ma'll be waitin."

"I thank the both of ya, you and Zenobia" he said, tears wellin up, but he wasn't gonna cry in front of a dame. "What's this I'm hearin about Jake? My old best friend tried ta whack my son?"

"Yeah, he did. He did when I was on special a job for The Dwarf, who had ta be the only one in the world who knew where I'd be that night. If Zenobia hadn't been fussin all in my ear right then, I woulda never dropped the keys, and if I hadn't dropped the keys…"

I paused, realizing her fussin had probably saved my life.

"Then Jake woulda whacked me, and then he probably woulda whacked Zenobia and the dog. And The Dwarf woulda had the microchip that night, which he then coulda used ta cut a better deal with The Management. In the end, the Ponzis woulda finally been outa the picture and the little shit woulda been an even bigger boss."

The room was silent as the three of us pondered how differently things coulda turned out.

"What's this about The Management?" my father asked. "I've heard of em. They're the *real* bosses. So how the hell would The Dwarf have *any* leverage with them?"

"That's where *I* come in, Mr. Ponzi," Zenobia cut in. "In his work, my cousin, whom they're all calling a traitor, innocently stumbled across some dangerous government secrets, which led to other secrets and so on, which he documented. I asked him if he could find *The Man* for me, and he did. So when the government found out he had accessed and copied sensitive files, he knew they were going to either kill him or lock him up for life. But before running to Venezuela, my cousin gave me a microchip he created that profiled The Management and identified *The Man*—the one man who was callin the shots, the one man who was running everything."

"The Management, yes," my father nodded, "but one man at the top of it all? That's impossible. The Management must have a committee or board or somethin like that."

"And at the top of that committee or board is *one* person," she asserted. "*The Man!* The proof of it is on that microchip, and that's why they all want it so bad!"

"But what difference does it make anyway, Zenobia?" my father said. "I mean, who *cares* if it's one man. And what would you do if you found im, providing he'd even *let* you find im? Believe me, some things are better left alone."

"When I *find* that bastard," she seethed, her nostrils flaring, "I'm going to look him straight in the eyes and tell him in no uncertain terms that he can kiss my ass! The nerve of it all! Trying to dictate every aspect of my life—*what I can talk about, my religion, my persona, my relationships, and having me throwing signs for him!*—turning me into a mind-controlled slave, a program, a predictable, obedient product! I'm going to tell that asshole shot-caller that he can order me *dead* if he wants to, because that's his call. And then I'm going to walk away from it, all of it, and damn the consequences!"

"It's the price of fame, Zenobia," my father said, his face showing rare empathy. "Or the price of success, whatever we wanna call it. I've seen it all my life, and in my experience, the only way out is in a rectangular wooden box."

That said, my father's expression changed.

"Welcome ta the family, Zenobia!" he smiled. "Are you comin for the last of the meatballs?"

The Ritz

The FBI knew where we were, but we still had to fly under the radar. The lastest report on *Celebrity Gossip* had us vacationing at an Anguilla beach resort in the Carribean, so no one expected us ta be comin north up the I-95. In spite of all that, we knew our whole plan would come apart at the seams if we were spotted anywhere on our way back up to New York, the logic bein that when you're talkin the FBI, the mob and The Management, invisible is better.

After much persecution and an apology, we finally pursuaded my cousin, Patrick, ta use his name and credit card ta rent us some wheels—in our case, a cherry-red Cadillac Escalade Hybrid four-wheel drive, complete with platinum trim, leather seats, 22" chromed multi-spoke aluminum wheels and a Bose® 5.1 surround sound 10-speaker system. Zenobia had all her unreleased songs loaded in the MP3, so alltheway back up ta Manhattan, we rocked her new album, at least three times!

Zenobia had special access ta all the Manhattan clubs and private spots, and we were tempted ta go out somewhere, but it was too risky with her, and we hadta make sure we would be ready for the meetin in the mornin with her record label, which was the first level of meetins with The Management. We knew Bubba King would be there, so between him and the label, we thought we'd get a pretty good idea about whether or not they'd be willin ta do business.

Even though we were careful, I still got the sense that someone was always right there behind us, watchin, just waitin for the opportunity ta strike. I didn't tell Zenobia about it, but I had a gut feelin, and my feelins were usually dead-on. I had ta assume that she made a phone call, maybe ta her parents or someone, and that told the mob all they needed ta know. If I called her on it, she'd deny doin it, so it became a matter of tryin ta stay one step ahead till we got ta the end of the road.

Usin Patrick's credit card, I rented a room at the Ritz-Carlton at Central Park in Midtown Manhattan, in the Premiere Parkview Suite. The place wasn't somethin *I* was used to, but Zenobia made herself right at home, takin the master bedroom, while relegatin me ta the livin room, which all by itself was bigger than my parent's house.

Once we settled in, she called the concierge and ordered some kinda spa package, the Caviar deal I think, that brought someone up ta give her an hour massage, followed by a ninety-minute facial. Diva that Zenobia was, the esthetician had ta be blindfolded when she did her procedure. After that, we ordered a little room service: standard surf and turf, along with two bottles of Napa Valley wine, a Chard and a Cab, followed by a bottle of Germain-Robin Alambic Brandy, the V 57 Single Barrel.

Zenobia was on the verge of getting some exclusive service ta come in ta do her manicure and pedicure until I stepped in, tellin her she looked better *natural*. I told her I had watched her change over the time from when we were over at the farm in Schenectady until that night. I said *as an everyman*, I thought she was much prettier without the make-up, without the nails and without hair extentions almost the size of Mystique.

"I could *never* let anyone see me like this, you know! Not any *real* person."

"Why not?" I sighed, shaking my head. "It's only now *you* look like a real person. They've turned you inta a product, makin ya think you *need* all that stuff. If you really *are* a mind-controlled slave like you told my dad earlier, then you can blame The Management for only *half* of that. The rest is your *own* doin."

"You really *think* so?"

"What?" I asked.

"You think I look just as good without the make-up and the hair?"

"Better," I insisted, takin her unmanicured hand in mine.

It was a moment. As she smiled at me, I could see the barriers weakenin. I could see it in her eyes, the true betrayers of the heart. She was fightin it, but we both knew she was startin ta kinda *like* me. When she knew I knew, she snatched her hand back, anger flashin in her eyes.

"I know what you're *thinking*! You're a pervert! No *way*! When this is all over, I'll give you the money I promised for killing that owl, but if you think I'll even want to *know* you after that, you're just jacking yourself off!"

"Well," I said, a little swagger in my voice, "after this is over and I *get* that million dollars, then maybe I won't wanna know *you*."

"Yeah, I know your type. All you want is some of my money, some of my fame and some of my..." she paused. "You want bragging rights, which you'll never get. You're not even my type."

"Oh really?" I asked, "What *is* your type?"

"Someone who's real," surprizin me, because she took the question so seriously. She spoke slowly, like she was releasing water from an overstrained dam. "Someone who can be great by being humble, powerful by sometimes being weak. Intelligence is my biggest turn-on. My type? Someone whose strength is in knowing his limitations, who has found that *something*, who has found that *cause* he can pursue with all his heart and energy. Someone who believes there's a greater plan and finds his place, who seeks the things that can't be found, a man who would die for honor."

"Ha!" I laughed. "Well good luck findin *that*? It's no *wonder* you're almost thirty and you don't have a man!"

"It's no wonder you have to tie women down and *torture* them in order to prove your manhood! I've known you were an idiot from the start, Michael. Doggie hit man? You kill helpless animals. You're pathetic!"

I could tell she was embarrassed cuz I laughed, but she was a little hurt too, cuz I made fun of her when she was exposin vulnerability, tryin ta share words that were precious ta her. I guess I just couldn't help myself. In an instant, though, it was like a cold front blew in. Her face, her voice—everything changed in the blink of an eye. It was the Blizzard of 1977 all over again!

"Of course, you *know* I was just kiddin."

"Let's just get this business over with! I was born with all my body parts. I don't need another asshole!"

It made for an awkward discussion when we had ta plan how ta handle the meetin with Bubba and the record label CEO in the mornin. I was askin questions, and she was givin me sarcastic, one-word answers. I guessed she wasn't *born* with a sense of humor!

"We sent the deciphered files ta Bubba, who no doubt shared em with The Management, so I would think that means The Management is sanctionin this meeting, especially since Dee Witty'll be there. You said he was just a mouthpiece for The Management?"

"Yep."

"Look, Zenobia—that was like the ninth or tenth question you answered with 'yep'! We're at a crucial point here. You don't have anything else to say?"

"Nope."

"Okay, I'm sorry. What I said was insensitive. I'm sorry I made that comment about you not havin a man."

"Oh I don't care about *that*!" she sighed. "You said I was almost *thirty*! I am *not* almost thirty! I just turned twenty-eight! *Twenty-nine* is almost thirty!"

I was never able to thaw the freeze, but we did agree on a few things: *twenty-nine* was almost thirty, we were gonna have our meetin in Dee Witty's office in Manhattan, goin in disguises, we were gonna park in Witty's space and take a private elevator ta his office, and the only people on the entire floor would be Zenobia, Dee Witty, me and Bubba, who was *not* gonna kick my ass or kill me.

Apparently, The Management checked out the files and was convinced we were the real deal: that one, we *had* the actual chip, and two, we had *deciphered* it. Considerations three and four woulda been that we were in separate negotiations with the FBI and the mob, both indicatin they'd be willin ta deliver big-time in order ta get their hands on the information on that microchip. It was maybe a game-changer.

Problem was, we didn't *trust* the FBI or the mob, but we weren't gonna tell Dee Witty or Bubba that. We figured we hadda make em believe that I had loyalties ta the FBI on accounta family, *while at the same time* I had loyalties ta the mob on accounta family. So at this meetin, I'd be an ass and come out against any kinda deal The Management offered, while Zenobia would kinda favor turnin the chip over ta them in exchange for her freedom.

Naturally, Dee Witty, the deal-maker, would try ta exploit the division between us and convince Zenobia that my loyalties were not with her. He'd call me a hired mob thug, who'd have no problem whackin her at the end if the family gave the order. Things would get dicey, and *that's* when she'd demand a face-ta-face with *The Man*, which I'd be in on. So we were gonna try ta set up a meetin where we'd be negotiatin at the very top—talkin ta *The Man*, but that particular meetin would hafta happen sometime after our meetin with the mob.

****

I was sleepin pretty good that night, with my mind made up about how I was gonna bring the business ta a finale, a conclusion that both me and Zenobia would be able ta live with. I thought my fatigue was gettin the better of me. I thought I was imaginin things when I heard a light tappin on the door and then the sound of someone tryin ta turn the knob. The tappin grew louder until it became actual knockin. Even Zenobia heard it.

"Michael, is that *you* or is that someone at the *door*? It's three-thirty in the morning!"

"Stay in your room! Let me deal with this!" I shouted in a whisper as I rose from the *couch*, wearin only my boxers.

The knockin had become more confident and forceful. Stayin way ta the far left side of the door, way outa the line of sight of the person on the other side, I shouted.

"Who's *there*? Who is it?—"

I had barely got the words outa my mouth when I heard the sound of an explosion and watched the door splinter from the force of steel shot, fired at close range. A second explosion obliterated the door handle before the person on the other side kicked the door in. I had no time ta go for my gun and found myself face ta face with him—Carlito the Ass.

"Michael Ponzi! I *told* ya I'd find ya and kill ya. Of course, me bein here is not officially sanctioned by The Dwarf, but ya stole my girl and you ran over my dad's feet with your car, on purpose! They don't even call him Jake the Ass anymore. They're callin him Jake the Schlep—a Jew word makin fun about the fact he can't walk the same anymore. It's your fault! This is for everything you've done ta me, Michael. I hate you! You're finally gettin what ya deserve!"

As he raised the gun, ready ta pull the trigger, we both recognized the sound of the safety bein released on the Glock, and we turned ta the sight of Zenobia, with the gun leveled toward Carlito's face.

"You shoot him, and I shoot *you*, bastard! Nevermind your bad manners, but we've come too far to have some dumb asshole break in here in the middle of the night and ruin things for us now!"

She approached him, unafraid, placing the gun at his temple.

"I'm not afraid to die tonight. Are you?"

With little contemplation, he raised his hands, shotgun in his right. In spite of the situation, we both noticed what Zenobia was wearin—some kinda sexy red camisole with tiny straps, the silk material just barely squeezing onta her beautiful breasts that wanted out. And her arms were raised ta hold the gun, something that made the bottom of the garment hike way up her shapely thighs. Yeah we were gawkin, but she was intense.

"Now put the gun down and walk your sorry butt out of here."

"You must be Zenobia," he muttered as he complied. "What *is* it with you, Michael? So now ya got the hot, bad-ass girls, like James Bond?"

"Does he have any other weapons on him?" she demanded.

After takin the shotgun outa Carlito's hand and tossin it out of range, I patted him down for extra guns or knives, but as always, the stupid shit had busted through the door too overconfident.

"He's got nothin else on him!"

She motioned ta him with the gun.

"Start walking before I *shoot* you in the ass!"

Waggin his head and cursin her, he left, but not thirty seconds later, he returned and threw somethin in the door, and that somethin caused a major, fiery explosion in the room. Before we knew anything, everything was in flames, from floor ta ceilin. There was no way out the front door, while out on the fire escape, we'd be sittin ducks for Carlito, who'd be watchin for us there, rifle at the ready. Our only choice was ta wait it out and hope help would somehow arrive.

So we went ta the bathroom, turned on the shower and stood in the cold stream and mist, prepared for the worst. Believe me—all hugged up against Zenobia in that wet sheer lingerie top, I wasn't complainin. Fortunately for us, the FBI was also followin, monitorin us, so when they heard the explosion and saw the flames through the windows, the response was immediate. Within minutes, firemen had made way for three agents to come in and find us. We watched as the flames consumed the room and threatened ta consume adjoinin rooms.

Salvaging what we could, we hurried out into the crowded hallway, where other hotel guests were runnin inta and trippin over each other to get ta the stairwell. Once we were downstairs, the

FBI agents escorted us ta our Cadillac Escapade and directed us ta one of their safe houses, where we'd be protected until the mornin. Inside, and doors locked behind us, I was angry, agitated.

"What were you *thinkin* back there, Zenobia, goin up so close ta Carlito! Do ya have a death wish? He could have easily overpowered ya, taken that gun and shot us both! Are ya tryin ta get yourself killed?"

"I don't care," she answered, sobbin. "I don't *care* if I die. What *difference* does it make? When was I ever *alive*?"

The Management

"Considering the amount of publicity there'll be when you re-emerge on the scene, Zenobia, this new album just might have the greatest debut of all time, and then, who knows? Wake up, *MJ*! Move over, *Thriller!*"

With a name like Dee Witty, ya'd expect to see a high-fashion-wearin black guy in sunglasses, with his own line of clothin, but that wasn't the case. His real name was Antonio López de Santa Anna. So with a name like Antonio López de Santa Anna in R&B music, ya'd expect ta see a Puerto Rican cat with light-skin, slick-backed hair and wearin overpowerin cologne, but this guy was *no* PR. It turned out he was Mexican. So with a name like Antonio López de Santa Anna and bein Mexican, ya'd expect him ta be someone from somewhere on the Texas border, but he was actally from south central Los Angeles, Compton born and raised.

Palmyra, a record label at Dee Witty's Music Recording Studio and Entertainment Company, took up one whole floor of one of the tallest buildins on Park Avenue in Harlem, his private office boastin a spectacular view of... well Harlem, I guess. The space was like a tourist attraction, with platinum records and framed pictures of stars all along the walls, glass cases fulla Grammy and Oscar trophies, awards on the walls, and a priceless art piece, made from Charlie Parker's once-favorite saxophone.

Almost dancin, Witty came around his huge, glossy desk, arms extended.

"I don't know where you been, girl," he said, embracin her, "or what *this* no good nigga's up to, but *lawd* it's great ta see ya!"

I was a little confused, but I was sure it wasn't the first time a Mexican had used *that* name ta describe a half-Italian/half-Irish guy in fronna black people! He shot me a cold glare, rollin his eyes toward Bubba, who sat there, massive muscles tensed, like a patient predator, ready ta pounce. Zenobia naturally had my back.

"Bubba, this is Michael Ponzi, the guy who shot you in the ass," she laughed. "You would not believe how many good jokes we've made these past few weeks out of *that* one! In yo ass!"

I briefly extended my hand for the introduction, but I snactched it back, realizing that with little effort on his part, he coulda tore the arm right off my shoulder.

"I really am sorry about that," I said. "I've *travelled* some, and I was just, just *standin my ground*, ya know. Zenobia was convinced ya were gonna whack us."

I cringed when he stood. I mean, he was built like my cousin's blue-nosed pit, except Bubba hadda be about six-ten. I could feel the heat of his glare as I continued.

"I was just tryin ta *stop* ya. I wasn't tryin ta kill ya. That's why I shot ya *there*."

"Well, you're *lucky* you're a bad shot and that bullet passed clean through one of his butt cheeks," Witty said, "Otherwise, it woulda been *over* for you the second you walked through that door. Now sit yo sorry, punk-ass down!"

Zenobia sat in a chair next ta me, across the desk from Witty, while Bubba stood in fronna the closed door.

"*Two* things are gonna happen today. One, Zenobia is gonna give me that microchip her cousin made and she's gonna make me believe there are no extra *copies* floatin around out there. And two, Zenobia is gonna get her ass back to work on *our* schedule, and if she plays nice for a year, we'll try ta forget that she *stole* from us."

He looked her dead into her eyes.

"Of course, that means you'll be on an even *shorter* leash, girlfriend. We got lotsa talented new girls comin up the ranks, so this is your last chance. You're getting old, anyway. What are you, thirty now?"

"She's twenty-eight," I interrupted, "and I think she actually came here taday, Witty, ta get ya *fired*."

"Oh, you got jokes, white toast? She's gonna get *me* fired? You two'll be lucky to get outa here with just an ass-kickin. I've already assured Bubba he's got five minutes with her... and ten minutes with you. Toast!"

"Yeah, well what you *ain't* got and you won't *get* is the microchip, cuz neither of us has it on us. So what's gonna happen after this meetin is that *your* boss is gonna ask ya if ya and Bubba secured the chip, ta which you're gonna hafta say *ya failed*. Then your boss'll somehow find out that Zenobia and me—we're in negotiations with the FBI *and* the mob, who are very motivated ta get what's on that chip, and they've been a lot nicer ta us than you and Bubba have been."

Dee Witty seemed to be caught a little off-guard by my statement.

"You mean you called this meetin and you don't have the damn *chip*, Asshole?"

"It's bein held by a neutral third party. Ya had ta know we'd hafta have some kinda leverage comin in here. If you want the the data on that chip, you and Bubba are gonna hafta slow your burn. Zenobia has already told me her first inclination was ta return what's on it back ta The Management, but after all this hard talk taday—I mean, ya just insulted her age! Ya called her thirty!"

"That was just *talkin*, Zenobia," Witty half-laughed. "She know me. She know she ma girl!"

"You called me *old*, asshole," she retorted. "I don't even want to talk to you now, and I'm not afraid of you or Bubba anymore. How about this: you tell your bosses I'll give *them* what's on the chip, but only if I can talk to someone more respectful, and only after they meet my special set of needs and conditions."

"Special needs? Oh now *you* talkin crazy," he laughed. "You of all people gotta know it don't work like that. You talk ta *me*, and *I* talk ta them. There ain't gonna be none of this *goin over my head* shit!"

"Take-it-or-leave-it, Antonio," she insisted. "I sent the set of needs and conditions to Bubba's email right before this meeting. You tell your boss and your boss's boss that we deciphered that chip, meaning we got the goods. We *know* who *The Man* is, and if *The Man* wants that information back rather than having it go to the FBI or the mob, then he needs to sit down and talk with us to make this deal in person."

Witty thought for a moment, and then he decided to call our bluff.

"Bubba, why don't you show Zenobia what we mean when we say *no one, absolutely no one, goes over our heads?*"

In an instant, the beast had her by the neck, liftin her, suspendin her mid-air, her legs flailin two feet off the ground. She gasped, her hands pryin at his fingers as she coughed and gagged, strugglin ta breathe.

"Go ahead! *Kill* her, and then kill *me*," I said, disguisin my panic and concern, "and if your bosses don't feed ya your tiny balls for *nixin* the last chance they'll ever have ta get that chip back—if your bosses don't make examples outa your two dumb asses, then the mob'll whack ya for steppin in between them and the best outcome they could have ever hoped for, plus you'll make the FBI's Most Wanted list, for sure."

Resolve fadin, Bubba eased his lock-grip on Zenobia's throat, allowing the tips of her shoes ta barely touch the floor.

"Truth is, it's no secret that you two are just peons—low-level flunkies in a global enterprise that's bigger than ya could possibly imagine, and ya have no *idea* about the important role ya could still play! Until now, ya've been expendible. You're most likely a *nuisance*, cuz you're so simple. *But on the level*—if you two end up bein the ones who make it possible for gettin all the damagin information on that chip *back* to *The Man*? Well then, ya could change your destinies."

I stood and spoke without turnin.

"*Per quadrum, Bubba!* Put Zenobia down. Put her down *now!*"

Still turned away, I heard her exhale, her body collapsing into the leather chair, along with a few choice curse words, a reference to God and the sound of labored breathin.

"I'm leavin a special condition of my own on the desk right here. I'll need it in two hours—very important. Tell your bosses Zenobia and I have a meetin with the mob tanite to finish up some personal business. Ya can tell em both the FBI and the mob want what's on that chip and they have offers on the table, but since Zenobia and I are fair and decent people and are willin ta forgive your rude behavior this afternoon, we'd like ta see the information gets returned ta its rightful owner. You tell em we want a meetin with *The Man*."

****

On the way out the parkin lot, we got spotted by New York City paparazzi—a crowd of maybe thirty flashin camera-whores and whormen, blockin the way and crowdin in around the Cadillac. *It was the last thing we needed before the big meetin!* After revvin the engine as a warnin, I floored the accelerator and screeched outa there.

When I looked back, there were two cars on my tail, but I figured if they were from that outfit out in California, mostly coverin that *Thirty-Mile-Zone* (TMZ) in Los Angeles, then I'd have no problem losin em in New York between Harlem and the Bronx.

Turns out I was right, but the bad part—we'd been made. It was only a matter of time before they caught up with us.

It would be hours before the big meetin, so we had ta find somewhere ta wait. I called Fat Tony, who was kinda like my older cousin. His real name was Antonio Pomodoro—*Pomodoro*, which meant "tomato" in Italian. He was Tommy's son, my Uncle Tommy Pomodoro's son. My grandfather told me, early on, when the family came ta America, Tommy's grandfather and friends used ta call him "rotten tomato" on accounta him goin ta jail at thirteen, and the name "rotten" just kinda stuck more than his actual last name did.

Everyone knew him as Tommy Rotten, and so little Antonio, when it came ta a nickname, wanted no part of *Rotten*. Because he was a kinda chunky kid, the natural thing was ta call him "Fat Tony," a name his domineerin ma started when he was in kindergarten. I guess she figured it was better than "Tony Tomato." Anyway, Tony stayed fat for a few years, but by the seventh grade he became obsessed with bein "not fat," and ever since then, he's been rail thin ta the point of bein unhealthy.

All that said, Fat Tony was very loyal to my family, like his dad and grandfather before him. So when I called him, he was glad ta have me come over, and then when he saw Zenobia with me, he screamed like a girl. Of course, that didn't mean he was gay, like I guessed his father had become, but it was a little odd—bein skinny and weekly aerobics just made him seem a little effeminate, that's all.

"Zenobia! I'm your biggest fan—next ta my girlfriend and our daughter, of course!" Tony swooned. "I just saw on TV that you'd been spotted in Harlem, and now you're *here*? I'm sorry. I'm just a little overwhelmed! It's been such a big story."

The kitchen table was covered with metal parts that looked like remnants from two or three AR-15 assault rifles and a couple Smith & Wesson nine millimeter handguns.

"Excuse this mess," he sighed, embarrassed, while reassemblin the weapons at incredible speed. "I was just puttin an order together. Please, sit down. A glass of wine?"

Seated and served a glass of *Primativo*, bread, *formaggella* and *scapece*, we talked for a few minutes.

"Looks like a big meetin tonight," Fat Tony said, snappin the last gun together. "I hear Marco Bello and all the resta the regional board'll be there. It's gotta be a huge deal ta get all them hairy grey balls over here. I hope you're bringin your A-game, Mikee. My dad and me, we got your back."

Fat Tony hadta go out for a meetin for about two hours, leavin me and Zenobia sittin at the table ta have one last conversation before goin over ta Vinny's.

"What was *that* about back there at the office?" she asked.

"What was *what* about?"

"You're always trying to play dumb, Michael, and most people let you get away with it, but you said something to Bubba in another *language* back there, and when you said it, he just froze and *dropped* me like you told him to. What was that?"

"That was nothin. It was just an expression my grandpa used when he was mad and tryin ta make a point."

"It seemed like *Bubba* understood what you said, though," she mused, "and Dee Witty too, because you took over after that. There's somethin else goin on with you. You're not the same dweeb I met that night at the Walfdorf."

"I was never a dweeb. I was just desperate ta save my father. You're not the same diva I met that night either. This experience has changed us both. Thank goodness it's almost over."

We sat in silence for a moment.

"So how is this all going to end?" she asked.

"Hopefully, we'll get everything we want. I'll get the mob off my back, and my dad'll be retired and safe, with full benefits. He and my ma can finally travel—go back ta the old country. And you'll get *The Man* off your back. You'll stop havin ta obey arbitrary orders, maybe get a little more freedom, artistic and otherwise."

"Yeah…"

"You don't sound very excited. What else do you want? Looks like this new album is gonna be the biggest ever in the history of music. You'll be at the top of your game, even more rich and famous! What else could any person want?"

"You wouldn't understand," she muttered, bowing her head.

"I could try."

"It sounds cheesy, so I know you'll make fun of me."

"I won't," I argued. "After all we've been through, I hope you realize you can *trust* me."

"Yeah? Well you seemed really concerned when Bubba was choking me out… you told him to go on ahead and *kill* me."

"Oh come on! I told im ta kill me too. I was callin Witty's bluff, and it worked. Hey, he let you *go*, didn't he?"

She was unresponsive.

"I'm listenin," I said, "and I won't make fun of you. What is it ya really want when this is all over?"

"I told you it would sound cheesy. I just want to be *happy*. I see myself in pictures all the time, and I'm *smiling*, but there's nothing, and I mean nothing, behind those smiles. It's just something I was trained to do. I look happy, but I'm not. Truth is—I haven't been happy for as far back as I can remember. That's it. Just for once I'd like to smile and *mean* it!"

It was an uncomfortable moment as I watched her eyes fill with tears and overflow.

"But you make a hundred million a year—you're one of the richest women on the planet. You're loved the world over and you're incredible at what you do! Doesn't *that* make you happy?"

"I knew you wouldn't understand. No. None of it is real. People tell me they love me all the time—on some days literally *hundreds* of times, but they don't love me," she laughed to herself. "They don't even *know* me! They've fallen for the ongoing publicity stunt *The Man* has turned me into, and if I don't get out, it's what I'll become: hollow, empty, a life without a soul."

Sniffing and dabbing her eyes, she looked up at me.

"You asked me what I wanted? I want to *walk away* from it, all of it. I've made enough money. I've received enough validation. I need to find a new path. I need to find my *soul*!"

Surprisin me, she reached over and grasped my hand, squeezin hard.

"And if finding my soul means I lose my life, then so be it. I'll die with a smile on my face, but I'll *mean* it."

Just then, somethin happened, somethin special between Zenobia and me. Sittin at that table at my cousin Fat Tony's house, we realized our fates were inescapably intertwined, for better or for worse. She was a woman who had lost her soul, and I was a man who had lost my sense of purpose beyond the past. We were two desperate, pitiful people who needed somethin from each other in order to find our way.

But there was somethin more—an intangible, an unpredictable, a passion between us, and at that moment, that passion caused me ta do somethin I wanted ta do from the first second I saw her at the Waldorf. And so takin up chance and fate, I took up her hand and kissed it gently. Eyes still moist, she smiled at me and nodded. Upon that signal, I leaned toward her, and takin her beautiful face in my hands, I kissed her, both of us realizing the die had been cast long before we ever met.

The Mob

Showtime! It was our intention ta get ta Vinny's late, so we got there at eight, when all parties knew the meetin was scheduled for seven-thirty. If mob meetins were anything, they were punctual. By the sheer number of cars and all the goons standin in fronna the restaurant and next ta some of the vehicles, everyone in the entire neighborhood knew somethin big was goin down that night.

Naturally, my concern was that The Dwarf was gonna *try* somethin, ya know, get the drop me or Zenobia or both of us so he could control the terms and the direction of negotiations. Fat Tony said he heard that Marcelino had told Carlito the Ass ta shoot me in the street like a dog if he could, so I wasn't takin any chances. When we got there, all the big bosses were a little miffed on accounta bein made ta wait. By then, I knew The Dwarf wasn't gonna risk upsettin em further by whackin me and makin the whole night a waste.

So when we got inside, the room was fulla family bosses. There was Dino Canto, the head of the D'Agostino family, and Skinny Legs Rufino, who ran the notorious Occhino family, and just barely alive was Don Aldoberto Toscano, the ninety-six-year-old boss of the Zacarria family. Of course, Don Adoberto was one of the bossiest bosses *in* the mob. Because of his age and connections, he could out-boss the Carzanos and all the rest of everybody if he had to.

But the face I was lookin for belonged to Marcelino's father, Marco Bello. At seventy-eight, I expected him ta look a little withered, but he was still incredibly good-lookin. In fact, the first thing Zenobia said ta me was, *who is that very handsome man over there?* Ta which I told her it was Marco Bello, once voted the best-lookin man in the whole state of New Jersey. Good lookin, yeah, but also one of the cruelest and deadliest. One of his nicknames was *aggiungi a morte*, for the snake.

On seein me, Marco Bello immediately smiled and summoned me.

"Young Michael Ponzi!" he said. "If you aren't the spittin image of your grandfather at your age, well then, I'm not Sicilian. Come here, boy!"

Takin me at arm's length, he hugged and kissed me once on each cheek. The Dwarf, standin in his shadow as usual, smiled at me and extended his arms for an embrace, which I ignored. The gesture did not go unmissed by all the bosses in the room—most of whom knew The Dwarf had put out an unsuccessful hit on me. I patted his head instead.

The restaurant was closed ta the public for the night, so everyone inside had a reason ta be there. Vinny's main dinin room was set with the big tables, the eight-person rounds with starched white tablecloths. Each boss had a table and was surrounded by essential personnel: a bodyguard, a lawyer, an accountant and a parliamentarian—someone well-versed in the rules of the business. There was a wife or two, here and there. No girlfriends.

Zenobia, who came in with me, stood out like, well like she was a rare black swan among a gaggle of snow geese, for lack of a better metaphor. Almost every person in the room, after all, was a man, Italian and loud, most of em over fifty with grey hair or baldin. And they were all lookin at her like she was the dinner. Feelin protective, I led her ta the table where my dad was sittin and put her next ta him, while I sat on the other side of her.

After we all finished eatin, Marco Bello stood again, callin the meetin to order.

"We are all here tonight upon the audacious request of young Michael Ponzi, who was late tonight. According to him, he has had the good fortune to come across a microchip that contains information which is of use and great interest to our families and our businesses, information we can use to secure our futures and the futures of our families for many years to come.

"For those of you who don't know him, Michael is the son of Dominic Ponzi, the Veterinarian, as I call him, and the grandson of Guido Ponzi, the original Brain, who was my best friend for many, many years.

"As I understand it, Michael has called us here tonight to make a deal that will involve him turning that information over to us in exchange for us giving him something *he* wants. The information in question will give us leverage in our dealings with The Management. In short, it will change the way we do business with them. It will give us a better hand."

Don Aldoberto Toscano was the first to nod, indicatin he wanted ta make an inquiry. After bein recognized, he bowed his head, listenin ta what his parliamentarian was whisperin in his ear, and then he spoke.

"This is good news. The Management demands more from us every year. I *think* that they are tryin ta put us outa business. A deal for that information would be a good thing. What is it that young Michael Ponzi wants?"

"That's just it," Marco Bello sighed, disgusted. "Until this moment, Michael Ponzi has not told anyone what he wants, except that he wanted this meeting tonight, and he insisted that we all had to be here. *Prepotenza!*"

"Then let's just ask him *now*," Skinny Legs interjected. "Ask im what is it that he wants, and let's *give* it to im. For information that'll get us a better deal with The Management, I say we give it to im, *whatever* it is!"

At that moment, Marco Bello shot me a look that said he knew what I was up to, along with a evil eye that told me he was gonna kill me first chance he got. He'd been around for awhile, so he was not one ta be tarried with. So affectin his million-dollar smile and summonin all his contagious charm, he turned on me.

"Michael Marco Ponzi—your grandfather named you after me. What is it that you *want* from us?"

For years I had awaited the moment.

"I'm not askin for much. I just want an apology."

"An apology?" Dino Canto laughed. "You want an *apology*? Who do you want an apology from, Michael Ponzi?"

I stood, ready ta launch.

"From whom? I want an apology from Marco Bello here."

The silent sound of confusion filled the air as all eyes in the room trained on the dapper old man standing there. But sly old fox that he was, Marco Bello was prepared for the moment and probably had been prepared for years. First, he smiled ta reassure his associates.

"This is all very amusing to be sure, but before we men of age yield the floor and our precious time to this *nipote* among us, I think we all need to know just who and what he is."

Marco Bello was a charmer. He had wrested control of the moment—*my* moment.

"A little more than a month ago, Michael Ponzi came to my son, Marcelino, for a job to continue in the veterinary arts of his family. My son figured he did it was because Michael's father, Dominic Ponzi, told us all one month earlier that he wanted to retire and travel back to Italy with his violent Irish wife. And because our families have always been close, Marcelino welcomed Michael to the family with no questions and open arms.

"Michael told everyone that he had been away at school, and after failing at being a writer, he had worked a few odd jobs that didn't pay much, and he had come back to the neighborhood because he wanted to be a part of the business and the tradition of our families.

"But it is what Michael Ponzi *didn't* say that matters tonight. We've all seen the stories on the news about him and his famous black girlfriend sitting over there, but what Michael *didn't* tell anyone about was the fact that one of those 'odd jobs' was as CEO of a company that did contract work for a secret government project involving clandestine data collection all around the world. And another one of those 'odd jobs' was as a negotiator in an American-Chinese joint adventure, worth billions of dollars. He even played a golf game with *Obama*! I could go on. So what we *do* know is Michael Ponzi is *not* who or what he says he is."

After gauging the expressions on the faces of his associates, Marco Bello smiled with growing confidence.

"Furthermore, when my son Marcelino got wind of the inconsistencies in Michael's story, he did some researching of his own. Michael said that over at Cornell he majored in English because he wanted to write novels, so he graduated with a mere Bachelor of Arts degree. But the truth is Michael Ponzi got two Phds over there at Cornell, one in Economics and another in International Relations, with honors—top of the class. So one's gotta ask: with all that going for him, why is it that Michael came back to the neighborhood, our neighborhood?"

I couldn't help it. I had to look at Zenobia, whose face signaled a sense of betrayal when our eyes met. She turned away in seeming anger as the old man continued.

"The Carzanos and the Ponzis—we go way back—to the very first day that Carlo Ponzi came to America. He was seated next to my father, Giuseppe Carzano, all the way on the long journey here. My good friend, Guido Ponzi, Michael's grandfather, was one of us. Dominic Ponzi, Michael's father, *is* one of us. But this one here, this Michael Ponzi—I say he is *not* one of us.

"Now I can't prove it, but I have it on good faith from a CIA rat whose name I cannot reveal, that Michael Ponzi never really wanted a job with the family, because he already *had* a job. Truth is that Michael Ponzi works for *The Management*. And this whole business about the microchip he came here promising to share with us. *That's* a lie. His whole reason for coming here in the first place, his reason for deceiving us, was to make sure we never got our hands on that information, so The Management could keep on *taking* from us."

The room erupted in angry murmuring as faces turned on me. The contempt in many of the old men's eyes was unmistakable.

"Michael Ponzi is a traitor to us all!" Marco Bello concluded. "*That* is why my son took action against him—to *protect* us from him!"

"Yeah, I was protectin us from *him*... and his father!" Marcelino the Dwarf echoed. "*Il Ponzis sono traditori!*"

With all eyes on me, I realized I had to turn it all around. There were difficult questions and charges to be answered, so I stood and took a deep breath, grounding myself, and began.

"I have to admit it: *that* was a very good and effective speech by Marco Bello. *Kudos* to him! He should have been a lawyer. Now, I know the charges he's leveled against me sound very incriminating, but believe me, you'll understand it all, by and by."

It was a steep hill, but it was climb or die.

"For those of you who don't know," I began, "I was very close to my grandfather, Guido. He was already in prison when I came along, so I got to know him in a different context than most kids know their grandfathers. He was there because he was convicted of murdering an informant, though most people knew that Guido Ponzi only dealt in animals. In all his life, he never killed a human.

"Anyway, I spent every Thursday with my *nonno*, from the time I was four-years-old until the day he died. Over all those years, he taught me a few things, but what I remember most is what he taught me about honor and the way that an honorable man should live. A man should love his family first, his friends second and himself last. That was exactly the kind of man my grandfather, Guido, was.

"So when he took that fateful trip to Cleveland, where he was charged, arrested and convicted for a murder he did not commit, a bogus conviction that put him in prison for the rest of his life, away from his wife and family, he did the honorable thing. He believed it was better to suffer the shame and humiliation of imprisionment—not to mention the financial loss and the loss of liberty—he chose to sacrifice his freedom in order to protect his family and friends.

"My grandfather wasn't a busybody, but he was very smart. He knew when something didn't *smell* right, but more than anything else, he knew the smell of a rat. So the way it was back then, he knew that somebody—one of us—one of *us* was working both sides of the street. My grandfather knew that *someone* was providing information to the Ness people in Chicago and to the Hoover people in New York and New Jersey. He wasn't sure who it was, but after a while, *nonno* started to zero in.

"But it just so happened that *right* when he found out who the rat was, there comes this ironclad murder charge against him in Cleveland, where the feds were telling him the only way to escape the conviction was to rat out his friends. That was something my grandfather never thought one time about doing. So he went to prison for the last forty-five years of his life because he was an honorable man.

"*That* my grandfather taught me! When I went to visit him every Thursday, he told me about the old days, about the old families and the old ways. *Valori della famiglia!* And one of the most important things I learned is that you've got to be loyal to your family and friends... to a fault. If Guido Ponzi had rolled over on his friends, everyone would have thought he was the rat in the first place, and the real rat would have gotten away again, like he aways has..."

"All right, enough!" Marco Bello shouted, his words quivering in anger. "We've heard enough of your bullshit, Michael Ponzi! *You're* the rat! And you're a proven liar! You came here under false pretenses to destroy us! All of us! No one in this room *believes* your idiotic story! I am sorry, *Signores*, to have allowed this *fugazi* to waste your time.

Marco Bello looked toward the door.

"Carlito! Get this piece of shit outa here! He's not worthy of another word!"

Carlito rose right away, glaring at me, his hand in his coat.

"*Stay* where you are, Carlito!" a strained, wheezing voice retorted.

All eyes in the room were averted to the source of the sudden contradiction, an old, hunched over man bein helped to his feet by an attendant.

"Don Aldoberto?" Marco Bello complained. "You can't *believe* this... this Michael Ponzi. He's a liar and a traitor to us all!"

"I didn't say I *believed* him, Marco," the Don explained, "but I want to hear his story nonetheless. We're all *here* tonight. Where's the harm? Let Ponzi speak."

Unable to voice a further objection, Marco Bello glanced toward Carlito, making a sign with his fingers, and resigned himself to listening with the rest.

"As time went by," I continued, "my grandfather became convinced that following in the family business was a dangerous course for me. He knew that, because of his and my relationship, the rat would never trust me and would surely come after me. That's why he used all the money he ever made in his life to send me to Cornell. *The rat is too powerful*, he said, and the only way I could save our family and *your* families—the only way I could save the people he cared about from further damage and manipulation was to put myself in a position to fight the rat from the outside."

"This *rat* you keep sayin! Who the hell is this *rat*?" Skinny Legs complained.

"I'll come to that. So with *nonno's* help and connections, I went through the measures when I was in college. It wasn't easy and it involved significant risk and personal sacrifice, but I eventually became a part of The Management."

"There! He *said* it!" The Dwarf interrupted. "He's The Management, and The Management is out ta control us! What more do we need to know? Carlito!"

Everyone paused to glance at The Dwarf momentarily before turnin back to me.

"I became a part of The Management because my grandfather said that too many good people had been hurt and someone had to stop him. He said someone had to settle family business, and that someone was me. *Nonno's* moment of truth is tonight. *Signores*, I didn't join The Management to hurt any of you. I joined to make things right."

I looked back toward the host.

"So as I was saying earlier, Marco Bello. I came here because I wanted an apology from you."

"An apology for *what*? For what, you little shit!"

"For what you did to my grandfather, Guido Ponzi, and to my family—you and the corrupt FBI agents you've been working with over all these years. *You're* the rat, Marco Bello! You set up my grandfather for a murder *you* ordered and someone *else* committed, and because my grandfather trusted you, you put him at the scene of the crime and stacked all the facts against him. You wrongly sent my grandfather to prison for life and did not help our family. I want an apology for that!"

"Michael, ah young Michael—" Marco Bello sighed, throwing up his hands. "Is *that* what your grandfather told you? Well, then I *understand* now! I understand why you are doing this. I would probably feel the same way in your place, but what your grandfather told you is *not* the truth. It was just a story he made up to save face before his grandson, when the rest of his family abandoned him."

"Bullshit!" my father interjected.

"The truth, I'm so sorry to say, young Michael, is Guido Ponzi was the rat," Marco Bello continued. "When I discovered what he was doing, feeding damaging information about us to the FBI in New York, I realized I had to do something. He was my best friend, so rather than calling him on it and getting him into trouble with all of you, I did the next best thing. Yes, I set him up to put him in a place where he could do our families no more harm."

He finally looked toward me, gesturing with extended hands.

"And if what I did hurt an impressionable grandson, a young boy who loved and believed in his grandfather and everything he was told, then I truly *am* sorry," he smiled. "So I sincerely *apologize* to you, Michael, for what you had to go through with that. But you have to realize this: you would have never *had* that special relationship with him if not for me. I actually *saved* your *nonno's* life."

"Don Aldoberto Toscano, Dino Canto, Skinny Legs Rufino," I called out, beginning my closing argument. "I honor your age and experience. I get the sense you know about The Management and what we are capable of doing. Coming here tonight, I knew the odds were stacked against me, so I knew I had to bring you something real, something concrete to convince you that my grandfather was telling the truth. Zenobia?"

Opening the briefcase placed before her, Zenobia began to stack the documents in the middle of the table.

"Those are *unredacted* FBI documents that contain the proof of everything I've told you tonight. For the last fifty years, Marco Bello and corrupt FBI agents have been working their own magic, for profit, power and revenge. It's all there."

I walked over to the table and retrieved three documents from the top, summarizing the first.

"Nineteen-sixty-eight—Paulo Roberto Toscano—caught red-handed torching a Manhattan construction project—convicted to thirty years on Park Row. FBI Informant: Marco Bello Carzano."

On hearing the name, the room erupted in murmuring and cursing in Italian. As soon as the sound died a little, I continued.

Nineteen-seventy-five—robbery, Atlantic City, three Brinks facilities to the tune of 2.4 million dollars—convicted, one Luciano Pashino, life in prison with no possibility of parole, because two guards were killed in the process. FBI Informant: Marco Bello Carzano, who secretly collected a two hundred thousand dollar reward."

"Hey, Luciano was my *nephew!*" Skinny Legs cut in, "my sister's *only* son. Broke her poor heart! She died that same year."

There was another abrupt eruption of commentary and complaining—this time with insults being directed toward Marco Bello, who was becoming visibly nervous.

"Nineteen-eighty-three—murder of federal judge Winston H. Cosgrove in Philadelphia—Marco Bello ordered it, but the only person charged was Benito Tomasi, who swore he wasn't even in the state on the night of the murder. That didn't matter—he was gunned down by a local crew before the case went to trial. Again, the FBI Informant: Marco Bello Carzano."

"Benito was my half-*brother!*" Dino Canto growled. "He swore ta me he wasn't there, but I didn't believe im!" He glared toward Marco Bello. "You set im *up!*"

"No, no!" Marco Bello protested. "Michael Ponzi is making all that up! He works for The Management for God's sake! They know how to *do* that stuff over there! They're settin me up! I swear he's lying! He and the broad probably typed those papers up themselves!"

He knew how serious my charges were, so he continued talking.

"The *other* thing I heard, though I didn't believe it when I heard it! He's *The Man!* Michael Ponzi is *The Man!* He's the bigshot, the one who's callin all the *shots* over at The Management. *That's* the only way he could pull something like this off! This whole thing's a set-up. He's trying to play you all for fools! He wants to *destroy* us all by turning us against each other!"

"Is this *true*, Michael?" the Don asked.

"Yes, Don Aldoberto. Everything I told you about what my grandfather told me and about what Marco Bello did is the truth."

"We'll deal with that later," he said, waving his hand. "I meant the part about The Management. Are you *The Man*, Michael Ponzi?"

I contemplated before answering, and I chose my words carefully.

"Don Aldoberto, on my very life, on the honor of my grandfather and my entire family, I swear to you there is no man at the top of The Management. It's something everyone wants to talk about, but it's just not the case. There is no man at the top."

I reached into my pocket for the note, which I had never read.

"Before he died, my grandfather wrote this letter to you, Don Aldoberto. I've had it all this time, but I never opened it, so I have no idea what it says. He told me to give it to you if you were still alive, or to Gionni, your oldest son."

"No! Whatever that letter says is not true!" Marco Bello pleaded. "He wrote that himself! Can't you see? They're trying to set me up! Those damn Ponzi's are the rats—not us! Michael Ponzi is *The Man!* It's the only way he could have gotten all that stuff! Don't you see?"

Approaching the old man, I gave him the letter, which he read in silence. After passing the paper to his parliamentarian, he strained to stand.

"My fellow families, this is a matter we need to take up in private quarters, far from the purview of the general eye and ear. It is long-neglected, unsettled family business that we must resolve tonight."

"No! It's not true! You gotta *believe* me, Aldo! Please!"

Don Aldoberto looked toward the suddenly not-so-distinguished host.

"Marco Bello—you will come with us immediately. My guards will escort you. In the meantime, Marcelino—you are relieved of all status and protection as a boss, effective immediately. Until further notice—Rotten Tomatoes—you, Tommy, will take his place, and Alphonso the Brain will be your lieutenant. The way I figure it, Rotten's the favorite uncle to a bigshot who works for The Management, so we've finally got a man on the inside. Bosses and family heads will meet at my spot in an hour."

Dénouement

With the meeting adjourned, the room quickly emptied. Everyone left, except Tommy Rotten's table and the table with Zenobia and my dad. When The Dwarf tried to sneak out the front door, one of Tommy's guys stepped in the way to block his exit.

"Stick around for a bit, Marcelino," Tommy called out. "I got someone comin by who really wants ta see ya."

To everyone's surprise, five minutes later, my ma busted through the door.

"Marcelino!" she yelled. "Marcelino Carzano! I *warned* ya! I told you if you ever tried ta hurt my son, I was gonna kick your ass much worse than I did when we were in the fifth grade!"

"No! No, Claire! It's not what you *think*!" Marcelino pleaded, backing. "What are you *doin* here?"

"You set-up my husband and then you tried ta kill my son!"

"No, that wasn't me! That was Jake! It was *Jake* who tried ta kill Michael!"

By that time, a panicked Jake had risen from his seat, trying to proceed as quickly as he could toward the front door. Doing that shuffling thing he did to move his feet, he wasn't getting far.

"I'll deal with Jake later. Someone put a *chair* in fronna that man!"

Marcelino made a break for it, dashing into the kitchen, but my mother was right behind him. I wanted to watch, but I couldn't. From where I was, I could hear the sound of face blows, elbow whacks and body slams coming from in there. And then it sounded like she was playing a drum solo with pots and pans, all over his head. *Bing! Bong! Boom! Bam!* Seconds later, we heard Marcelino's gut-wrenching scream and the sound of some kinda bone, cracking, and then he was whimpering.

"Okay, now someone bring me in Jake!" she called out. "I'm a little winded, but I got a Bialetti saucepan in here with his *name* on it! Tommy?"

I sat next to Zenobia, both of us trying to ignore the sounds and violence coming from the kitchen.

"So now you *know*," I sighed.

"You are one big liar, Michael Ponzi!" she sobbed. "You are the worst person I have ever met in my whole life! I *hate* you!"

"Zenobia, you don't understand."

"Of *course* I do. I trusted you! You set this whole thing up from the beginning. Nothing about you was real, Michael. Every story, every explanation, every *word* you said was a lie, and knowing that, you let me open my heart to someone I *thought* I knew… and cared about—knowing you were completely someone else!"

She stood, looking toward my dad.

"Mr. Ponzi, I was watching your face when you found out. He had you fooled too. Neither of us deserved to be lied to. Thank you for inviting me to dinner tonight."

"In light of the circumstances," my father comforted, "he really *had* no choice."

"I told you that first night, Michael," she sighed, taking the Cadillac keys from her purse. "You *always* have a choice!"

And saying that, Zenobia launched her knee into my nuts with all her dance-athletic rhythm and might—a very solid shot that made even my father groan in empathy. I dropped to all fours, waiting out that initial surge of pain. My personal agony, along with all the noise from the kitchen made it impossible for me to think straight.

In all the commotion going on, Zenobia left so fast that I didn't get a chance to warn her. But suddenly I remembered Marco Bello and the hand sign he gave to Carlito across the room.

"Oh no! *Zenobia!*"

I jumped so abruptly that I upended the tabletop and had to scramble over the chairs on my way to the door.

"Someone *stop* her!" I yelled toward Tommy Rotten's men as I rushed out.

When I got to the corner, the Escapade was still there, but then I thought I saw the brake lights come on briefly.

Baroom! Baroom! Baroosh!

The violent, earth-shaking explosion was immediate and deafening—a huge, bright orange fireball replacing what had once been a vehicle, with Zenobia inside. Apparently she didn't suffer, but she never stood a chance. She died instantly. All along the street, car alarms were going off and the windows of nearby buildings were shattered.

That's when I saw him. Carlito Soranno was standing at the corner on the adjacent street, watching the conflagration, his arms crossed, laughing, completely fascinated. When our eyes met, I smiled to mock him, leaving him dumbfounded and angry, and he was just in the process of flipping me the double-bird when three FBI agents came up behind him and arrested him for the apparent murder.

Nevertheless, my heart sank to the pit of my gut. I fell to my knees and wept. I could not believe she was gone, just like that. My father and one of Tommy's guys came up behind me, helping me up to my feet.

"It was my fault!" I groaned. "I should have *warned* her. I should have stopped her! I should never have let her go, but she was so angry with me that I could never have made her stay."

"That's right," my father agreed. "She was too angry. She didn't wanna stay. She *hated* ya for lyin ta her. What a waste!"

"I never wanted to lie to her, but what else was I going to do? You were right, Dad. In this case I did *not* have a choice. Yes, I could have *trusted* her. I could have told her everything from the beginning, but I had to make her believe what it was necessary for her to believe to play her part."

"I think you're in shock," Tommy's bodyguard offered. "Ya couldn't stop her. Ya didn't know. I'm sorry, Mr., Mr. *The Man*."

"Because I had this family business to finish, I couldn't share everything with anyone! I never even told Zenobia that I was in *love* with her!"

The news spread like wildfire on the Internet and on television, with station after station issuing announcements of Zenobia's death in a fiery Hoboken explosion. The world and celebrities were soon to weigh in, making Zenobia even more popular in death that she ever was while alive. There were candlelit vigils for her all across the globe, and it seemed every major radio station played a tribute to her in the first few hours. I stayed, watching the Escalade, until crime scene investigators came to remove the body and took it away for autopsy.

I hardly slept that night. All I could remember was the flash of anger in Zenobia's eyes at the table and the very real kiss we shared just before the meeting. I remembered her last words to me: *you always have a choice.* And finally, I remembered the words of the song she sang after dinner at Uncle Joe's. That song just kept going through my head, along with rememberances of my grandfather.

****

So I was having a little lunch with my parents the next day when there was this knock at the door. My ma went to answer it, and when she returned, Lolita Cardulo, *aka* Lola Fox, was with her. Sheesh! As a *bona-fide* celebrity, Lolita was better-looking than ever, especially after whatever cosmetic procedures she had done in southern California. She was a living doll, and apparently she was signing major deals in Hollywood.

"I'm sorry about your girlfriend, Michael," she consoled. "From what I hear, Zenobia was a classy broad who cared about other people. She really helped a lot of the younger performers comin up. Good person. Too bad she's dead."

"Yeah," I grumbled. "Mom? Dad?"

Slow to pick up on hints, my parents sat there an additional two minutes before realizing Lolita and I wanted some privacy to talk. A little put off for being excluded, my ma insisted on a trip to the mall to shop for the Italy trip, which they were going on in two days.

"They're *finally* gone!" Lolita sighed. "*Quickie* on the table, for old-times sake?"

"Really?" I laughed.

"Oh come on! Ya know I ain't *like* that! Are you crazy?" she groaned. "Ya were just an itch with me that needed ta get scratched, Michael Ponzi, and while I hafta admit you're a great scratch, I'm actually here ta tell ya I'm movin ta Los Angeles."

"Los Angeles? And *that's* why you're here, to tell me that?"

"Well, let me be honest, Michael. Word's out that you're part of The Management, if you're not *The Man* himself. You of all people know how it works. So I came ta ask, 'What advice do you have for me, your boyhood wet-dream fantasy?'"

"Well, Lolita," I began, "you have the prospect of an incredible career before you. You'll be rich, famous, wanted, envied, imitated, idolized, sensationalized and worshiped. All you have to do is want it. And who wouldn't want that?"

"Some of that's already happenin," she smiled.

"Yes, I'm sure it is, Lolita, or Lola. But if you're going to reach the top, somewhere along the way, you'll also be told to do some things that go against who you are, or were—all that your family stands for, if you even remember. You'll be tested, tamed and turned every which way until you are turned inside out and completely broken down. Then you'll be reconstructed and reprogrammed, fashioned into a product that can be reliably sold, traded, reprogrammed or eliminated at someone else's pleasure. It's the cost of ambition, the price of fame. If you really want to reach the top, you have to be prepared to lose your soul."

I stood, because I felt emotion welling up. All I could think of was Zenobia.

"My advice to you, Lolita Cardullo: Ya got a lot goin for ya. Get out before it's too late!"

****

Before leaving town, I went to the hospital, where both The Dwarf and Jake were recovering. They were under indictment for multiple murders and other felonious acts and crimes, so there were two guards stationed outside the door. Marcelino's left leg and right arm were in traction, while he had bandages and an icepack on his head for the headache caused by the concussion. Jake was in a little better shape, though he had visible damage to his elbow and a broken jaw, and he was missing the bottom row of his silver teeth.

"Lolita told me the two of yas wanted ta *talk* to me?"

"Yeah, Michael," Marcelino whispered, struggling to breathe. "You're *The Man*, Michael! Ya had me fooled the whole time. So anyway, I was hopin ya could check and see what's goin on with my father. No one's seen or heard from im since that night. That ain't like him, ta be off the radar for so long."

The Dwarf could not hold back his tears.

"I know ya don't owe me anything, Michael, ya know, especially after Jake and Carlito tried ta kill ya and I didn't help ya with your own father. But you said family meant somethin ta you that night, and what you said was touchin ta me. So I'm beggin ya, for the sake of *my* family, will you please find out about my father? I'm worried maybe he ain't comin back."

"I'll check for ya," I nodded, "but *you* of all people know how these things work. If nothing else, he'll go down in mob history."

"That's what I'm afraid of!" Marcelino groaned.

Reaching an arm and hand up from the bed across the room, Jake the Schlep grunted.

"Michael, my *son* did not blow up that singer in that car," he strained through his wired-shut jaw. "He was sittin nexta me all that night. Someone *else* rigged her car."

"You're right. I know that," I assured him.

"Then who? What are ya talkin about?" he pleaded, looking into my eyes, and then he understood. "You mean *you*, Michael? *You* killed Zenobia? *You* blew her up?"

My lack of a response turned both mens' faces toward me.

"Why?" Marcelino asked. "I thought she was your girl, the *black* chick ya always wanted."

"Business concerns—loose ends. Wasn't the first, and won't be the last. I think I loved *that* one, though. Yeah, I think I loved her."

"Then you hafta *tell* em, Michael. Tell em over at the FBI!" an agitated Jake insisted. "They're blamin Carlito for that. The world hates im, includin her fans—all the minorities and the young people! Please! Carlito's gonna go ta prison for the rest of his life if ya don't help!"

"I don't know how to tell you this, Jake," I smiled, wagging my head, "but I'm sure somewhere along the way, Carlito did *somethin* to deserve that sentence."

"So tell me, Michael Ponzi," Marcelino called out as I stood, ready to leave. "Was there ever *really* a chip, or was that all part of some game?"

"Oh, there was a chip all right," I answered, "but there was never anything *on* it. I just let everyone *believe* there was."

I approached his bed, sat and explained in a quiet voice.

"In the end, all the information that all the parties ultimately got came from the *other* parties involved, who provided me with specific information that I requested in exchange for specific information that they themselves wanted—information that I was getting from the other parties involved. It's a little complicated—something from nothing."

"A *Ponzi* scheme!" Marcelino blurted without realizing what he had just said, and then he made the connection, nodding.

"*Genius! Pure genius!*"

Coda

When I got back to the farm outside Schenectady, little had changed. Uncle Joe and his sons were working as hard as ever in the fields, and Margaret was living at the house full-time, helping with the cooking after she finished her homework. I made sure I arrived near the *end* of the workday, so I could put in an hour at most and still enjoy one of Aunt Mary's incredible home-cooked meals.

After dinner, the menfolk sat on the porch as Uncle Joe lit his pipe. There was Shadrach, his brother Joab, Stanley and me, each of us with a cigar. Feeling a little guilty about killing Bubo, I kept one eye up, still worried about the wrath of his wife.

"So how did you two meet, anyway?" Joab asked.

"Who? Me and Michael here?" Stanley laughed. "We met just kinda by accident when I was going to school at Cornell. It was random, but he ended up being my mentor and coached me until I graduated with a Performing Arts degree. Turned out that, in addition to his other degrees, Michael had a Master's in acting, and in languages. Anyway, out of the blue, I just ran into him in New York last month, a couple days before I brought him here."

Uncle Joe did not mince words.

"So Michael, I take it you're here to *see* her?" he said between puffs.

"Yeah," I answered. "It's been a long time. Too long."

"You mean Ebai?" Shadrach cut in. "Ebai thought you were never going to come back. She's *married* now! She's married to *Kal-El* now. My father's building them a house on the property and starting them out with a farm. They're at Granma Ollie's tonight."

"Really?" I blurted, surprised.

"Hey, Ebai said she waited as long as she could," Stanley explained. "You didn't come *back* for her."

"I was gone—what? Two *weeks!*" I sighed. "That's a woman for you! What a—"

I remembered just then that it probably wasn't a good idea to talk trash about a man's daughter on his porch with him still sitting on it.

"What a *disappointment!*"

"And all this time I thought *Stanley* was the actor!" Uncle Joe chortled. "Somehow Michael, you don't seem too disappointed.

****

I got up early the next morning and started walking. Miss Ollie's place had to be a good three miles away, but the place where I was headed was another five. I took my time, practicing along the way what I would say and how I would say it, so it had to be about eleven when I arrived at the cozy house sitting way back off the road.

The mostly brick structure seemed clean and modern for the area, with a well-kept lawn in the front, surrounded by a freshly-painted white picket fence. I hesitated as I opened the creaking gate, uncertain about what to expect. The kitchen window at the front of the house was open, and on the windowsill: two freshly-baked, homemade apple pies. There was a table on the porch with two empty glasses and a frosted pitcher of lemonade, a large chunk of ice floating inside.

I knocked briefly and took a seat on the porch swing, looking around at the pots with plants and the starter beds with seedlings. A moment later, the door creaked open and there she was. She looked different, in a flattering way—no make-up, no fingernail polish, her hair pulled back in a ponytail.

But what I noticed most about her that day wasn't anything physical, though in a way it was. What I noticed was her smile, which had less to do with her face and more to do with her spirit. She *meant* it on that day. She was free, and if she hadn't already reclaimed her soul, she certainly was on her way to reclaiming it.

"Wonderful funeral, great soloist. Believe me, there were a lotta tears," I offered.

"I watched it on my smart phone," she said. "It's not something most people ever get a chance to do."

"Just think of it like this: for all intents and purposes, you're in *heaven* now."

"I *am*! What do you think?" she said, sitting next to me, motioning toward the surroundings.

"It's definitely you! How do you feel?"

"Reborn! I never believed this could be possible. I never thought you could pull it off."

"Well, it took some doing and some expense. I had to kill Zenobia, which meant staging the actual event. Then I had to put in an Oscar-winning acting performance and alter lab results and legal documents—plus what it cost to buy you out of some of your more *expensive* contracts. In all, it cost you at least twenty-five million, but since projections have you making close to one billion dollars during the first year after your death, I'm sure you won't miss it. And just so you know: it'll cost you three million a year to *stay* dead. Of course, there are less expensive ways to 'opt-out,' and some of them less than voluntary—you know—Amy, MJ. But I think you'll be very happy with your decision."

"Good to know. You are very clever man, Michael. I take it you've *done* this kind of thing before?"

"Yeah, I have," I answered, staring forward. "You *know* Elvis?—"

"Elvis Presley!" she interrupted. "You mean *he* isn't dead either?"

"No, he's dead all right," I sighed, "but he didn't die until just two *years* ago. Real good guy, but we had the hardest time keeping him a secret, you know, until he got older. I played poker with him at least once a month for those last three years. Some kinda poker player *he* was! Presley payed me to let him win!"

"Anyone else?"

"Well, Elvis was pretty good friends with Sam Cooke through the years. They went fishin on occasion. Sam *liked* fishin, and if you didn't know any better, he'd sandbag you at the pool table and take all your money."

"You're kidding me! Oh, okay. So I *gotta* ask, what about *Tupac?* What about all those rumors?"

"You mean *Makaveli?*" I laughed. "That's what *we* call him. Oh yeah, we were able to help *him* out too! He wanted to walk away from it all, just like you did. He's got a real big place that he calls *Gangsta Paradise*, complete with his own state-of-the-arts music studio. He's *still* trying to do music, still trying to release new songs. We're always telling him he can't *do* that, though he's managed to slip a couple by us."

"But I saw his uh, his *autopsy* on the Internet," she protested.

"Take a look when you get a chance. *Yours* is on there too!"

"Eew! I think I'll pass on that!"

"But Makaveli," I continued, "he doesn't live far from Biggie. Biggie's place is uh… what does he call it? Yeah, *Big Pappa's*, I think. Big surprise, huh? They've made up, probably because there aren't many folks on *this* side, and they're basically the only two serious rappers so far. They've got an arrangement where they play *golf* together on early Saturday mornings."

"They golf? Wow! This is so hard to believe! You really know these guys. They never really died? They're still around?"

"You'd be surprised at how many of the *beautiful people* and one-percenters decide to 'opt out.' It's an adjustment. Of course, they can still travel and go places, but it's very expensive because of the risk involved. Most of them have nice homes, so once 'the death' is sold and locked in, we can make arrangement for visits from friends and relatives. Sometimes you *can* win, even when you lose."

I rose to stretch my knees and pour two glasses of lemonade. The sun was on the porch, and it was getting hot. Looking back over at her, I smiled, my heart confirming that, yes, I was in love with her.

"Finally, to make things a little better—four times a year we throw these parties we call 'Esoterica,' for anyone who's opted out and who wants to go. We spare no expense. I remember one year, must have been 2004 or 2005—at the height of his popularity, we booked Dave Chapelle to perform, because he swore he was opting out that May, but then he changed his mind at the last minute. Talk about a mess!"

As I sat next to her, I could hardly contain myself. At that moment, I was ready to opt *myself* out and beg her to make me the world's happiest man by marrying me. It was too soon though. If nothing else, time was on my side.

"Just between you and me, I think Tupac's lost a step or two. Ya know how it goes: ya eat with Biggie, ya naturally gain weight, so Tupac's sportin a little belly nowdays, and he's gotten kinda *conservativ*e as he's gotten older."

"Conservative? Tupac?"

"Well, yeah. I hate ta be the one to put the word out, but they tell me he watches *Fox News*! They say he *really* does. And get this," I whispered. "I don't have any direct proof of it, but I think Tupac voted for Romney."

****

We sat most of the afternoon talking, dancing around the subject. I couldn't read her because there was something *different* about her. She seemed more relaxed, more at peace with herself and everything in her new world. As the sun, in its downward trajectory, reached toward the horizon, I knew I had to start talking or start walking.

"What are you going to call yourself?"

"Zenobia. It's the name I was born with. I don't have to become someone else to be happy. I'd rather find peace with who I really am."

"Well, Zenobia, I have to admit—I *am* falling in love with you. I have been since from the beginning. I want a life with you."

"You do?" she asked, surprised.

"More than anything I've ever wanted before."

"I don't know," she shrugged. "At the end of the movie, Frank Farmer kissed Rachel Marron and headed off for the next *job…*"

"Yeah, but you said it that first night—*I'm not Kevin Costner*, plus we never got a chance to have our *Bodyguard* moment."

"You're on the couch tonight, Michael. You might be *The Man*, but you're still going to have to take me out on a real date where you're spending real money and putting in some real effort. Did you think you could just *walk* over here and sweep me off my feet? I hardly even *know* you."

"We were together every day for over a month, and you don't think you know me?"

"I didn't know you were with The Management. And if you hadn't told me everything right before that meeting at Vinny's, I would have never forgiven you for lying to me in the first place."

She smiled, sipping the last of her lemonade.

"And one thing I do *know*. My cousin was right. You lied that night when you told all those mob bosses that you weren't *The Man*. You swore on your grandfather's and family's honor that you were not *The Man* when I know you are, because *someone's* got to be *The Man*. My cousin showed me the proof."

"Okay," I said. "First I'm going to kiss you and then I'm going to make it all make sense."

"That's fair enough."

It was a wonderful kiss. Our lips touched for a quick kiss the first time, and then it was on—lips locked, tongues entangled, heads tilted this way and then that way, her hands claspin my face, my neck, my shoulders—my fingers runnin through her hair, massagin her neck, her back, her butt—Whoa! *Big* mistake!

"*Excuse* me!"

"I'm sorry. I just got a little carried away."

"You're forgiven, but return your hands to the PG-13-rated position, now!"

I quickly complied.

"I kinda like you too," she smiled. "Now tell me the truth: are you *The Man*, Michael Ponzi?"

"No, Zenobia. I am not *The Man*, but I'll admit I'm close. And I didn't lie that night when I swore on my own life, on the honor of my grandfather and my entire family that there is no man at the top of The Management. I didn't lie because I was telling the truth. There is no man at the top."

"What? You're not making sense!" she interrupted. "I saw the proof..."

"Because the person at the top of everything, the one person at the top of The Management, that person is a *woman*—a little common mistake made by all you people with bullshit sexist attitudes. No question about it—a woman—because women are just *better* at getting complicated things done, period. The world's a new place, and in it *The Man* is now a woman."

"A *woman!*" Zenobia exclaimed. "*The Man* is a woman? So who *is* she?"

"*Think* about it, Zenobia," I smiled, "because you already know."

"I do?"

"Of *course* you do. Just think of the most powerful woman in the world—the most powerful woman in the entire *history* of the world, as we know it. Doesn't take long for the name to come to your mind, does it?"

"No. Her name came to me just like that! It's unmistakable!"

"Then you *have* your answer. *The Man* you've spent all this time looking for—*The Man* they're *all* looking for—is that *woman*," I smiled. "Welcome to the real *New World Order!*"